PRAISE FOR JOR

"Barnes illuminates places that too often remain hidden. He expertly reveals the complexities of mental health care systems while crafting a captivating story of recovery and hope. Above all, Barnes' empathy for his characters shines through. No one is reduced to their diagnosis, or addiction, or tragic past. Late Blight in the Ko'olaus eviscerates stigma, resists easy narratives, and invites the reader along on an unforgettable journey, one that society often pushes to the margins or out of view entirely. A stunning, revealing, and necessary read."

VINCE GRANATA, AUTHOR, EVERYTHING IS FINE: A
MEMOIR

"Late Blight in the Ko'olaus is a clear, well-written book that grabbed my attention from the first page and held it there until the last. Avery West's story of reintegrating into society after spending years in a mental hospital will instill a sense of empathy in the reader for people who live with the stigma of a mental disorder. There was more than one character in the book that I've met a real-life counterpart to, which made me appreciate the book even more. Jordan P. Barnes has captured the challenges those of us with mental disorders face daily. At times in the book, it felt like all was lost, but Mr. Barnes has written a story of hope. That, in itself, makes it a worthwhile read."

MEAGHAN HILARY, AUTHOR, GENTLY DENTED: INSIDE
THE MIND OF A BIPOLAR SCHIZOPHRENIC

"With rich details and vivid Hawaiian imagery, Jordan P. Barnes explores a critical question: is it better to be a captive in a place that is safe, but predictable, or free in a world that is full of risks, but also possibilities? Late Blight in the Ko'olaus is about mental illness, recovery, and the healing power of nature, but most of all, it is about the courage it takes to start over."

"Jordan hits the nail on the head with every book he writes, adding yet another brilliant addition to the discussion on recovery and mental health. His compassion comes through on every page in his trademark way of educating while entertaining from cover to cover."

"Barnes skillfully crafts a story of the deep suffering of psychiatric illness and substance use disorder. He brings us into a world we all need to know and understand more about. His empathy shines through in this compelling and realistic novel and leaves us with hope for healing and recovery in the aftermath of even the most devastating of circumstances."

"Late Blight in the Ko'olaus is a must-read for anyone who wants to gain a personal understanding of the struggles of living with schizophrenia. Written with real-world wisdom and sage advice, this moving story provides a glimpse into the current standards of care and protocols within the mental healthcare system. Whether you're a professional in the field, or just looking to understand someone close to you, this book is a powerful and insightful read."

LATE BLIGHT
IN THE
KOʻOLAUS

LATE BLIGHT
IN THE
KOʻOLAUS

J O R D A N   P.   B A R N E S

Island Time Press, LLC.
Kailua, HI 96734

Cover Design and Illustration by Riad www.gorillabrigade.bigcartel.com
Book Layout by Jordan Barnes www.JordanPBarnes.com
Edited by Jessey Mills www.JesseyMills.com
Narrated by Ryan Haugen www.RyanHaugen.com

DEDICATION

For Kourtney and the fire in your sky

BY THE SAME AUTHOR

ONE HIT AWAY: A MEMOIR OF RECOVERY

- Winner of 2020's "Best Book of the Year" award from Indies Today
- Winner of the Nonfiction Cover Design award from The Book Designer
- Finalist for the 15th Annual Book Awards in the Addiction & Recovery category from the National Indie Excellence Awards (NIEA)
- Finalist for the 2021 Independent Author Network Book of the Year Awards in the Spiritual/Inspirational category
- Recipient of the Book Readers Appreciation Group Medallion

BRIDGETOWN: A HARM REDUCTION NOVEL

- Finalist for the 2021 Indies Today Book Award Contest
- Finalist for the 16th Annual Book Awards in the Addiction & Recovery category from the National Indie Excellence Awards (NIEA)

- Finalist for the 2022 Readers' Favorite Book Award Contest in the Social Issues category
- Finalist for the 2022 Book of the Year Awards from the Independent Author Network in the General Fiction and First Novel (over 80,000 words) categories

RULES TO DIE BY: FROM HEROIN ADDICTION TO LIFE IN LONG-TERM RECOVERY

Available for free at www.jordanpbarnes.com / rulestodieby

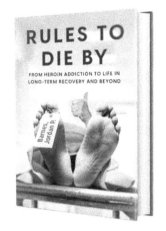

RULES TO DIE BY

FROM HEROIN ADDICTION TO LIFE IN
LONG-TERM RECOVERY AND BEYOND

Barnes,
Jordan P.

What does a life in long-term recovery look like, and how does one make the most of it?

Award-winning author and recovery advocate Jordan P. Barnes reflects on his decade-long journey navigating a life in long-term recovery from all mind and mood-altering substances.

Having distanced himself from a hopeless condition of body, mind, and spirit, Barnes spent the better part of the past ten years navigating the traditional twelve steps and fine-tuned what worked best for him in his personal program of recovery.

What emerged was *Rules to Die By,* a short read, 15,000-word manifesto comprised of 12 reflections on the practices Barnes has employed to maintain a life worth living. These constructs and observations are broken down into relatable, digestible chunks designed to offer invaluable insight into one man's journey from heroin addiction to life in long-term recovery and beyond.

Download your free copy today at:
www.JordanPBarnes.com/rulestodieby

CONTENTS

AUTHOR'S NOTE

This book touches on the critical role of forensic therapy in our communities, specifically relating to mental health and reintegrating people into society from psychiatric facilities and treatment centers. It is not intended as a substitute for the medical advice of physicians. The reader should consult a physician in matters relating to their health, particularly concerning any symptoms that may require diagnosis or medical attention, such as thought, mood, behavioral or substance use disorders.

If you or someone you love needs help, know that resources are available and that you are never alone.

Substance Abuse and Mental Health Services Administration (SAMHSA): For general information on mental health and to locate treatment services in your area, **call SAMHSA's National Helpline at 1-800-662-HELP (4357)**.

Health Resources and Services Administration (HRSA): HRSA works to improve access to health care. The HRSA website has information on finding affordable healthcare, including health centers offering care on a sliding fee scale.

Centers for Medicare & Medicaid Services (CMS): CMS has information on its website about benefits and eligibility for mental health programs and how to enroll.

The National Library of Medicine (NLM) MedlinePlus: NLM's website has directories and lists of organizations that can help identify a health practitioner.

"Sometimes when you find yourself in a dark place you think you've been buried, but you've actually been planted."

—UNKNOWN

LATE BLIGHT
IN THE
KOʻOLAUS

1

SEPTEMBER 29TH

A tormented Avery West peered through the darkness and grappled with a thought that had throbbed in his mind for hours, if not days. It was an obsession he could not shake, a plan festering in his mind as his remaining time ran thin. Every ounce of him wished it hadn't come down to this—that there could be another way—but he had ruled out every plausible alternative he could think of. At last the time to act had come, and with actions always speaking louder than words, he knew exactly what he needed to do.

Avery kicked his sheet off his torso, slung his legs over his bunk and planted his bare feet on the cold floor. He sat there in silence, massaging his temples and allowing his eyes to adjust to the darkness. When he pushed off his bunk, his mattress creaked beneath him, disturbing the familiar drawn-out snoring of his ever-present roommate. Avery froze and steeled his breath, then bent an ear toward the sputtering. From beyond his vision, he listened to Marv snuffle and flop in his bed, then mumble intelligible makings of something perturbed.

He stood there in silence, thinking how far he had come since first entering the system as nothing but another name on another caseload. Remembering the world he left behind, the same one

he wanted no part of, Avery recalled the fallout from his undiagnosed and untreated schizoaffective disorder and the mess he
left in his wake. Then, closing his eyes, he saw the years burn in
his mind—a mind that always imagined this day would come—
a mind that refused to ever go back.

Avery listened patiently until Marv's buzzing resumed, then
turned around and felt his way through the darkness toward his
nightstand. His alarm clock read a quarter past midnight, and he
picked it up, measuring the weight in his hand. Red light
engulfed his face, so he capped the display with his palm and
tiptoed across the room.

For a moment, he listened to the rise and fall of Marv's chest
as he approached his bed, then cocked the alarm clock above his
head and brought it crashing down with all his might. The clock
exploded on impact, shattering into shards of plastic and
circuitry that rang through the night, stopping time cold in its
tracks. Marv reacted instinctively, shooting out of bed in a panic
that sent his sheet billowing in the air. Tumbling onto the floor,
he protected his head and hesitated for a heartbeat before scram-
bling toward the door. His hand searched for the knob, and the
instant he found it, he cranked the door open to escape.

"Wait!" Avery begged as a flash of light from the corridor
flooded into the room. "Please don't get help yet. At least not
until I'm done here."

"Done here with what?" Marv flipped on the lights and held
the door open with his heel. He stood there naked except for a
pair of briefs and socks and fought to catch his breath. Marv
stared at his roommate with eyes ringed in shadows, then raked
thick fingers through his wild beard and cleared his throat.
"Avery, what in the fuck is going on here?" he demanded, dragging the question out as he spotted the clock Avery had shattered on the floor.

"Trust me on this, Marv, I have nothing against you. But we
both know that if I told you my plan, you'd try to stop me."
Avery took a step back and raised his palms to show he was no

threat. Taller than most, he had a paddler's physique with broad shoulders, toned arms and strong hands. In his forties, his light-brown skin showed signs of sun damage, especially around his hardened eyes. Large bags sat beneath his eyes, carrying a certain pain. His thick, wavy hair—once naturally dark—showed signs of early graying that paired nicely with his hazel eyes.

"I'm so confused. Stop you from doing what?"

"Take a wild guess." Avery circled his bed, casually flipped his mattress onto the floor and reached for his pillow.

Marv whistled as the pillow sailed into the corner, then he walked over to his dresser and grabbed the first shirt he could find. "All I see here is you destroying our room," he said, slipping into a vintage Iron Maiden tee. "Have you been staying on top of your meds?"

Avery rolled his eyes as he passed his desk, nonchalantly toppled his chair and picked up a coverless sci-fi novel he had lost interest in ages ago. He tore the title page from the book and tossed the crumpled wad over his shoulder. "Why is it that anytime anyone does something out of the ordinary, everyone immediately assumes they went off their meds?"

"I can't say for certain, but it may have something to do with us living in a mental institution?"

Avery walked over to the windowsill and picked up his black prayer plant. He ran a finger across a silvery blue leaf, admired the emerald blotches on either side of the midrib and then kissed the pot goodbye.

"Don't you do it," Marv said. He took a step forward and held up his hand. "I know you well enough to know you'll regret this tomorrow. Whatever your goal is here, there are better ways to get what you want than—"

"If you know me so well, you'd know it's not what I want but what I don't want." Avery cocked his arm back, closed his eyes and sailed the plant across the room.

Marv winced as the pot shattered against the wall but he kept his eyes fixed on Avery. "You didn't have to do that, but since you did, I hope you know you leave me with no choice. Either tell on yourself or I will because you're not taking me down with you."

Avery opened his eyes and wiped them dry. "I did what I had to, now it's your turn." He turned his back on Marv, walked into their bathroom and locked the door behind him.

Scooting forward in her driver's seat, Lauren glanced through her salty windshield and admired the forest lining the ragged Koʻolau mountain range. With the coming of dawn on the east side of Oʻahu, stirrings of sunlight infiltrated the inhospitable, knife-like ridges that disappeared into a lingering cloud cover.

Lauren's sharp emerald eyes flashed between the road and the cliffs as a crosswind from her open window whipped her hair across her heart-shaped face. She brushed the black strands away and cursed as she bounced violently in the torn seat of her Wrangler. Lauren glanced in her rearview mirror at the two-lane road snaking behind her and registered the newest pothole brought to the surface by a recent flash flood. Moments later, it disappeared behind a bend, but not before she committed its location to memory, hoping to avoid a future surprise down the road.

Turning her attention back to the road ahead, Lauren wondered what a new day at Hale Maluhia would bring. She came to a stop as she approached a moss-covered sally port of the psychiatric hospital and, with her free hand, flashed a delaminating employee badge to the security guard before swapping it for a cup of coffee.

A retired marine, Cap had an alertness born from a high-stress career full of pressure, precision and a fair share of pain. Clean cut and shaven, he had a full head of silver hair, bushy eyebrows and cold eyes. As Lauren's first and last human interaction at the start and end of each day, he also had a special place in her heart.

"For me?" he asked as he received the drink with both hands. "I appreciate it, but you know you didn't have to."

"I know, but I wanted to," Lauren said, tilting her head out her window. She smiled calmingly and stared at Cap for a moment. "Promise not to take this the wrong way, but you look like you could really use a nice, long vacation."

"Vacation?" Cap asked, turning to his coffee. "What's that? And where does one even go when home is paradise?" He set the cup down and squinted at his wristwatch. "Trust me, the only place I want to go to right now is home to sleep, but you know I can't abandon my post just 'cause my replacement is running late."

"What's gotten into him lately?" Lauren asked.

"Beats me," Cap said, a bit annoyed. "But what I do know is that if he doesn't start taking his job seriously, they'll find someone else who will."

"Is this something you need my help with?"

He turned away as another car pulled up behind Lauren. "No, not yet," he said, punching a button that set an old wrought-iron gate into motion. "Let me try talking with him once more and see if I can't appeal to his senses. God bless him, he's got a family to feed."

"Then maybe he should act like it." Lauren shifted into gear and passed the gate as she entered the Hawai'i State Hospital. She took her time easing over a series of speed bumps, then turned into the asphalt parking lot and backed into her reserved stall. Lowering herself down onto the side steps of her Jeep, she waited while a late-model Toyota eased into the stall beside her.

From her vantage point, Lauren watched as her secretary collected manilla folders from her passenger seat and took her time getting out.

"Need a hand?" Lauren asked as she jumped down and

circled Gail's car. Before Gail could refuse, Lauren placed her coffee in the crook of her elbow and pulled Gail's door open.

Gail flashed a weathered smile and clutched the paperwork against her frail torso as a breeze billowed her sun dress. White hair swirled about, revealing sun spots on her high cheekbones. Once the breeze passed, her bangs dropped and settled like curtains. She stepped aside to allow Lauren to close the door behind her, and as the two of them headed for the steps, Lauren insisted on taking a load out of Gail's arms.

Swiping her badge at the entrance, Lauren allowed Gail in first, then followed in stride through a long, tiled corridor that ran parallel to the Step-Down Ward. The ward housed several low-security patients in a community program, most of whom lived in anticipation of the day they could reintegrate back into the community.

The two women hooked a corner at the end of the corridor and entered a cramped office they shared. Gail took a seat at her desk and began completing the last round of monthly court letters for each patient in the program, a continuation of the work she brought home last night. Lauren headed to her desk in the back corner and began digesting a nursing report left for her by the night shift crew.

The report read like cliff notes on the previous night's events. Lauren scanned the text for potential fires waiting to be extinguished and held her breath when processing that Dylan's younger brother had been in a car crash in Las Vegas. Fortunately, the brother was both alive and stable, but knowing Dylan, he could take it either way. Lauren then noted that Kalani had yet another med refusal and made a note to address this developing pattern with the treatment team before it became a habit. Several patients returned on time from their field trip to an off-campus AA meeting, and those who stayed behind were recorded as baseline, which was always a good sign. Everything else seemed to be business as usual until she digested the last note.

She rubbed her brow and read the note on Avery a second time before rising to her feet and starting for the exit. As she passed Gail's desk, a lanky Psychiatric Security Attendant knocked on the open door.

"Mornin' Lauren. Mornin' Gail." Sam rubbed his dark wrinkled hands together and flashed a seasoned smile. "Before I punch out, I wanted to drop in and see if you reviewed last night's report?"

Lauren placed her hand on the edge of Gail's desk and nodded. "I did and I'm actually on my way to check on Avery now. So I saw you were around during his outburst?"

"I was in the community room when it popped off and was the first PSA on scene." Sam scratched his beard and smiled at Gail, undeterred, who continued with her work. "I'm not sure what to make of it. It's so out of character for him."

Lauren slowly shook her head. "Was Marv in the room when it happened?"

Sam nodded. "He's the one who brought it to my attention, but he wasn't involved as far as I could tell."

Lauren smiled and pushed off the desk. "I'm going to check on him. I have an idea what this is about."

Sam nodded and stepped back into the corridor. "Want me to escort you? In case there's another outburst."

"I appreciate that, but it's not necessary."

"You sure? Even though he wasn't violent last night, he was destructive, and we both know there's a thin line between the two."

Lauren waved him off. "I'm sure we'll be fine. Knowing Avery, he's lashing out at the process, not at me, you or any other person in particular."

"Suit yourself." He waved goodbye to Gail and started down the hall.

Lauren followed at a distance as Sam's heavy boots clunked along the tile. He punched a code into a keypad, and a brief flash of natural light flooded the corridor as he exited the building.

Lauren listened for the door to lock behind her before making her next move.

Without pause, she donned a smile and entered the Step-Down Ward and moved with a purpose to the far back corner where a hallway led to Avery's room. But there was no hiding in the bright lights, and she made it less than ten feet before someone tugged on her sleeve.

"Aloha, Aunty Roberts. Do you have a sec?"

Lauren smiled, knowing that being called Aunty was a sign of respect for one's elders and had little to do with her being thirty-seven. She first heard the term back home in Las Vegas—a city hailed as the "ninth island" by many locals from Hawaiʻi—but it wasn't until she moved to Oʻahu six years ago that anyone thought to use the word on her. "What's going on, Krystal? How are you holding up today?"

Krystal bit her lower lip and held out a piece of paper. "I'm good. Hoping you won't mind signing my money slip."

Lauren took the form from her hands and clicked a pen but paused to inspect Krystal's shoes before scrawling her signature. "This is for another pair? Those look like they still have at least six or seven lives left in them."

"They do, but I figured I'd treat myself to something special. My birthday's right around the corner and a girl needs to celebrate."

Lauren didn't remember as much as she wished she could. Tracking thirty-plus inpatient clients along with a hundred outpatient clients tested her limits. "I'll tell you what," Lauren said, signing the paper. "Take this and sleep on it. If you still feel like it's a good use of your money in the morning, why not treat yourself? You deserve it."

Krystal took the paper and spun on her heels, but by then, a small group had swarmed Lauren and began bombarding her with everything from field trip itineraries to requests to contact their attorneys.

Rising to his tiptoes, a bony native Hawaiian man in his mid-twenties peeked over the crowd and interlocked sinewy hands over his buzzed black hair. His tank top flaunted a petroglyph of a surfer inked into his arm by someone still perfecting their craft. Beneath his boardshorts were a pair of cheap slippers that displayed slightly yellowed toenails picked short rather than clipped.

Kalani continued to skirt the sidelines, nervously vying to get his word in. His uneasy brown eyes darted around the room, and every time he opened his mouth to speak, someone else beat him to it.

"Miss Roberts," he said once everyone dissipated. "I wanted to ask again about tapering off my meds. I know you want me to stay on Depakote, but—"

"Kalani, you've been here long enough that I shouldn't need to explain how this works. I'm more than happy to present your request to the treatment team, but remember, we don't allow anyone to taper off meds in a low-security ward in case things go sideways. That's not to say it will or won't—I'm a therapist, not a doctor—but it's still our policy and there's no way around it."

Kalani stared off into the distance.

"If that's something you're okay with, we can bring it up at our next weekly meeting. Just know what you're asking for because our policies are non-negotiable." Lauren waited for him to make eye contact, and when he finally did, she spotted a dash of uncertainty in his eyes.

"Let me think about it," he said. "I like it here."

"And I enjoy having you here, too. Come find me when you make your decision, and I'll do my best to get you where you want to be, assuming it's in your best interest."

As Kalani retreated to the game room, Lauren cut through the dayroom and headed toward the back of the ward. She passed room after room before approaching the end of the line, knocked on a steel door and waited to be let in. When no one answered, she announced her presence and opened the door.

Lauren held her breath as she casually inspected the bedroom. The space felt reminiscent of most college dorm rooms, except the beds and dressers were bolted to the floor to prevent the making of forts or a possible barricade situation. No curtains over the windows meant no curtain rods to hang oneself from, though blankets and sheets were allowed, as evidenced by them strewn across the floor. Avery's mattress lay folded on the ground next to remnants of books and fragments of a terracotta pot buried in a shallow grave beneath loose dirt.

"Avery?" she called out, stepping forth into the space.

Marv sat up in his bed. "I tried to stop him," he said, placing his novel on his pillow. "But someone wouldn't listen to reason, *would they?*"

Avery stepped out of the bathroom, working his hands against each other. "I already apologized, Marv. What more do you want from me?"

"It's not that I want something *from* you. I want something *for* you, and it all starts with you admitting you're scared of moving out."

"Hi Avery," Lauren said. "I had a feeling that's what this disturbance was about." She took a step forward and picked up a splayed-out Moleskine sketchbook. She turned it over and began flattening a wrinkled page when Avery stepped forth and removed his book from her hands.

"I'll take that," he said.

"What a beautiful drawing." Lauren watched him close the book, peeked into the bathroom and frowned upon seeing his beloved black prayer plant wilting in the sink. "Is it true?" she asked, leaning over so Avery could see her face. "Are you having second thoughts about moving on with your life? Because if you are, that's okay. But this"—Lauren waved her hand at the mess— "this isn't."

Avery opened his mouth but stopped short of responding.

Lauren lowered her voice. "Would you rather head back to my office to talk about it?" She turned around and motioned to

Marv. "Or I'm sure we can have some privacy if you prefer to stay here."

"It's okay," Avery said. "This is Marv's room, too. He can stay if he wants."

"In that case, why don't you tell me what's going on?"

Avery stared at the shattered pot in the corner and barely pieced together a response. "What happens if I don't want to move out?"

Lauren smiled. "Avery, you've been in this hospital for six years, and much longer than that if you count your time spent at the hospital before pleading NGRI. You know the process and understand that transitioning into community housing has always been part of the plan."

"But what if I don't want to?"

"I'm confused." Lauren crouched and picked up a shirt from off the ground. "If you're asking about not going to your upcoming interview at the sober house, then I'd suggest searching for an alternative placement immediately, which includes getting it approved by the review boards, your treatment team and lastly, the court." She placed his folded shirt on his dresser and reached for a pair of pants.

Avery smiled nervously and leaned against the wall. "And what happens if I can't find an alternative placement?"

Lauren folded the pants over her arm and studied his face. "Securing community housing is part of complying with court orders and your treatment recommendation. Is there a reason you don't want to go to this particular sober house?"

Avery stared at the ground. "Not that I can think of."

"Don't forget that part of moving out means moving on," Marv said. "That means being more of a father to Bri and being more involved in your grandson's life."

Avery glanced at Marv like he had taken a cheap shot.

"I have to say he's right. They would love nothing more than that," Lauren added. "Not to mention we both know you don't want to lose your conditional release privileges, which is *exactly* what will happen if you can't secure placement in community housing. You're also looking at revocation of pass privileges, and even possibly getting bumped back into the medium security ward. No one wants that for you, Avery. And for your own sake, I hope you don't want that for yourself, either."

Avery started pacing, stopped himself and sat down on his bunk.

"If you don't know what you want, trust me, that's okay." Lauren approached and squatted beside him. "It's natural to be apprehensive, but you can't let it overwhelm you. Making progress is the driving force of this program, and moving on with your life is what you've spent the better part of these past six years working for, right?"

Avery fluttered his hands as though he didn't have the answer.

"Come on, give yourself credit. You've made it through the highly assaultive ward, where you saw your fair share of excitement," Lauren reminded him. "There's so much progress for you to be proud of. You've completed competency restoration and have shown you can function both in here and out there. You've made it to the final phase of the self-medication program, which reminds me, I should do a med check since I'm here."

Avery stood and headed to the foot of his bed. After a brief struggle with the combination lock on his wooden footlocker, he fetched a plastic pill organizer and passed it to Lauren. She skimmed her finger across a week's worth of flaps and handed it back. "Looks good, but I'm not surprised. You're doing the damn thing, Avery. The hardest part has come and gone, and the sooner you accept this and navigate transitional housing, the sooner you're literally home free."

"But then what?" Avery's gaze skipped over Lauren and landed on Marv.

"Then you live your life," Marv said in a neutral voice.

Avery shook his head. "Easy enough for you to say, but how can I be certain I've really changed? It's one thing to keep it together when I'm under lock and key, but out there . . ." He took a deep breath and winced. "Out there, it's different."

"You're right," Lauren said. "It is different, very different, but nothing you can't handle. And trust me, if I didn't believe that you stood a fighting chance, we wouldn't be having this conversation." Lauren bent down, picked up a crinkled Aloha shirt, gave it a shake and passed it to Avery. "You have until tomorrow to make up your mind, but if I don't hear from you between now and then, I'm going to step out on a limb and assume you made the right decision."

2

SEPTEMBER 30TH

"So what's the plan?" Avery asked. "Are you just going to hang out here until I'm done?"

Lauren nodded and killed the motor. "I've seen these interviews go either way; it all depends on who's home, how well they take to you and how many questions they have." She pulled out her phone and unlocked it. "As for me, I'll be with you in spirit and waiting right here for you when you're done. I have a ton of calls to make so take as long as you need."

Avery popped the door open, stepped down onto the curb and hesitated before closing the door and leaning into the open window. "I feel like I should lean on you for sage advice or something."

Lauren stroked her chin. "I don't know if it's sage or mugwort, but I'll tell you what I tell all my people: just be yourself and you'll be fine."

"That's it?"

She looked at him with the kindest of eyes. "That's my cool, calm and collected way of not stressing you out needlessly, though if you're asking me to expand a bit, I would remind you we've worked with each other for six or seven years now. In that time, you've changed drastically, and even if you can't see it when you look in the mirror, I assure you others can. That means people who knew you in your past life will see your progress because they know how far you've come, but people you meet moving forward will only know the man you are today. One thing you have going for you is you're a good man with a kind heart—even if it is a little rough around the edges—and if you want others to believe in you, all you have to do is be yourself. So long story short, just do you and you'll be fine."

Avery took a deep breath. "I'll do my best."

"I guess that's all you can do." Lauren glanced up from her phone. "Trust me, you'll do great."

"I sure hope so." Avery thumped the side of his fist against the door and started up the narrow driveway.

He approached the beige, two-story home with a stroll and took in his surroundings. A decaying picket fence surrounded a patchy yard where someone took pride in raking the dirt to resemble a Zen garden. A feral rooster in the shade of a palm tree pecked at a pebble and spat it out. At the end of a long driveway blotted with oil stains, an open-air carport bursting with bikes, mopeds, surfboards and boxes gave off classic hoarder vibes.

As he approached the front steps, Avery noticed that while the house seemed dated, it also appeared well cared for by the tenants. Beyond the flaky paint and other home improvements that fell to the landlord, the home seemed tidy and presentable, save for the overflowing ashtray on the porch. A Filipino whisk broom made from the midribs of palm leaves leaned against the wall and Avery's back hurt just from looking at it.

Avery paused, turned back to the yard and procrastinated further by admiring a lone plumeria tree. A galaxy of fallen milk-white flowers peppered the grass, their petals wilting and rotting away. His eyes gravitated toward the trunk where the surrounding soil was soaked from a recent watering. Instinctively, he looked back to Lauren for a final push of reassurance but her face was buried in her phone.

Behind him, a screen door banged and Avery spun around.

A short, beefy Hawaiian man who had seen better days took his time shuffling down the steps. "Whatever you're selling, we no like," he joked, then clapped at the rooster to shoo him away. As the man approached, he scanned Avery up and down and reached out to shake his hand. "I take it you're here for da kine?"

"I am, and appreciate the opportunity." Avery maintained eye contact and shook the man's hand. "You must be Mr. Akoni?"

The man flashed a toothy smile. "Only to the judge and my parole officer. Uncle Earl is fine, and I'm glad to see you're on time. It doesn't make you a shoo-in, but you're off to a good start." After running his hands through his receding hair, Uncle Earl turned and motioned to the front door. "Well, what are we waiting for?"

Uncle Earl headed up the stairs and added his rubber slippers to a massive pile of footwear. Avery followed in his footsteps, kicked off his shoes and closed the door behind him.

"If you don't mind, let's get the interview out of the way and save the house tour for later." Uncle Earl held out a hand and motioned for Avery to step into the living room.

Avery sheepishly entered the room. A folding plastic chair sat idly in front of a TV and faced two mismatched sofas. He silently counted seven residents in all, five split between both couches and two on the floor, their backs against the wall.

Uncle Earl gestured toward the chair. "In case you can't tell, we saved that one for you."

Avery nodded and made himself as comfortable as possible.

"Even though you're all technically required to be here, I want to thank everyone for making it," Uncle Earl said, pacing near the entrance. "I trust we're all doing well and want to introduce Mr. Avery West. He's interviewing to be our next housemate."

Avery raised a hand from his lap and waved, then turned his attention to a gecko skittering across the ceiling.

"Before we start, I should point out that there's more of us than what you see today," Uncle Earl said. "Both Otto and Terrence are at work, so they don't get a vote this time around." He raised a finger and started with the stocky Japanese man sitting to Avery's far left. "Avery, I'd like you to meet Kātisu. Sitting next to him is Haunani and sitting next to her is—"

"Nani is fine love," a māhū woman said. She stiffened and adjusted a spaghetti strap with a smile.

Uncle Earl cleared his throat and pointed to a heavyset Samoan man in his late twenties that filled the rest of the first couch. "Next to Nani is Atonio aka Tino, then we have Rod and Gil, and finally sitting on the floor is Nigel and Berto, Nigel being the sunburned one."

Berto flashed a Shaka along with a set of golden incisors.

"And since we've already met," Uncle Earl continued, "let's get right into it. Now, my main goal with these interviews is pretty straightforward; I want to see that you're a good fit for us and that we're a good fit for you. Sounds good?"

Avery nodded. "Of course."

"Perfect. Then, as House Prez, I guess it makes sense to start with me." He jammed a fat thumb into his chest. "Uncle Earl. Addict. I'm originally from Puna, but I intend to stay on Oʻahu until it spits me out." He wiped his mustache with his hand and nodded at Kātisu.

Kātisu uncrossed his forearms and pulled on the armrest to sit up. His midnight eyes locked onto Avery's and he twisted his beard as he spoke.

"Kātisu. Convict. Nothing against this place or these people, but I can't wait to get the hell out of here."

"Geez, so angry," Nani said. She leaned away from Kātisu and gave Avery her undivided attention. "I know you nevah foget, but once again I'm Nani, which means beautiful flower in Hawaiian. I'm also the Treasurer, so no be late on rent, keh?" She side-eyed Berto while elbowing Kātisu. "And unlike Ebenezah

Scrooge ova hea, I, for one, love dis place." She placed her palm on her chest as if making an oath. "And you will too, especially if you coming from prison, 'cause you can come and go as you like, cook your own meals whenevahs and holoholo all day long. Talk about livin' da dream, plus you get to cruz to the beach. You do like the beach, yah?"

Avery shrugged.

"Perfect, cuz you get Kalamas, Flagpoles, Lanikai—all up da road. Den there's Nalo, Makapuʻu, Baby Maks, Sandys, Cockroach Bay, Chi—"

Uncle Earl raised a hand. "Nani, if you don't mind, we still have a lot to get through."

Nani raised her pointer finger, turned to Avery and whispered, "And no foget China Walls."

Tino chuckled and smiled at Avery. "Howzit. Like Uncle Earl said, I'm Tino. I'm from Maui and—"

"Hey, me too," Avery said, leaning forward. "Sorry, didn't mean to cut you off."

"No worries. It's always nice to meet someone from back home. What town?"

"Kihei."

"Killah. I'm from Lahaina. So what school did you go to? Baldwin High?"

"Maui High, until I dropped out," Avery said. "But that's another story."

"I bet." Tino turned to Rod, who introduced himself before passing the torch to Gil. Though the oldest in the bunch, Gil's loud outfit spoke of being young at heart. From his tie-dye shirt to billowing hemp trousers, he appeared at peace with himself, the universe and his fleeting place in it.

Gil shifted in his seat and pinched his lips together. His flecked, sky-blue eyes reflected a weathered kindness. "Aloha," he said. "It's nice to meet you. I go by Gil, and I guess I'm from nowhere in particular." He broke eye contact and studied the cramped living room with apparent dismay. "Unfortunately though, I appear to be stuck here for the time being since I had a terrible public defender, and nowadays it seems you really get what you pay for."

Avery wasn't sure how to respond, so he thought it best not to.

The last two men on the floor took it upon themselves to introduce one another. Berto got a kick out of the experience, relishing in the insults cast by Nigel and returning them in kind. Despite at least a twenty-year gap in age—though not in maturity—Avery related to their bond and immediately presumed they were roommates.

Uncle Earl let the charade play out a little longer before ending it. "Now that you know a bit about us—perhaps more than you'd like to—what brings you here?" he asked.

Avery swallowed and rubbed a hand on his thigh. "I guess I'm hoping you all will take me in as one of your own."

"I understand you're interviewing to move in, but what I meant was . . . *what* brings you here? No one ups and moves into a halfway house just for fun. Are you on probation? Parole? Are you homeless and looking to get off the streets? Or maybe you're transitioning to community housing from inpatient treatment?"

Avery wiped his mouth. "Yeah, something like that."

"'Something like that' doesn't really tell me anything. Can you be a bit more specific?" Uncle Earl asked, noticing Avery eyeing the exit. He stepped to his left to cut off Avery's view. "You alright?"

"Define 'alright.'" Avery pulled his knees together and turned to face Uncle Earl. "Sorry, I'm not used to being put on the spot. It's a lot to take in."

"Unfortunately, that's the nature of an interview, but hang in there. I know it can seem intimidating but it doesn't have to be. We're all friends here and we've all been in your seat."

Avery scanned the room and Nani caught his eye as she

exhaled a deep breath while motioning for him to do the same. He closed his eyes and pictured a blistering shadow on the sun, then filled his lungs with an expanse of stale air.

"I've been under lock and key for some time now," Avery said, opening his eyes. "It's been a rough ride, but I think I'm at the point where I'm prepared to move on with my life. However, in order for me to do so, I need to secure community housing." He leaned back in his chair and hoped they found his statement satisfactory.

Tino took it upon himself to break the silence. "Where were you held? MCCC?"

Avery shook his head. "I left Maui when I was about your age. I figured too many people back home will never step foot off that rock, and I refused to be one of them."

"Fair enough," Tino said simply.

"So you came here from Maui?" questioned Kātisu. "Why would anyone in their right mind swap one rock for another?"

"Why wouldn't they?" Tino wondered aloud. "I made the same move myself and there's not a lot of other options when you live in the most isolated land mass in the world."

Avery knew Tino's heart was in the right place, but he didn't see the need to be defended. He cleared his throat and addressed Kātisu. "I moved here with my daughter when she was four. Her mother wasn't doing her any favors and we both needed a fresh start."

"And where'd you end up?"

"Makiki to start, but we moved all over the island trying to keep our heads above water."

"And then?"

"And then what?"

Kātisu cocked his head. "Where were you locked up? OCCC? FDC? Halawa?"

Avery leaned back in his chair. "It gets complicated."

"Not to someone who knows the deal."

Avery took a shallow breath and wet his lips.

"How long were you incarcerated for?" Kātisu asked.

"About seven years, give or take."

"Where? Here on Oʻahu?"

Avery nodded.

"Seven years straight?"

Avery nodded again.

"Then that takes both OCCC and FDC off the table."

Tino leaned forward. "What are you talking about? Get choke guys doing hard time at the detention center."

"Yeah, but he said 'straight' and most federal detainees get shuffled around every few years. They're always getting shipped to the mainland and wind up at Victorville or Dublin or wherever." Kātisu turned back to Avery. "At the FDC, what floor and which side were you housed in?"

Avery leaned forward. "I served time at the Oʻahu Community Correctional Center."

"Not seven years you didn't," Kātisu said hotly. "OCCC houses pretrial defendants, but at the end of the day, it's still a jail. Any sentence longer than a year and you're taking a ride to the valley, the same valley where I just served an open five." He squinted and crossed his arms. "Halawa Correctional Facility is big, but not so big that we wouldn't have crossed paths before. So where were you really?"

"Nuff already," Uncle Earl said, pushing off the wall. "Avery, this needs to be an interview, not an interrogation. Don't forget you came to us so help us help you and please don't make us work for it. All we're trying to figure out is who you are and where you came from."

"Don't say Halawa," Kātisu warned. "Unless you were in the SHU or PC the whole time, but if that's the case, I want to see paperwork cuz I don't rock with chomos or rapists."

"Kātisu." Uncle Earl held up a hand to calm him down. "Avery, there's no reason to make this difficult. If any group can relate to where you're coming from, it's us right here."

"Not if he's one sex offender."

Nani held out a palm. "We mek mistakes, but we not mistakes, keh?"

Avery eyed the exit once more. "I'm sorry and don't mean to be difficult. I'm just not sure where to start."

"You can start by answering the question," Kātisu demanded as anger flashed over him. "Because now I think you're hiding something like one rat."

Avery flinched and leaned forward. "No, of course not."

"Then who are you? Because I can google you right now or tap into the coconut wireless and find out what you're hiding." Kātisu placed an iPhone on his armrest and tapped the screen. "It's all public record."

Avery stared at the phone and sat in his chair. He waited for the right words to formulate, but nothing came.

Rod broke the silence first. "Don't forget there's a fourth option—Hale Maluhia."

"The Loony Bin?" Berto asked, turning to face Avery. "You lōlō?"

Nigel reached out and smacked him on the arm.

"Knock it off, you two." Uncle Earl turned and studied Avery's face, then took a step forward and looked out the window. "I thought I recognized your friend. She brought someone here for an interview back when I first moved in. She's your therapist, right? What's the first part again?"

Avery glanced at the window. "She's a forensic therapist."

"Which makes you NGRI."

"Wats dat?" Nani asked.

"Not guilty by reason of insanity." Nigel wrapped his arms around his knees and leaned forward. "What was your crime?" he asked. "Murder?"

Uncle Earl turned and observed Avery.

Avery shook his head.

"Are you sure?"

"I'm positive."

Uncle Earl rubbed his forehead and closed his eyes. "Look, you might have all the time in the world, but we don't. Why not just tell us what you're guilty of so we can get to the house vote and make a decision?"

Avery crossed his legs and thought for a moment. "Technically speaking, I'm not 'guilty' of any offense because an NGRI plea is an acquittal."

"But you were still sentenced, right?"

"Yes, then I was remanded to the hospital."

"I've heard all I need to, which wasn't much. My vote is no." Kātisu rose out of his seat and headed for the exit. "On second thought, my vote is actually fuck no."

Uncle Earl held out a palm to cut him off, but Kātisu brushed past him and stormed out of the room. Turning back to face Avery, Uncle Earl said, "Normally, I would ask you to step outside while we take a house vote, but in a case like this, I see nothing to vote on. What it comes down to is this—if you can't be honest with yourself, I don't see how you can ever be honest with anyone else. Good luck out there."

Avery avoided all eye contact as he rose out of his chair and headed for the exit.

"These things happen," Lauren said, "and you're not doing anyone a favor by beating yourself up over it. Part of life is navigating the highs and lows, and the only way you'll ever make it through them is if you keep moving forward."

Avery continued to stare at his reflection in the window as the Jeep barreled down the road. "How am I supposed to move forward when I just botched my one shot at moving out? Where do I even go from here?"

"Back to the hospital to regroup and once you're ready, you work the phones and try again."

"Try again?" He let out a heavy sigh. "What's the use?"

"I'm not even going to dignify that with a response."

Avery twisted to face her. "But you just did."

Lauren smiled and turned down a side road.

"Seriously though, I knew this would happen. What a waste of time. I should have known they wouldn't want anything to do with me."

"Oh, I highly doubt that. Otherwise, why would they have offered you an interview?"

Avery folded his arms over his stomach. "I never stood a chance. Had I led with where I was coming from, they wouldn't have let me set foot inside the house. But when I hold back and hope they'll take the time to get to know me, I'm shown the door because I'm seen as being manipulative."

"I think you're looking at this situation all wrong." Lauren changed lanes and veered into a rundown parking lot. "This is all part of the process. For some, it's easier than others, but whatever your path is and wherever it takes you, we will get through it together. That said, all this fatalistic talk like it's the end of the world is getting you nowhere." She let the motor die, popped her seatbelt and grabbed the door handle. "Sorry if that comes off as disparaging. You have every right to be upset, and it's human nature to get lost in hindsight, especially when things didn't pan out how you hoped they would. In the end though, you took your shot, and that's what really matters. Also, don't forget that if anyone understands why you went in there the way you did, it's me. Had the roles been reversed, I can't say for certain that I would have approached the interview any differently."

Avery sat there for a moment, then popped open his door. "Why am I sensing you brought me somewhere to cheer me up?"

"Maybe because you know me too well?" Lauren got out and circled the hood. "How's Bubble Tea sound?"

Avery shrugged.

"What's wrong?" she asked. "Not feeling it?"

"I think I have a hard time feeling anything right now."

"That's too bad, though it's on me if you change your mind." Lauren led the way through the parking lot with Avery clambering behind. When they approached a small storefront, she held the door open and waited to see his reaction.

A bell dinged against the glass and Avery side-stepped a wet floor sign. He studied the illuminated menu behind the counter, then glanced at Lauren. "Say I did want something, do you have any suggestions?"

"That's the spirit." Lauren touched her chin and scanned the offerings. "I would say you can't go wrong with Honeydew or Winter Melon."

"What about the lychee? I used to lean over the fence and pluck those off my neighbor's tree every summer."

"Can't go wrong there, especially if it takes you back." Lauren placed their order with an elderly Thai woman and motioned for Avery to join her at a small table. "I really am sorry that things didn't work out the way you had hoped back there, but try not to let it get you down. I have no doubt that you'll find a place eventually and all will work out."

"But what if it doesn't?" Avery asked.

"It has to."

"What makes you so certain?"

Lauren tapped the table. "Because you've done your time and you deserve it. You're not gravely disabled and there's no reason you can't make it on your own, especially with a strong support system and treatment plan. You've also responded well to treatment, been med-compliant and haven't experienced an episode in how many years?"

"Longer than I remember."

"Exactly, so there's no rational reason to extend your stay. Remember, the system is far from perfect and as much as we love having you around, we don't want to keep you forever. Not to mention, we have a continuous flow of new patients needing a place to stay and we need somewhere to put them."

"But what if the court revokes my conditional release because I failed to secure housing?"

"Miss? Your order."

Lauren jumped out of her seat and grabbed their drinks. She returned with extra napkins and placed Avery's tea in front of him.

Avery took a sip and nearly choked on a tapioca pearl. He raised the cup to inspect the sunken balls swirling in the slurry. "So what if the court revokes my—"

"That won't happen, or at least I'd be very surprised if it did. Of course, no one can guarantee what the courts will or won't do, but that's why we keep moving forward and plugging away. No good fighter ever wants to leave it in the hands of the judges, right?" Lauren took another sip and nodded approvingly. "What I can guarantee, though, is that I'll have your back as long as you're in the fight. As long as you don't give up, I'll be in your corner." She took one more sip and dabbed her napkin on the corners of her mouth. "Actually, who am I kidding? Even if you toss in the towel, I'll still fight for you."

Avery glanced down at his drink and took a sip. He chewed on another pearl and when he thought back to the last physical fight he had been in, the memory left a bad taste in his mouth like sucking on pennies. It didn't matter that the incident led to him getting help or meeting someone like Lauren with an endless commitment to him. As a result, he lost years of his life, and no amount of support would ever make up the difference.

Upon returning to the hospital, Avery thanked Lauren and told her not to worry about him. He kept his head down and cut through the communal areas, refusing to answer any and all questions. Then, bypassing his room, he steered straight for a heavy steel door leading to an open-air courtyard.

High above him, a cluster of Java Sparrows swooped through the late morning sun. The flock bounced between swaying palms and copper gutters, occasionally colliding in midair as they bill-clicked between them to woo one another. Avery leaned against the door and watched them feed off each other's energy before disappearing behind the rooftop.

The chatter of approaching patients broke his concentration, and he turned to spot two women walking laps around the perimeter. To avoid any possibility of small talk, he crossed the courtyard seeking solace in the only place he knew he could find it.

The flimsy greenhouse door squeaked open as Avery entered the building and he stepped on a disinfectant mat to sanitize his shoes. An older man in the middle of watering the plants glanced to see who had joined him and lazily waved with his free hand. Though Avery worked in and managed the greenhouse alone, policy demanded a vocational supervisor during all work hours, and that's where Benny came in. Despite what the staff implied, the mandate was less about accountability and more about the handling of sharp instruments such as secateurs, sickles and shears.

In his late sixties, Benny was a gentle giant with droopy eyelids, wrinkles everywhere and the look of a life well lived. His unofficial uniform consisted of cargo shorts and a knitted Polo shirt which looked far too hot for the day. He would often pass shifts without rising from his seat except to move out of the sun, and even then he moped about, clutching his chair behind him as though afraid someone might steal it out from under him.

Benny sauntered over to the spigot and turned off the hose. "Didn't expect you to be back so soon," he said.

"Yeah, me neither." Even though Benny had his back to him, Avery looked away and forced a smile. "Thanks again for helping out in my absence. I'm sure the plants appreciate it as well."

"You're welcome." He finished coiling the hose, turned around and thumbed his belt. "So, will you tell me how your interview went or make me find out through the coconut wireless?"

Avery's voice went flat. "It went about as well as expected."

"You don't sound too excited. Want to talk about it?"

"No, not really. Not when it won't change a thing."

"Well, if you change your mind, you know where to find me." Benny walked over to his seat and groaned as he took some weight off his feet. He stretched for a novel under his chair and delved again into his own world.

Avery navigated toward his workbench in the back and told himself that since the work never ended, the surrounding work could wait. He swung a leg over his wooden stool, kept his back to Benny and the door then thought about his future.

Aware he possessed a personality type prone to depression, Avery tried not to imagine the worst-case scenario but he couldn't quite help himself. Taking it a step further, he compared both outcomes of him staying put in the hospital and him moving out, and for the first time he imagined himself growing feeble in the institution like Benny. He wondered what value he placed on the safeguards of being a patient and if those protections outweighed the sacrifice of life passing him by. Then he debated the alternative of moving out and taking himself with him and what it would mean if he fell flat on his face.

It was an interesting debate, but one he didn't think to fruition because the outcome of his interview meant no illusion of choice remained. He couldn't move out with nowhere to go—that much he accepted—but to go from not wanting to move out to not having the opportunity gave him pause long enough to question his heart's desire. At that moment, he realized securing housing had little to do with having a roof over his head, making Lauren happy, complying with his treatment recommendations or even appeasing the judge. Instead, he realized it was about reclaiming his story and his role in the lives of those he loved. It was about his daughter and grandson being able to visit him without driving through a sally port.

And now that he could see the forest for the trees, he realized what he had lost. He understood he would beat himself up over this missed opportunity for days to come. But rather than run from it, he welcomed the self-loathing. Knowing the pain would keep his mind busy, he rested his head on his crossed arms and fell into the age-old trap of feeling sorry for himself.

3

OCTOBER 7TH

One Week Later

Avery opened the door to his room and looked down at Lauren standing in the hallway.

"You got a minute?" she asked.

He stepped into the hallway and closed his door behind him.

"I know it's been a hectic week," she said, "but I wanted to check in with you and see how things are going. Any updates?"

He ran his fingers through his wavy hair and peered down the hall. "All things considered, I'm hanging in there, but as far as making any progress, I honestly don't know what to tell you." He dropped his hand and leaned against the wall.

"How many places have you called?"

Avery thought for a moment. "Enough to be discouraged."

"That's not good. Here, take this." She removed a piece of paper and unfolded it. "Maybe it'll help you get back on track. It's a list of all the housing options I could find. Some are stepping stones and some are better than others."

He scanned the paper, then tried to hand it back. "I've already tried my luck with most of these places."

"But not all of them?"

Avery sighed, then glanced at the list again. "No."

"Good. That means you still have your work cut out for you."

He winced and bit into his lower lip. "I don't know, Lauren. Your optimism is normally infectious, but I don't see the point in trying anymore."

She shot him a determined look. "To me, that sounds a lot like you're giving up. I hope that's not the case, not with how far you've come."

"Honestly, I don't know how far I've come. My earliest memories here are blurry at best."

"Which to be fair, isn't uncommon." Lauren moved a bit closer. "In my experience, most patients struggle with processing their thought disorders, especially near the onset of their condition—to the point where they lack the capacity to even comprehend they are ill. Regardless, you have every right to be frustrated, but what you don't have is the luxury of giving up on yourself. Therefore, it is my professional opinion that you do yourself a favor and get your head back in the game."

He flapped the paper against his calloused palm. "I can't help but think it's all a waste of time, but if it'll make you happy—"

"Don't worry about making me happy. This is about your future, not mine." She pointed at the paper. "Those aren't just random numbers you're holding. That's the next step in your treatment plan, which is key to you playing a bigger role in both Bri and Micah's lives. Isn't that what you want?"

He softened at the thought of his daughter and grandson. "I'll make a few calls but I can't guarantee I won't get discouraged."

Lauren studied him for a moment. "Sounds like a plan, and if you could use a bit of moral support or ever want to use my office phone to have some privacy, just say the word."

"Thanks, but I'm sure you have your hands full with a million other things."

"True, but if you change your mind, let me know."

Avery watched Lauren disappear down the hallway for a moment before taking off in the opposite direction. He kept to himself until he reached the dayroom and moved with a purpose toward a lone square table in the far corner. With the back of his hand, he brushed a few magazines aside and reached for the corded phone.

He started with the third number from the list, having already been supposedly waitlisted by the first two locations. After the sixth ring and no answer, he gathered his thoughts to leave a message, only to discover the voicemail inbox was full. So he hung up and drew an ominous question mark next to the number.

Someone approached Avery from behind and tapped his shoulder. "Got time for a game?" Kalani asked. "I've been practicing my Scandinavian Defense." He rattled a box of chess pieces and tried to place it in Avery's hands.

Avery refused to take the bait and instead reached for the phone. "Try me again after dinner. In case you can't see, I'm a little busy right now."

Kalani leaned over his shoulder and studied the list. "You thinking of moving out?"

"At this point, what I think doesn't seem to matter."

"Either way, you deserve it." Kalani placed the chessboard down and motioned for the list. "May I?"

Avery picked up the game and pressed it back into Kalani's chest. "Not right now. I have momentum on my side and can't afford to lose it."

"You sure? Maybe I can save you some time?"

Avery shifted in his seat. "How so?"

"A lot of those 'sober living homes' are flop houses in disguise. Why waste your time trying to get into a place notorious for taking advantage of its residents?"

Avery placed the game down and slid the list to Kalani.

"Can I see your pen?" Kalani asked, then scratched out a third of the phone numbers and tore one from the page. "You're better off dying in here than moving into that hellhole. My cousin stayed there for a few months after being paroled and hated every second. I hear the owner is a real slumlord who belongs in jail, and it's not like the housemates were any better. If they weren't constantly loaded, they were stealing from each other and you don't need that drama in your life." He returned the list to Avery and searched for a partner to play against.

Avery reached for the phone and dialed the number anyway.

"Hello, how are you? My name is Avery West, and I'm calling from Hale Maluhia State Hospital. I'm a patient here and need to secure housing that satisfies the level of care mandated for my court-approved discharge. I'm wondering if you have any openings available and if so, could you tell me how to apply?" He gave it a moment, then released his breath in dismay. "What about a waitlist?"

The man on the other end hung up before Avery could thank him for his time. Then, frustrated, he called another number and asked for the name of the person who answered before he introduced himself. He did this with the logic that some semblance of accountability would humanize his experience. Yet when the rejection came, he took it as personally as before, further losing faith in the promise that he would be kept in mind if something opened up.

Of all the gatekeepers he spoke with, only one gave him the time of day, though the questions felt somewhat disingenuous. The man asked a series of invasive questions about Avery's disorder, each phrased in a manner that laid bare his stereotypes. Avery found himself explaining the critical differences between schizoaffective and dissociative identity disorders—and how they aren't the same—but cut the conversation short when asked how he could guarantee he wouldn't torch the house with the residents inside.

Rising to his feet, Avery made the long trip back to his room with a pang in his belly and an overwhelming desire to sleep through dinner.

4

OCTOBER 10TH

Kalani picked up his plastic chair and held it overhead as he weaved through the dayroom. He pardoned himself and bumped knees until he finally reached Avery, then placed the chair next to him and skipped the small talk. "What happened last night?" he asked. "You left me hanging. I thought we'd squeeze in a few bullet games after dinner, but Marv mentioned something about you refusing to get out of bed."

Avery kept his voice low as Lauren began taking roll call. "Bullet games are fine for honing concentration and instinct, but not so much for learning. If you're deep diving into established chess theory, it's best to take your time and think things through." He raised his hand when Lauren called his name. "Otherwise, you're bound to make the same mistake repeatedly and never improve."

"Fine, let's play a few regular games after the community meeting. You can be White."

"Appreciate the offer, but I'm only here because I have to be. The moment I'm free to go, it's off to bed."

"Come on. How do you expect me to improve my rank if I can't get any practice in?" Kalani turned at the sound of his name and waved at Lauren.

"I suppose one option is to play with yourself. If anyone gives you grief or tries to up your meds, just tell them that's how Bobby Fischer taught himself the game." Avery cracked a smile and glanced around the room. His best guesstimate of no less than thirty souls in the mix seemed conservative. "How is it that with all these men and women, not a single one of them wants to play with you? Marv has never turned down a game, not as long as I've known him. Same goes for Dylan, Holly, Krys—"

"Krystal won't play with me until I pay her back, and for the rest of them, what's the use?" Kalani shuffled his feet on the floor. "I've given up on Holly ever learning the rules and Dylan can't sit still long enough to make it through an end game. Call me old-fashioned, but I see no point in shooting fish in a barrel."

Avery scanned the tightly packed dayroom and questioned the logic behind the barrel analogy, specifically why anyone in their right mind would waste a bullet on a fish that's already been caught. Spiking the brain with a dive knife would be just as quick and save destroying the meat with entrance and exit wounds. He then wondered whether the resulting shock wave from a bullet breaking the surface would send the whole shoal to meet their maker, only to conclude he had too much time on his hands.

"How are we all doing today?" Lauren asked, commanding everyone's attention as she and Sam addressed the room. The pair stood shoulder to shoulder in front of a picture window that looked out onto the courtyard. "Thank you," she said as the chatter calmed down. "That makes our jobs a lot easier. As always, Sam and I will do our best to get through this as fast as we can, so please do your best to stick with us. And before we start, I have some bad news to share this week, so as always, would you like it now or later?"

Lauren gave the room a moment to vote and used a finger to count about twenty hands in favor of hearing the bad news first. "In that case, I'm sorry to say the field trip on Friday is canceled because we have not one, but two PSAs out with the flu."

The room booed, and Sam motioned for everyone to knock it off.

"Boo all you want," Lauren said, "especially if you want me to skip the good news altogether." She flipped a page and smiled as the room grew quiet. "Much better. So the good news is we're rescheduled for next week Friday. The tickets are transferable, though we'll probably have to pick a different movie. As soon as I get the lineup and showtimes from the theater, we'll take another vote."

A man in the back of the room raised his hand. "I have to work next Friday. Does that mean I'll get a refund?"

"Or a voucher, just let me know what you prefer. Any more questions?" Lauren scanned the room. "Next up is everyone's favorite—vocational news." She flipped a page on her clipboard and searched the crowd for a face. "Congratulations, James. I know it's been a long time coming, but you're starting in the warehouse next week. Please find me after this meeting and we'll get you squared away. Now, where's Kalani?"

Sam pointed him out, and Kalani gripped the edge of his seat.

"You asked and we listened. Effective immediately, you're the new greenhouse assistant until Avery moves out and you take over."

Lauren glanced up from her clipboard and met Avery's stare. She winked assuringly and flipped a page.

"Wait. Does that mean I'm out of the laundry room?" Kalani asked.

Lauren nodded without looking up. Once she took requests for haircuts, Kalani scooted his seat closer to Avery. "Did you hear that? Your future replacement. Who would have thought, Boss?"

"I'm not your boss." Avery rubbed his eyes and let out a weak laugh. "You requested to come work in my greenhouse? Why?"

"Have you ever worked in the laundry room?"

"No, but you can't kill a pillowcase if you don't know what you're doing. Do you even know the first thing about horticulture?"

"No, but how hard can it be? Especially with such a great teacher."

Avery turned to face him. "You should have asked me first."

"But you would have said no."

"Exactly, because I need a qualified replacement to take my place, not someone like you. No offense."

Kalani jerked his head back. "You don't think I'm up for the job?"

Avery opened his mouth to respond but knew words wouldn't change anything. So instead, he listened to Lauren explain the details of the upcoming Super Bowl party and raised his hand to contribute five dollars to the pizza party. Kalani followed suit, and Avery pulled his hand down.

"I thought you just said you owed Krystal money."

Kalani took his hand back and cleared his throat. "What do you have against me?"

"You may think that's the case, but keeping a greenhouse in order is not something you pick up overnight. It takes knowledge and passion; you either got it or don't. Besides, all jobs pay the same minimum wage, so why switch?"

Kalani sat up tall. "Because I figured I could make your life easier and learn a thing or two while I'm at it."

"What makes you think you can make my life eas—"

"Thanks again for your time," Lauren said, shoving the clipboard under her arm. "I'll see you all back here next week. Same time, same place."

Avery got up to leave.

"Wait, one more thing before you go," Kalani said. "Care to make a bet for Sunday? I'll cover the spread."

Avery drew his head back. "One, I don't bet, and two, how can you possibly cover anything when you're broke?"

5

OCTOBER 11TH

"Morning, Boss." Kalani entered the flat arched greenhouse as the door bounced on its squeaky hinges. He hadn't stepped foot into the structure before, though like most of the population, he had peered through the polycarbonate panels in the past out of curiosity or boredom.

Avery looked up from a tomato plant and pointed his pruning shears at Kalani. "I'm not your boss and stop right there." He kicked back his stool and skirted past Benny, who pulled his leg back to let him by. As Avery approached Kalani and pointed to the sanitizing footbath mat by the door, Benny returned to his book and leaned back in his chair.

Kalani looked at the mat, down at his slippers and back to Avery. "I don't understand."

"That's to disinfect and sanitize your shoes . . . which are where?"

Kalani wiggled his toes in his slippers. "Is this not a garden? We always go barefoot in the lo'i."

"This may be a garden, but it's also a workplace," Avery said.

"No problem. Want me to run back to my room and grab my boots?"

"No. Just sanitize those and please dress appropriately next time." Avery watched Kalani step out of his slippers, hold them by the straps and swish them in the thin solution one at a time. "Be sure to do this before you or anyone else enters the growing area. I know it's not perfect, but it's better than nothing."

Kalani stepped back into his slippers and began walking through the workspace. Rows of plants and flowers lined the three-tiered shelves that ran the length of each wall. Grow beds bursting with edibles filled most of the usable space beneath hanging plants that wept droplets of water onto the walkway below.

Avery squeezed around Kalani and returned to the seeding table in the back. He finished pruning the stem and inspected his work with a keen eye before setting the plant aside.

Kalani dropped his elbows onto the table and watched as Avery dipped his shears into a solution. "What's that? Oil?"

Avery shook his shears dry and held them out for Kalani to see. "Isopropyl alcohol. Helps to prevent the spreading of disease pathogens from one plant to the next."

Kalani reached across the table and grabbed the tomato plant. "Don't look diseased to me."

"That's the idea, and your first lesson; it's good practice not to trust what you can and can't see with your eyes." Avery took the plant back and reached for another tomato starter.

"So, what are we doing today?"

Avery clipped a leafy stem off the plant and held it out for Kalani to see. "We call these suckers or side shoots," he said. "I'm pruning them so they don't grow out of hand and slow the development of the fruit."

"What fruit?" Kalani asked, standing up. "I thought tomatoes were vegetables."

"It depends on who you ask, but the prevailing wisdom is they're both." Avery picked up the pair of tomato plants and placed them on a shelf, then turned around and wiped his hands on his apron. "Let's move on. We have a lot to get through today."

Kalani beamed with excitement. "So you've finally decided to teach me everything you know?"

"No, but I'll teach you what I can with the time I have left and hope you soak it up. Just do me a favor and don't make me repeat myself; I would hate for the med team to see me babbling and adjust my meds on account of you." Avery cracked a smile, returned to the table and sat on his stool.

"What changed your mind?"

Avery studied his hands and began scraping dirt from beneath his fingernails. "As the head plantsman here—or I guess *only* plantsman, really—my job is so much more to me than growing edibles for the kitchen or raising orchids to sell to the public. This vocation is therapeutic and gets me moving in a space where I belong. It gives me a chance to get my hands dirty in a good way, and boost serotonin levels, all while caring for something other than myself. I've grown a lot in this greenhouse, and figure you can too, as long as you put in the work." Avery paused and admired what he had built. "I thought about this a lot last night, and my fear is this attitude of yours where 'everything will work out in time' will be your downfall if you let it. So I suggest the sooner you become a realist the better because you won't make it if you kick back, let Mother Nature run her course and hope for the best."

Kalani planted his feet in a wide stance. "I can do that," he said. "Especially since I felt no purpose in the laundry room. Some people thrive in the mundane, and good for them, but that's not me. I go stir crazy in there. The workload is borderline maddening, and I can only spin my wheels for so long before I get burned out." Kalani rapped his knuckles on the table. "I'm here to work, and you can count on me."

Having liked what he heard, Avery kicked back his stool and began giving Kalani a tour that quickly branched out into a crash course. First, he pointed out where things belonged and the importance of staying organized in a cramped space. Then he threw the book at Kalani, starting with plant identification, including scientific and common names and ending with an overview of traditional propagating techniques. Next, he made Kalani get his hands dirty as they touched on everything from soil structure to soil additives to nutrient deficiencies and fertilizer mixes. Then the pair turned to pests and diseases, and Avery ended by driving home basic nursery hygiene and making Kalani parrot everything he heard back to him.

Kalani leaned against a shelf and wiped his brow. "I had no idea how complicated your work is, especially when you make it sound so easy."

Avery stretched and cracked his knuckles. "Don't forget, this is how I made my living long before I got sick and ever stepped foot in a hospital. So I think it's only natural I picked it up where I left off." He reached around Kalani and unhooked a watering wand from the wall. "The last thing I'll show you is one of the most basic but important parts of the job. Do you know how to properly water a plant?"

Kalani stared at the watering wand. "A few hours ago, I would have said yes, but now I suspect it's more complicated than I imagined."

Avery's face softened. "Not complicated, you just have to know what you're doing and why." Avery grabbed a plant from the shelf, removed the nursery pot and showed the root system to Kalani. "You can often tell the health of a plant by the location of its roots. If the roots are gathered up here at the top, that would suggest to me you overwatered the plant. And if they're grouped down here at the bottom, I'd bet the plant was consistently underwatered."

"I thought you didn't bet," Kalani joked.

Avery returned the plant to the pot and switched on the water. "Plants drink mainly from the root system, so it's best to flood the soil until water drains out down here. And you see this?" Avery ran his finger over the percolating dirt. "These bubbles are a sign the plant is dry; they're caused by an exchange of air and water." He shut off the water and wiped his brow dry. "I also prefer to water earlier in the day because it's cooler for all parties involved, but to each their own."

Avery glanced at Kalani and realized his attention had drifted. He opened his mouth to say something when the door cried open.

"How's it going you two?" Lauren propped the door open with her heel and stuck her head in the greenhouse. "Hopefully off to a good start."

Avery turned around and shrugged. "I guess it—"

"I love it here," Kalani said. "And Bossman is a born Kumu."

"Yes he is," Lauren said, smiling at Avery. "Just a friendly reminder; you may want to clean up. Your visitors are checking in as we speak."

Avery's eyes sparkled as he tamped down his hair. "I'll be right there. Thanks."

Avery tapped the wand as the door bounced closed and turned to face Kalani. "I have found the key to making this all work lies in you finding a balance and giving these plants only what they need. No more, no less, and remember, there's a reason it's said that water is the greatest power on the planet and with great power comes great responsibility." He tapped the wand in his palm a few more times then handed it to Kalani. "Before I go, I feel like reminding you once again that these plants mean the world to me, but I won't. The last thing I want to do is get all sappy on you."

Kalani buried his face in his palm.

"Hey, no shame in the pun game." Avery twirled his shears on his thumb and walked over to Benny. After handing them over, he brushed his hands clean and adjusted his shirt. "I'm off to see my daughter and grandson again. How do I look?"

Benny finished his page and examined Avery. "A little rough around the edges, but I've seen worse."

Avery nodded and pushed the door open. "Thanks, Benny. I'll take that as a compliment."

. . .

A waft of dust billowed from Avery's jeans as he smacked his thighs and approached his daughter and grandson waiting for him on a bench. In one hand, he carried a long, thin gift wrapped in a contractor's trash bag.

"Please, don't get up," he said as Bri ignored him and wrapped her arms around his neck. She pecked him on the cheek and whispered something into his ear before sitting back down.

"Never in a million years would I forget," he said, forever amazed at the beautiful woman she had become. Bri was hapa haole—half Hawaiian and half her father—having inherited the best of her mother's features, from her flowing black hair to her deep obsidian eyes. She was short like her mother, with full lips and a radiant face that had a sweet fire to it. Her skin looked more beige than brown, and though she carried herself well, her clothes—loose fitting and breathable—were selected more for comfort than style.

Avery crouched on the pathway and leaned the gift against the bench. He turned to his grandson and reached to brush his bangs out of his sun-beaten face, but the boy turned away toward the comfort of his mother.

Micah avoided eye contact with his grandfather and focused his attention elsewhere. He studied his surroundings, transfixed on a lone palm tree swaying in the courtyard. "What's that for?" he asked.

Avery turned around and traced Micah's finger with his own. He pointed at a short metal band cinched around the trunk. "You mean the metal belt up there?"

He nodded. "I see them everywhere."

"I'm not surprised. That band is needed when they build palm trees. How else would they lock the two halves together?"

"Nuh uh!" Micah cocked his shoulders and leaned forward. "What are they *really* for?"

Avery briefly turned his back to the boy before spinning back around. His upper lip had curled under itself, revealing bared top teeth and a slick of drool leaking from his forced overbite. "Maybe those rings keep us rodents from climbing the trunk and making a nest up top?"

Micah broke a smile and sat up straight. "You lie!"

"Aʻole Micah." Bri crossed her arms and gave him the look.

Avery fixed his lip and crouched down. "You know, I used to climb trees way taller than that when I wasn't much older than you."

"I wanna see."

Avery craned his head back and squinted. "I suppose I could, but what's the point in climbing a coconut tree when there's no coconuts up top?"

Micah raised his hand to his brow. "Oh yeah. Where'd they all go?"

"Good question. My bet is the groundskeeper beat us to them."

"Does he share?" Micah asked.

Avery chuckled. "I don't think so, at least not with us. No, he removes them long before they ripen and become dangerous, especially to old men like me who like to nap in their shade." He glanced at Bri and then back to his grandson. "Which reminds me, do me a favor and never play under coconut trees, okay? I don't know if you know this, but more people die each year from falling coconuts than shark attacks."

Micah tugged on his mom's shorts. "Mom, is that true?"

Bri rolled her eyes. "I've heard that before, but I think you have far better things to think about. Especially on your birthday."

"You mean like presents?"

"*Ding ding ding!*" Avery said. "I'm so glad you said something." He dropped to a knee, grabbed the bag from the bench and undid the knot. Then, he reached inside and removed a wet cutting with a growth of roots at the end.

"You got me a walking stick?" Micah laughed and looked up from his gift. "Why?"

Bri gently nudged him.

"It's okay," Avery whispered. He reached out and placed the cutting in the boy's hands. "It's not just any old stick; this one is magical."

Micah grabbed the base of the stick and instinctively pointed it at his grandpa. "Alohamora!" He giggled, tried once again and inspected the tip. "It doesn't work."

"I said it was magical, not a wand." Avery reached for the gift and rolled it back and forth in his palms. "This is called a cutting, and it's from a very special plant known as the Crown Flower. Have you ever heard that name before?"

Micah rocked backward on his heels.

"It may not look like much now, but here's what you do . . . assuming your mom says it's okay. When you get home, I want you to find a place in your yard that gets the most sun and dig a hole the size of a coconut. Stick this end with the roots inside, backfill the hole with soil and give it a nice watering. Water it a few times a week to start—not too much, not too little—and if everything works out, by this time next year you should see your first flowers bloom. Can you guess what comes next?"

Micah took the cutting from his grandpa and twirled it in his hands. "I don't know."

Avery pressed off of his knees and stretched his back. "Repeat after me: *Danaus Plexippus*."

Micah screwed his face. "Is that another spell?"

"Even better. It's Latin and translates to 'sleepy transformation.' But do you know what else it means?"

Micah shook his head.

"Monarch *butterflies*. Once the cutting takes root and grows leaves, butterflies will swarm your yard and lay eggs all over them. Then, the larvae will hatch and caterpillars will munch on the leaves until one day they all hang upside down like bats and transform into a chrysalis. Do you know what that is?"

The boy shook his head.

"It's where butterflies come from. Give it some time, and

soon, you'll have more butterflies than you know what to do with. We can also go over collecting and raising the caterpillars inside to protect them from predators like the Bulbul birds, but first, you have to grow the plant."

Micah turned to his mom. "Can we go home and plant it? Please?"

"Of course we can, but right now we're enjoying our visit. Also, since we're renters, it will have to go in a pot if that's okay."

"But Grandpa said it has to—"

"Actually, I think that's an even better idea," Avery said. "That way, if you ever have to move, you can take it with you." He opened for a hug and Micah charged into his arms. "Happy birthday, Champ. I'm proud of the fine young man you're becoming." He let go and gave the boy a healthy thump on the back. "Go on and play for a moment, but remember to stay in sight."

Avery sat down on the bench next to Bri. "Thanks again for making it. It means the world to me to be involved in his life. And yours, too."

Bri smiled and patted his knee. "Don't be silly, Dad. There's no need to thank me. Micah wanted to come, and I wanted to bring him. And how sweet of you to get him a gift, especially such a thoughtful one. I've always loved that part about you."

"What part?" Avery asked.

"The part where you always gave the best gifts. Remember that Jackson Chameleon enclosure you built me for my sweet sixteen? I must've played with that for years and—"

"Hey, Mom!"

Bri turned to see Micah walking circles around the coconut tree.

"Can I climb this tree?" he asked, slapping its trunk. "Since it's safe to play under?"

"Oh, sweetie, I don't think that's allowed and it's just us here so there's no reason to show off." She waited for Micah to accept her decision and turned back to Avery. "Where was I? Oh, right? About that—"

"I'm sorry for being difficult, Brianna." Avery took a deep breath and dropped his shoulders. "For being difficult when I drank, and for my actions that followed."

Bri jerked her head back. "Where did that come from?"

"Just now when you brought up your birthday, it brought back some mixed emotions." Avery's eyes searched hers and he spotted a flash of confusion. "You don't remember what happened, do you?"

"I do, and it was great. It was great, wasn't it?"

"Of course." Avery smiled and turned away. "There's something else I meant to bring up but didn't want to mention in front of Micah. I've had a minor setback, and I don't see myself moving out anytime soon. I had an interview that didn't pan out and finding a place willing to accept someone like me is proving harder than I expected. I hope you're not disappointed."

"Disappointed?" Bri waved him off. "You know we can't wait for the day you move out, but you have to trust the process, right?"

"That's what they say. By the way, how's Tristan doing?"

Bri shrugged. "Hard to tell. We're still separated and don't speak much."

"So he's not involved in your life at all?"

"No he is, but in his own way. For example, he called and sent Micah a birthday card, which was thoughtful of him, but Micah needs more than that. He wants his dad back and needs him healthy."

"I take it he's still drinking?"

"Who knows? For his own sake, I'd hope not, but I'm not playing that game anymore with him. I don't have time or energy to police anyone. I already have one kid and I'm Micah's mom, not Tristan's."

"I don't blame you, and that's coming straight from the mouth of an alcoholic." He reached out and squeezed the top of

Bri's hand. "It's a rough go being in a relationship with an alcoholic who's actively drinking, and no one deserves that level of anger, frustration, resentment and pain, especially not when young children are involved."

The two of them sat there for some time discussing things they both already knew to be true. Having grown up the daughter of an alcoholic father, Bri expressed how actions spoke louder than words. And Avery, mindful not to reopen old wounds, reflected on his shortcomings as a man who put his drinking ahead of his family. He knew he couldn't change the past any more than he could forget it and felt grateful Bri didn't hold it against him even though she had every right to.

In time, their conversation slowed. "Why do these visits always go by so fast?" Bri asked.

"Probably because they're too short," Avery said. "Also, the next time you talk to Tristan, tell him he can reach out to me anytime. If he needs a sponsor or someone to take him to a meeting, all he has to do is say the word and I'll make it happen."

"I'll let him know, but I won't get my hopes up." Bri motioned to Micah to get ready to go and the child frowned. "But in the meantime, try not to worry about him or us. Whatever happens, we'll be waiting for you along with a wonderful life with your name on it. All you need to worry about right now is keeping your head in the game and praying that everything will fall into place."

Later that afternoon, Avery entered the game room and tuned out the lively voices of the broadcasters calling the last minutes of an NFL preseason game. A crowd of patients with little in common sat in angst and mismatched chairs in an oddly shaped semicircle around the TV. Whoever the losing team was, they had their fair share of die-hard fans rooting for them and holding out hope, the loudest in the bunch sporting a homemade jersey made from an old shirt and sharpie.

He made his way over to Marv, who sat as far away from the commotion as humanly possible while maintaining a line of sight with the game. Avery pulled up a chair, sat with his back to the TV and helped Marv align the rest of the remaining chess pieces.

"Do you ever wonder where fandom begins and ends?" Marv asked as he watched a replay of the field goal. "Or is it just one more sickness that plagues us?"

Avery lined up his pawns and glanced over his shoulder. "It's not something I've cared to think about. Live and let live works for me."

"So you don't find it strange that we live in a state that can't point to an NFL team in either conference, yet somehow those two knuckleheads bleed black and yellow?"

"I find a lot of things strange." Avery opened with his queen and waited on Marv. "You don't?"

Marv brought his knight out, held it for a moment and let go. "Something's off with you. I can tell."

Avery advanced his pawn a square and rubbed his temple. "Micah turned five today, and during my family visit Bri brought up a wonderful childhood memory from her own birthday."

"And?" Marv went to move a piece but changed his mind. "Do you have something against fond memories?"

"Nothing about that day was fond." Avery captured Marv's pawn and set it aside.

Marv returned the favor. "Care to share?"

Avery thought momentarily and moved, advancing his knight to control the center. "Bri brought up her sixteenth birthday but seems to have conveniently forgotten the part where I confiscated and destroyed half of her gifts because I thought they were hiding tracking devices."

Marv grunted and made a move.

"It doesn't make sense," Avery said. "How could she forget?"

"Maybe she didn't."

"You think she's trying to protect me in case I've forgotten?"

"I know how much she loves you, so sure, that's one possibility."

"You think there are others?" Avery pushed a pawn forward and challenged the center.

"Sure. Why not? Our minds are clever little buggers, aren't they? I think we're all outfitted with any number of systems in place to protect us from trauma." Marv reached out to accept the trade on principle. "I feel like you should know this."

"Don't go there," Avery said, returning Marv's stare. "I meant on the board. It's too early in the game."

Marv withdrew his hand. He scanned the board and took his time before nudging his bishop out.

"So you think she may have blocked the memory out on purpose?" Avery asked, taking his turn.

"Not necessarily. If hidden memories are a real thing, and that's what's going on here, then it's likely beyond her control."

Avery didn't look up from the board. Marv had made a mistake but didn't realize it, and as Avery calculated his response, he uncovered a line of attack that led to an unavoidable defeat. It wasn't any old checkmate either, but a humiliating trap that forked Marv's king and pinned the queen not once but twice.

He snuck a look at Marv and admired his confidence but also knew that once shattered, Marv would rather slip out the back door than request a rematch. And as competitive as Avery could be, he had studied the game long enough to know that sometimes the best moves were the ones no one saw coming. So he reached out and sacrificed his knight.

Marv pointed at the piece. "What's going on here? Is this a trap?"

"Only one way to find out. Now, tell me more about these hidden memories."

Marv captured the knight and tapped the piece on the table. "I'm no scholar, but from what I understand, it's a concept Freud came up with to explain how memories go poof. The brain shields itself and buries unwanted experiences in a protective mechanism to suppress memories or something like that. But it's also hotly debated amongst scientists so take it with a grain of salt." He placed the captured knight next to the board.

Against his better judgment, Avery made another intentional blunder. "So is it chemical, or—"

"Don't know."

"Can it be reversed?"

"Couldn't say." Marv's eyes lit up as he captured another piece. "Sorry, not sorry."

Avery rubbed his temple. He thought about many of the schizophrenic episodes he'd had over the years and what little he had to show for them. The memories were there—if only a blur—but to think Bri's trauma had been so overwhelming that she blocked it out felt beyond unnerving.

"Earth to Avery? You okay?"

Avery stared into space.

"It's not possible for her to forget you, if that's what you're thinking. But also, don't forget that just because you were manic for any period of time, that doesn't mean you weren't a decent father. If anything, you were probably a ton of fun to be around most of the time, so she has all of those memories to hang on to."

"I don't think that makes me feel better."

"Well, it could have been worse. You weren't abusive and you never laid your hands on her, right? So don't beat yourself up over it. Look, you and I both know that when paranoia over-takes our thoughts, we become internally preoccupied. If anything, I bet Bri had no idea what you were thinking most of the time you were manic."

Avery reached out and moved his king out of harm's way. "Micah is growing up so fast. I don't want him to keep seeing me like this."

"That's one way to look at it. Or you could be grateful that at least you have visitors. Many of us aren't so lucky. Check."

Avery cut Marv's queen off with a pawn. "I am grateful, but evidently it's not enough. I'm doing everything I'm supposed to do, but no doors seem to be opening up."

"Check." Marv took the pawn and scooted his chair closer. "Just keep doing you, which is about all you can do."

Avery looked up and tipped his king over.

"What just happened?" Marv asked.

"That's me resigning."

Marv stared at Avery's toppled king. "Which means I win?"

"Which means you win. Good game."

Marv stood up and hunched over his masterpiece. "After how many years, I can't believe I can finally say I beat you."

"Rub it in if you want, just know it happens to the best of us." As Marv stood there, Avery began boxing up the chess pieces, folded the game board and slipped the cover on the box. "If you don't mind, I'm going to go back to our room to reflect on where I went wrong."

He got up, left the box on the table and patted Marv's shoulder as he slipped by.

Once back in his room, Avery sank into his bed with his shoes still on and stared at the ceiling. He knew what was coming; the familiar crash following a family visit always seemed to get the best of him. Looking inward, he couldn't help but see himself in a new light, a light that dimmed the lives of others by simply existing. He was a burden by imposing his reality on his family and a burden for forcing them to meet him halfway. Feeling naked, he pulled his blanket out from beneath him and wafted it over his torso. He lay there trapped in his own body with nowhere to hide and nowhere to go, then rolled onto his side and let everything go dark.

6

OCTOBER 18TH

One Week Later

Avery moaned, flopped onto his side and stretched his blanket over his head. At first, he hoped to ignore the tapping sound that had roused him from his sleep, but as the knocking persisted, Marv, who had been isolating himself in the bathroom, flushed the toilet and answered the door. A flash of light entered the room and faded as the door clicked behind him, only to return a second later when he returned to the room.

He reached out and tapped Avery's shoulder with the novel he had been reading. "Psst. Hate to wake you, but Lauren's at the door."

"I don't care. Do me a favor and tell her I'm not here. I have no plans on getting out of bed today."

"She knows you're here so I think it's a little too late for that. Besides, I have a feeling you want to hear what she has to say." Marv nudged Avery's shoulder again, then crossed the room and flicked on the light. "Don't make me drag you out of bed, because you know I will."

Avery cursed, flipped onto his back and kicked his sheet

away from his torso. Barefooted and half asleep, he moped to the door and felt some bone in his spine pop in place.

It took a moment for his eyes to adjust as he entered the hallway, but as promised, there stood a beaming therapist bouncing on her heels before him.

Avery looked down at her and pulled at his eyes with his palms. "You look like you have good news."

"Good for you, but bad for someone else," Lauren said. "I just got off the phone with Mr. Akoni from the sober house. Someone there recently relapsed, which means they have an immediate opening."

A flood of thoughts sloshed inside Avery's head and he clung to the first thing that floated to the surface. "Did he say who?"

"No and it doesn't matter."

"So, what does this mean for me?"

"It means you should call him back and hear him out. He definitely has some questions, but I won't ever speak for you without your permission and a written release."

Avery stared at the floor. "What questions?"

"Just the usual. Are you rehabilitated? Are you violent? Could I vouch for you and guarantee you aren't a danger to yourself or others?" Lauren rolled her eyes. "One thing I did say is that I don't see how anyone could make that guarantee for another person, since we all have a breaking point. He had more questions, but I protected your privacy and told him I can only speak for myself."

"So he doesn't know about my crime?"

Lauren shrugged. "That's another one I can't answer. It's possible he may since your case is public record, but anything he knows didn't come from me." She handed him a Post-It with a phone number and motioned down the hall. "Why don't you come to my office and return his call?"

Avery stuffed the number into his pocket and tugged on his pajamas. "I don't mind using the community phone, but first let me finish waking up. I want to be thinking clearly before I say the wrong thing."

"Fine, but please don't sleep on this opportunity. There's a reason I came to wake you up; second chances are hard enough to come by." Lauren turned to walk away and paused. "Also, don't forget you have a family visit today."

Avery returned to his room to collect his thoughts. It had been a week since he last saw his daughter and grandson, and though Bri wouldn't hold it against him, he wished he had some progress to speak of. Yet something held him back and after mulling it over, he realized he wasn't keen on talking to the same people at the sober house who had turned him away.

It turned out to be Marv, of all people, who helped Avery push through his apprehensions by suggesting he put his ego behind him and get over himself. So with a fire in his belly, Avery dressed like he was running late, slipped out the door and made his way to the community phone in an alcove near the dayroom.

Uncle Earl answered on the second ring, despite the call coming from an unknown number.

"Aloha. Earl speaking. Who's this?"

"It's me, Avery. I just spoke with Lauren and she said—"

"Avery, it's good to hear from you. Mahalo for calling, especially with the way things ended last time. I know it's not the outcome either of us had hoped for, and for what it's worth, I apologize. Either way, I should have offered a vote and have since realized that issues I've had in the past with others from the hospital probably impacted my judgment. That wasn't fair to you, and that's not why we're here." Uncle Earl paused only long enough to clear his throat. "We're here to 'provide an opportunity for every recovering individual to learn a clean and sober way of living.' So if it's okay with you, I'd like to extend an opportunity to have you return and interview again, with one caveat—please be honest with both us and yourself. No games or beating around the bush this time."

"I have no problem with that," Avery said, then wondered when being dishonest and not forthcoming became the same thing. "Just let me run this by my therapist and make sure there's no objection from the treatment team."

"Please do, because not only do I believe we can help you be successful, but you can help us be better prepared to deal with people like yourself down the road."

Avery sensed the muscles in his face go slack. He wasn't sure how to respond, so he went quiet until Uncle Earl killed the silence.

"You know, since it's just you and me, do you mind if I ask what your charge was?"

"Assault."

"Can I ask what kind? Are we talking about verbal, aggravated or sexual?"

"No, nothing sexual. Just your classic assault in the second degree." Avery considered going into detail but thought better of it.

"That's it?"

"There's more to the story, but if it's okay with you, I'd rather go over the details in person."

"If you say so. In that case, we have a house meeting in two days. If you can make it, great, otherwise I'd appreciate you letting me know since we can't afford to sit on an empty bed."

"You got it."

"Perfect, and call anytime. If I don't pick up, feel free to leave a message." Uncle Earl paused for a moment. "There's one more thing. Every decision we make in this house comes down to either policy or a vote, and if the house votes you in, I hope you can help me prove that I made the right decision. Otherwise, it will make it that much harder for us to accept future applicants from the hospital."

Avery cleared his throat. "I'll do my best. Thanks."

After saying their goodbyes, Avery hung up the phone and crossed his arms behind his head. He sat there in silence, replaying the call in his mind. To be offered a second chance was beautiful, yet a pang in his gut told him he was overlooking something. For years, the only people in his life who believed in him were Lauren and Bri, so the idea of anyone else going out on a limb for him didn't quite sit well, especially when he couldn't imagine why.

Avery released his hands and folded them between his knees. By giving Uncle Earl the benefit of the doubt, he could picture a perfect world where the interview went his way, a way that would allow him to put this place behind him, closing a painful and perplexing chapter of his life. Then he squared the circle, imagined the worst-case scenario and immediately wished he hadn't.

Micah offered up a hug with far less hesitation than Avery expected.

"Any trouble planting your cutting?" Avery asked.

The boy nodded. "At first it kept falling over, but I planted it deeper and it stayed."

"Good. I take it you have a nice big pot for it to grow into?"

"Oh yes," Bri said. "Filled it with a good potting mix and whatever those little white rocks are called."

"Perlite? That should be fine, just don't forget to stay on top of your watering." Avery smiled at his grandson, then turned to Bri. "You know, I have grounds privileges, and this section of the hospital is an open campus. Why don't we take one last look at the greenhouse since it could be the last chance the three of us can see it together. Would you like that?"

Micah grabbed his mom's hand and nodded.

"Then say no more. Follow me."

The three of them crossed the courtyard and filtered into the greenhouse. Micah gravitated toward the footbath mat and became entranced by his newfound ability to walk on water.

Avery walked Bri over to Benny and reintroduced her by name in case he forgot.

Bri turned back to the door. "Aʻole Micah. That's not a toy, and if you make a mess, guess who's cleaning it up?"

Avery tapped her shoulder to insist the boy was fine, but Micah took the hint and reconvened with them in the walkway. The trio walked toward the back of the space where a pleasant aroma of citrus extract hung in the air. Kalani waved, then returned to scrubbing a buildup of dirt and pollen from the windows. Micah spun in place and admired a sprawling cucumber vine creeping along an overhead trellis.

"Hey Kalani, got a sec?" Avery asked.

Kalani dried his hands on his apron and flopped his towel into a bucket.

"I know you've seen them around but I'd like you to meet my daughter Bri and my grandson Micah. Micah here is culti-vating his own green thumb and if all goes well, will be a budding lepidopterist in no time." Avery patted the boy's head and noticed Kalani looked lost. "The more people we have who study butterflies in this world and fight against habitat loss, the better off we'll all be, especially now that Monarchs are back on the endangered species list."

"I think that's great," Kalani said. "About you studying butterflies, not about them being endangered again."

Micah reached behind his mom and tugged on Avery's pants. "Do you mind if I look around?"

"Go ahead, just stay close and be careful."

Kalani undid his apron and tossed it on a hook. "Tell you what. Why don't I give you my first ever tour? I could use the practice."

Bri thanked Kalani and watched him guide Micah toward the front of the greenhouse to show off some seedlings. Then, she turned her back to them and took a moment to admire her father's hard work. "I love what you've done with the place. It's almost unrecognizable from the last time I saw it."

"Not too shabby, huh? It's almost impossible to imagine leaving it all behind after all this work."

"But is that not the natural cycle of things?"

He shrugged and placed the stool in front of Bri. "If it is, it sure doesn't come naturally to me."

Bri sat down and listened to her father recount his earlier phone call. He took his time walking her through his initial interview—if he could call it that—and how Uncle Earl offered him a second chance, but he wasn't sure he should take it. As he spoke, he realized he couldn't put his sense of rejection behind him, even when it appeared to stand in the way of a brighter future.

"What about this is so upsetting to you? Are you embarrassed at how it played out?"

Avery thought for a moment. "I don't know what I am. It almost reminds me of being the last kid picked on the playground. By that point, it no longer matters because no one wanted to play with you in the first place."

"That sounds a bit extreme." Bri reached out and patted her father's forearm. "Besides, anyone who takes the time to know you will love having you around."

"And there's the catch. A lot of people out there won't take the time to get to know someone like me. Maybe it's best that I hold out for another option where I can start fresh."

Avery heard the door creak and sat up as Kalani entered the greenhouse. His back went stiff. "Kalani, where's my grandson?"

"What do you mean?" Kalani asked, looking around. "Is he not with you? I just ran to the lua and told him not to leave. I assumed he'd make his way back to—"

Avery flew past him and burst through the door. He spun in place, scanned his surroundings and desperately hoped to see the boy. When he finally spotted Micah sitting on a patient's knee, Avery scrambled across the courtyard in a fit of fury.

"Get off of him," Avery demanded, startling the young child. He grabbed Micah's arm and snatched him off the patient's lap.

The craggy-faced patient raised his palms and rose off the bench. "We were just—"

"Back the fuck up, Harold." Avery shoved the patient with his free hand and passed the boy off to Bri.

"Come on, man," Harold whispered. "There's no reason to overreact."

Avery turned back to face his family. "Go on. I'll be right there."

Bri pressed her lips together as she slipped an arm around Micah.

"It's okay," Avery said. "Go on. I'll be right there."

He waited for them to walk out of earshot, then turned back to Harold. "The only reason you're still breathing is that I won't traumatize my family. But if you ever even think about putting those miserable hands of yours on my grandson or any other child again, you won't live long enough to regret it. Understood?"

Harold gripped the edge of the concrete bench and nodded.

On his long walk back to the greenhouse, Avery told himself that this was no world for his family to navigate. He met his family at the greenhouse door, along with Benny and Kalani.

Kalani opened his mouth to speak. "Boss . . . I'm so sorry. I didn't mean for—"

"That was my fault," Benny said, pulling Kalani's hand down. "I assumed the boy went outside to catch up with Kalani."

"It's not your fault," Avery said as he opened the door. He let Bri and Micah in first, but Benny reached out and grabbed his wrist to hold him back.

"A word," Benny whispered.

Avery let go of the handle and watched the door bounce close.

"Family comes first," Benny said. "I get it, and as far as I'm concerned, you're not in any trouble. But just to be on the safe side, why don't you hang tight while I go inside and round up any sharp tools? Not that I'm not saying you'll do anything stupid, but best to be safe."

"I have a better idea. If it's okay with you, I'd rather save you the hassle and call it a day."

Benny nodded. "Sure thing. Gimme a sec and I'll round up your family and send them out."

As Benny entered the greenhouse, Avery spun in place and scanned the courtyard. He hoped he hadn't scared Micah by reacting the way he had, and as he beat himself up over it, he heard the door squeak behind him and listened to the footfall of his family approaching.

"Hey," Bri said, touching the small of his back. "Is everything okay?"

Avery turned around and smiled. "Fortunately, yes."

"Sorry, Grandpa," Micah said, his voice catching in his throat. "I didn't mean to make you mad."

Avery hunched down to the boy's level. "No, you didn't make me mad. It was just a misunderstanding and it's not your fault."

The boy looked across the courtyard to the empty bench. "Kalani said that man's sick, but I don't think he looks sick."

Avery glanced at Bri, then back to Micah. "You can't always tell that someone is sick just by looking at them. That's also why you never wander off, okay? Especially here."

"Okay."

After hugging his family goodbye, Avery retreated to his room to imagine a world beyond the confines of the institution that defined him on every level. He remained there until dinner rolled around and imagined a full stomach would quiet the rumblings in his belly, but he only picked over his meal before scraping the plate clean into a waste bin.

Avery—in no mood to sleep—gravitated toward the game room and its soothing late-night ambiance. Near the entrance, two men sat cross-legged on the floor with a Kōnane board between them while a third waited to challenge the winner. In the center of the room, an odd quartet of patients stacked mahjong tiles into walls as they prepared to start a new round. Nearly out of earshot and tucked away in the back corner, six men playing Texas Hold 'Em pretended not to gamble.

Despite an indifference toward tennis, Avery started toward the TV when a Chinese woman with a bent frame yelled out to him from across the room.

"Avery, could you be a dear and take over for me?" Carol asked with the voice of a crow. "Just for a bit while I grab my meds from the med window."

He glanced at the mahjong table and held up a hand. "Normally I would, but I'm not really in the mood."

"I won't be long, and you know the game can't go on with three players." She struggled to rise and patted the back of her chair. She motioned for him to sit down when he walked over and squeezed his shoulder as he slumped into her chair. "Thanks again, Darling. You're West Wind. Zhù nǐ hǎo yùn."

Another woman at the table smiled at Avery as he made himself comfortable. Her arms and wrists were laced with a kaleidoscope of hypertrophic scars. Surprised to see Keilah back on the ward, Avery sorted his hand, removed a flower tile and set it face up on the table. While waiting for the other players to get their hands in order, he made eye contact with Keilah.

"What happened?" he asked.

"Isn't it obvious? I violated the terms of my conditional release and they reeled me back in."

Avery tipped his head to the side. "I'm sorry to hear that."

"Why are you sorry? You didn't do anything wrong." Keilah finished arranging her tiles and placed them face down.

The dealer motioned for Avery to help himself to the flower wall, then discarded a tile in the center of the table to kick-start the game. "Nine circle."

"Pung!" Keilah picked up the piece and placed it in her scoring pile with two matching tiles from her hand. "I hate to say it, but it's not as easy as it looks out there," she said to the group. "Forget what the staff says; our kind isn't wanted or accepted anywhere." She discarded a tile. "East Wind."

The older man to her left drew from the tail end of the wall and discarded the tile.

The dealer picked the piece up and returned it to the man. "You have to call it when you play it, Bob. Remember?"

"Oh, right, right." Bob placed the tile back onto the table. "Six . . . whatever you call that."

"Mánzi," Avery said, taking the tile from the discard table. "And pung." He matched the tile with two from his hand and set them aside. "What do you mean we're not accepted anywhere?"

Keilah didn't bother looking up from her hand. "I mean just that. No one I worked with wanted to work with me, and no one I lived with wanted to live with me. So naturally, I hid my past because I never felt safe in sharing." When her turn came, she played a tile. "But when the truth came out—as it always does—I was accused of being deceptive. It felt like regardless of what I said or did, I couldn't win."

"It can't have been that bad," Bob said. "One bamboo."

The dealer picked up the tile and handed it back to him. "No Bob, that's a flower."

"Who are you to say what it was or wasn't?" Keilah asked Bob. "Name the last time you had to 'feel someone out' to unearth their opinions on the mentally ill?"

Bob took a tile from the flower wall and added it to the center. "Eight circle."

"That's what I thought. You've been here so long, you have no idea how it feels to be judged by everyone you meet, and sometimes, even by people you've never even met or talked to." Keilah turned back to Avery. "Our kind will never be accepted because we will never be trusted, and nothing we say or do will change that."

Avery furrowed his brow. "Seems a bit harsh."

"That's because the truth hurts. Look, if you think people will treat you any differently now that you're diagnosed and 'treated', trust me . . . they won't. It could be years since your last bout with mania, doesn't matter. You know the saying, 'Do the crime, do the time?' Well, that doesn't apply to us and nothing anyone here says or does will ever change that."

Avery looked down at the dead tiles before him and calculated his next move. "I'll be transitioning to community living soon, so time will tell if your experience translates across the board."

Keilah drew a tile and added it to her hand. "At the very least, I think you'll see that there's a lack of support out there for all of us." She discarded a tile and propped her elbows on the table. "We have it made here. I couldn't wait to come back and beat you all at mahjong again."

Bob picked up her discarded piece and laid down a run. "It's starting to sound like you came back here on purpose."

"But doesn't everyone?" Keilah glared up from her hand. "I can tell you all this much; I sure as shit didn't get high for the fun of it."

The table went quiet for a moment. Bob spotted Carol returning and laid his tiles face down as she passed behind him.

"Where are we?" Carol asked as she swapped places with Avery.

"It's your turn," he said. "Oh, and as a side note, apparently none of us will ever be accepted by anyone anywhere."

Carol cocked an eyebrow. "Says who?"

The other players turned to Keilah.

"What?" she said. "Would you rather me lie to you?"

Carol shook her head and took a tile from the wall. "I've spent my whole life unwanted and labeled as a danger to myself and others, so if you think I give two shits about what anyone thinks of me now"—she placed the tile in front of her and exposed the rest of her hand—"you don't know who you're playing with. Good game, everyone."

Avery watched the four of them flip the pool of tiles face

down and shuffle the game pieces before them with eight colliding hands. Every so often, a piece would flip over, and they'd all look away until it was reshuffled back into the fold. He wished them luck, took the long way back to his room and said little to Marv, who was reading in his bed. Then, stepping inside the bathroom, he closed the door behind him and transferred his weight to the sink with the heel of his hand. His toothbrush sliced through running water and he let the water run while he brushed his teeth.

Staring at himself in the mirror, his thoughts ran to what he had heard earlier and he wished he hadn't sat down at the table. Keilah's words dredged up a deep uneasiness and a sickly feeling washed over him. He thought he might be getting sick. *'Our kind isn't wanted or accepted anywhere.'* She's just one person, and though the experience she described aligned with what he had long feared, he told himself his mileage might vary.

Wishing the feeling away, he switched sides and told himself not to brush so hard. Over the sound of running water, he heard Keilah's voice again: *'Our kind will never be accepted or trusted and nothing we say or do will change that.'* He stopped brushing, bared his teeth in the mirror and watched a trickle of blood seep from his puffy gums. Then he spat into the sink and watched pink saliva dribble down the drain. Licking his wounds, he scrubbed his toothbrush under the running water with his thumb, splashed a palmful of water around the basin and, for better or worse, decided to call it a night.

7

OCTOBER 19TH

A startled Avery snapped awake from a terror and peered into the hollow darkness. His hand—numb from sleeping on it—only regained feeling as it crept toward his throat. Then, without making a sound, he parted his mouth and drew the pads of his fingers across his slick teeth.

"Do you mind?" Marv whispered.

Avery exhaled, sunk back into his pillow and turned to face the blackness. "Sorry, I didn't mean to wake you."

"You didn't. Is everything okay?"

Since he couldn't see anything, Avery closed his eyes. "I had a dream that I lost my teeth."

"You mean a nightmare?" Marv's voice hung in the air. "How? In a fight?"

"I don't remember. They were just . . . gone." Avery touched his teeth again. "What do you think it means?"

Marv grew silent for a moment. "Sounds to me like your anxiety is getting the best of you."

Avery rolled onto his back and knew Marv was right. "I get that moving out is inevitable, so why am I so torn about it?"

"Because you're afraid of something. What though, only you can say."

Avery turned back onto his side. "Long before I was forensically committed, life as I knew it was unbearable. Today, things are so good, I can't imagine—"

"How can you compare life today to life back then? You were undiagnosed and untreated, remember? You didn't have meds or a support system educated in mental health. You didn't know what warning signs to look for or what to do when you saw them."

Avery pushed off of his pillow and sat up. He thought about the bright side of living in the hospital and all he would leave behind. Not only was his rent and food covered, but he could always locate someone to turn to when he needed it most. He had all the health care he could ask for, haircuts on demand and even a fully stocked pharmacy within arm's reach. As Avery's eyes adjusted, he looked down at his empty hands. "Maybe I'm afraid of leaving this all behind? Or maybe I'm not? I'm not sure, to be honest."

"Then think harder," Marv said bluntly. "Are you afraid of stigma? Moving to somewhere less familiar? Are you afraid of relapsing?"

"Maybe that's it," Avery confessed. "Minus the part about relapsing. There's nothing I miss about drinking."

"Doesn't matter what you think, the fear could be buried alive in your subconscious."

Avery thought long and hard, embracing the silence. "What if it's bigger than all of that? What if I'm nervous about this interview because it puts the fate of my future back into my own hands?"

"And you're saying you can't handle it?"

"I don't know what I'm saying, but you should be able to relate. You've said it yourself a million times; you want to stay here forever."

"I'm a different case. I'm the definition of institutionalized and there is no light at the end of my tunnel."

"Just because you're institutionalized doesn't mean you're

damned to live here forever. If you really wanted to, you could move out."

"I'm a *murderer*, Avery. Do I need to say that again?" Marv's words darkened the room as something in him changed. "What kind of life would I have out there under lifetime supervision?"

"I don't know. I guess we'd both have to move out of our comfort zones to find out."

Marv took a moment to respond. "If I could have a normal life like what you're facing, I'd consider it, but that's not the case here. And unlike you, I don't have a family that wants or needs me around. If I did, I'd be more willing to embrace the idea, but when you kill your own mother—God rest her soul—it has a way of making Christmas and Thanksgiving dinners a bit awkward."

Avery made out the still silhouette of Marv idling in his bed. "You were sick, Marv. It's not like you meant to—"

"That doesn't change a thing."

Avery heard the footfall of Marv crossing the room. A moment later, the lights flicked on.

"My family has every right to hate me even though we all sat through the same courtroom proceedings together. It doesn't matter whether I was paranoid, delusional or manic; in the end my poor, innocent mother is gone, and she's gone because of me." Marv sat on the edge of his bed. "No one cares that I needed help. If they did, you'd think at the very least they'd be happy to see me getting better."

Avery hesitated. "I can't imagine how hard that must've been for everyone."

"Of course you can't, but that's my kuleana to deal with. Now enough about me. You have your own family to worry about."

"But what about my family here?"

Marv made a show of looking around. "What family? You mean your precious plants?"

"I've poured my heart and soul into my work and Kalani's

not ready to take over yet. I can't just abandon them and hope for the best."

"It sounds to me like you're making excuses. Kalani will be fine. Plus, won't Benny be around for him to fall back on?"

"Benny? Benny's great and all, but he's about as useful as a log. I'd say the most Kalani can ever hope to get out of him is a second-hand Louis L'Amour book."

"I find it hard to believe he hasn't picked up something in all these years. But if it'll make you feel better, I'll do what I can to keep an eye out for him."

Avery dismissed the idea with a flip of his hand. "No, that doesn't make me feel better, not when you probably know even less about plants than him."

"But I know how to call you if we need help," Marv said. "And I have another thought; your interview's tomorrow, right?"

Avery nodded.

"Call me crazy but I feel like if you didn't care about this interview, you wouldn't be so anxious about it. Besides, if the treatment team didn't think you could handle it, they wouldn't have given their blessing for you to go back for a second shot."

Avery's chest hitched. "I don't know. I guess I can see that."

"You guess? This is your shot to take your life back, Avery. Don't downplay it, especially when you're one of the lucky few."

"Lucky?" Avery cocked his head back. "What do you mean?"

Marv got up and walked over to the door. "We both know that across the country, most people with severe mental illness never see the inside of a hospital. They either end up on the streets or in jail, if not both, but you've been offered the opportunity to get better. Run with it." With a flick of a finger, the room returned to darkness. "Now, if you don't mind, we both need to get some sleep."

Avery leaned back in his bunk. "Do you have a big day tomorrow, too?"

"I wouldn't call it big. Just a funeral."

"I'm sorry to hear that. Who died?"

"Some aunt I never grew close to. Growing up, she was always off her rocker, though now that I'm older, I have a better idea why. Perhaps we were closer than I ever imagined."

Avery covered his body with his sheet and turned onto his side. "Funeral aside, it will be nice for you to get a break from here. I can't remember the last time you went out on a pass."

"I wouldn't call it a break. I'm going to come across a lot of people who would rather see me in that box than her."

"Who cares? You're going there to honor your aunt, not to impress the guests. Besides, I imagine you've grown so much in these past twelve years you'll be unrecognizable."

"Somehow, I have a feeling no one will care. But again, if no one out there wants to see me succeed, who am I to hurt them all again?"

Avery opened his mouth to respond but Marv cut him off.

"I know you can't read my lips right now, but that was a hypothetical question," Marv said. "Just in case you couldn't tell."

8

OCTOBER 20TH

Uncle Earl greeted Avery at the front door with a warm smile and stepped aside to let him enter. Avery heard voices from the living room tumbling into the foyer. Realizing they were waiting on him, he fixed his collar, straightened his shirt and combed his fingers through his hair. Then sensing Uncle Earl bringing up the rear, he entered the room and took his seat in front of everyone.

The chatter died down and all focus turned to Avery, who motioned that he had something to say to the room. "I feel like before we get started, I should open up with an apology for not being as transparent as I could have been the last time I was here." He paused not for emphasis but to change his tone since his words sounded practiced. "I never intended to be deceitful or dishonest, and for what it's worth, please know I've always struggled with talking openly about myself and my past." Avery considered whether to expand further, but after reading the room, he left it at that.

Nani clasped her hands in her lap and winked at Avery.

Avery turned to Uncle Earl. "Where would you like me to start?"

"I leave that entirely up to you."

Avery rubbed his palms together and nodded. "As I

mentioned last time, I was born and raised on Maui and had a typical upbringing compared to most of my friends. Being from Maui, when I wasn't in school, I spent the better part of my childhood in the ocean, either bodyboarding or diving below. Life was simple back then, but something in me changed toward the end of high school, something I couldn't put a finger on. Eventually, I dropped out and struggled with alcoholism as my sickness went unchecked."

Tino raised his hand. "When you say 'sickness,' what exactly do you mean?"

"I have what's known as Schizoaffective disorder. It's a broad term used to describe a condition that combines schizophrenia, a thought disorder, with any number of mood disorders."

"Like multiple personalities?"

Avery turned to Nani. "You're thinking of Dissociative identity disorder, and no, I don't suffer from multiple personality states. When I say mood disorders, I'm talking about Bipolar type I or II, or in my case, depression."

"Oh. Sorry," Nani said, pursing her lips. "So das why you stay in the State Hospital?"

"Yes, but don't be sorry."

"If you don't mind, can we back it up a bit?" Uncle Earl asked. "What happened with your disorder that led you to drop out of high school?"

Avery repositioned himself in his chair. "Nothing, which was precisely the problem. Back then, like most people with this condition, I had no idea what I was working with and no one around me did. This delayed the proper diagnosis along with years spent in denial."

"So no one knew what was going on with you?" Otto asked.

"People knew something was wrong, they just weren't sure what. I mean, they all saw the red flags and hospitalizations along the way, but my drinking convoluted everything. People who knew me thought I needed help for alcoholism, and while they weren't wrong, the story had more layers than met the eye.

But since I wasn't ready to quit drinking, I left Maui to get away from anyone who cared enough to tell me what to do."

"What about yourself?" Uncle Earl asked. "Didn't you recognize you needed help?"

Avery went silent for a moment. "Yes and no, because with thought disorders, it's often hard for the afflicted to register something's off. Understand, because I believed I was thinking clearly, I saw no reason to listen to anyone else."

Nani raised her hand. "But eventually you found out what was wrong."

Avery turned to face her. "I did, but I'm what they call a 'late bloomer.' While I dealt with my fair share of disturbances early on, I attributed them all to alcoholism. It was only when I experienced my first deep episode of psychosis in my early thirties that it clicked, but by then it was too little, too late."

"I take it that's when you committed your crime?" Uncle Earl asked.

Avery began picking at his cuticles. "When the psychosis hit, I tried to quiet it as I usually did with the bottle, but my girlfriend at the time had enough of my drinking. This led to yet another fight, a neighbor calling the police and ultimately, me getting hauled in for assault."

Kātisu shifted forward. "You put your hands on a woman?" He turned to Uncle Earl. "Like I said when I first moved in here, I refuse to live with rapists or wife beaters, period."

"You'll have your turn to vote as you wish when the time comes."

"Hold on," Avery said. "I'm not a wife beater. I never laid hands on her."

Kātisu cocked his head. "Then who got assaulted?"

"That depends on who's telling the story. Since it was a DV call, the police had to remove one of the parties by law, and for obvious reasons, they chose me. It probably had something to do with me believing a demon possessed my daughter's mother and my delusion that she and the cops were all conspiring against me. Either way, I tried to flee, which led to me getting tackled and fed a mouthful of dirt. I'll never know how, but somewhere in the tussle and confusion of it all, I managed to bite an officer's finger."

Nani uncrossed her arms, studied her housemates and turned back to Avery. "Das all? All you did was nibble on someone?"

"It wasn't just someone. I bit a police officer, and that's Assault II with the entire weight of the law behind it."

"I'm confused," Uncle Earl said. "You've spent how many years locked up, all because you *bit* someone?"

"Going on seven, but in order for it to make sense, you need to have an idea of how NGRI works. Since I was delusional at the time of my arrest, they took me to jail, then immediately transferred me to the psych hospital for a fourteen-day eval. That segued into comp rest, which, because of the severity of my case, took a few cycles to work through."

Silence fell over the room until Nani's inquisitive mind spoke up. "Wats comp rest?"

"Competency restoration. It exists to ensure defendants can understand the charges levied against them. Each cycle runs for ninety days, and since they wouldn't rule me competent to make my plea in court after the first cycle, I returned to jail to restart the cycle. In my case, it ended up taking three cycles and a forced med order from the court before I finally leveled out and was stabilized on meds. Then, I had my day in court and pleaded NGRI after the prosecutor refused to drop the charges since the victim was a cop."

"That doesn't make sense to me," Otto said.

Avery shrugged. "What part?"

"All of it. If you're deemed competent, how do you end up pleading Not Guilty by Reason of Insanity?"

"An NGRI plea is based on my mental capacity at the time of the crime. Because of my condition, I lacked *mens rea*, otherwise known as a guilty mind which is almost always needed to prove someone guilty of a crime."

"So you got off?"

"Look at me. Does it look like I got off?" Avery scooted forward in his chair. "Not by a long shot. No, anytime someone pleads NGRI, they get handed the maximum sentence according to the sentencing guidelines. Also, it's not a guilty plea, but a postponed acquittal."

"I'm so frickin' confused." Nani wiped her brow with the back of her hand. "Are you lōlō or not?" She heard her own question and looked up at Avery. "Sorry if dats one bad word."

"I've been called far worse but no, in my mind, disturbed, deranged, ill, insane, it's all the same—a way to describe something we can't understand. But the main thing is I am now diagnosed and treated, meaning my condition is managed and I can live a normal life."

"Well, as an addict in recovery, I can relate to being insane," Nani said. "I think we all can. Welcome to the club."

Avery smiled and turned to Uncle Earl.

"I can't imagine what you went through on your journey to get to where you are today, and I admire you for your strength to be so candid with us." Uncle Earl paused and scratched his forehead. "So unless anyone has questions, Avery, why don't you step outside and give us a moment to talk this over and take a house vote?"

Avery nodded and pressed himself out of his chair, avoiding eye contact as he slipped out of the room. Once outside, he stepped into his shoes and rested against the railing, feeling the sun's warmth on his neck. He gripped the wood beneath him, and his fingernails found loose paint that he picked nervously while waiting to learn his fate.

9
NOVEMBER 21ST

One Month Later

"Is it just me, or did this past month really fly by?" Lauren nudged Avery with her elbow and waved to Cap as she stepped on the gas. "You excited?"

He lowered his sun visor and watched the sally port fade into a distant memory. "I can't believe I'm really moving out."

"Why not? You've been working toward this moment for years, and now it's time to carpe diem." She swerved into the oncoming lane to dodge another pothole.

Avery checked on his belongings in the backseat and adjusted the plant that fell over. "Tell me, how does one seize anything when they can't get past the overwhelming feeling that they're forgetting something?"

Lauren eased up on the accelerator. "Do we need to go back?"

"No, I'm not talking about anything material." Avery's eyes shifted nervously as he studied the long road ahead. At the same time, he subconsciously bounced his knees in place and folded his hands between them. "Or maybe I don't have the slightest clue as to what I'm talking about."

She cruised to a stop at a red light and turned down the radio. "Just a friendly reminder that you're making a big change so it's normal to experience big feelings. Don't forget we've worked hard to ensure you're not being tossed to the wolves. Your ducks are in a row and I'm confident you know what you need to do to succeed."

"Then why am I drawing a blank?"

Lauren looked around for a second. "Maybe you have road-blocks up, but I bet if we take a trip down memory lane, we can jog that memory of yours. How's that sound?"

"Like you've done it before."

Lauren chuckled. "I have, and it works every time. Now, to start, we've confirmed you have no outstanding legal issues, correct?"

He nodded.

"Your ID is valid and you have your monthly bus pass on you? The one you swore up and down you wouldn't lose?"

Avery patted his wallet through his pants and saw where she was going with this. "I do."

"Then I say we're off to a good start." Lauren blew through the intersection and entered Kāne'ohe town. She fought traffic for a few blocks, pointed out a grocery store, then slowed as they passed the Windward Federal Credit Union. "Any questions about accessing your new checking and savings accounts?"

He shook his head as they continued down the main drag a bit before hooking a right onto a side road.

Lauren pointed out her window as she skirted a Mom-and-Pop pharmacy. "Here's where you come to refill your prescriptions, and I've personally confirmed that you're officially transferred to Medicare so there's no risk of a lapse in coverage."

Avery leaned out his window and murmured, "Open 9 A.M. to 5:30 P.M."

Lauren turned onto a side road that led into an aging residential neighborhood and decreased her speed as the streets grew tighter. "I know we've beaten your relapse prevention plan to death over the years, but how do you feel about going over it one last time, just for—"

"Shits and giggles?" Avery rolled his eyes. "Let me guess: you're going to ask me to rattle off what warning signs I should keep an eye out for, and when I say 'missing appointments, refusing or forgetting to take my meds, losing sleep, hyperventilating, rambling incoherently, missing showers and talking about impending doom,' you're going to ask if I forgot about 'chest or stomach pains due to tenseness' and I'm going to say 'no, I was about to get to that but you didn't let me finish.' Then you'll want to change the topic but I'll beat you to it by firing off coping strategies like, 'taking a hot shower, going for a walk, talking to family, gardening and so on,' until you cut me off and tell me it sounds like I know what I'm talking about."

Lauren nodded approvingly and said, "I'm glad to see I've taught you well."

The homes they passed were built on top of one another with measly yards with battered roofs blistered by the unforgiving Hawaiian sun. On the right-hand side, Lauren pointed out a nondescript church while keeping the car moving so as not to impede traffic. "And you know where to go to catch your AA meetings, right?"

He admired a concrete shrine gleaming in the sunlight. "Seems less ominous during the day."

Lauren swerved into a dead end and came full circle. "You've got this, Avery. Knowing where to go and then actually showing face is more than half the battle. The only thing left to do from here is to schedule your upcoming intake appointments, but I had to wait until you switched insurances before I could make those calls."

Avery leaned back in his seat. "Maybe we did cover everything?"

"I think so, but even if we're forgetting something, we'll take care of it when the need arises and keep it moving. That's not to say you won't face challenges, but as long as you stay on top of the things that have kept you sane and sober, you're going to be fine. Plus, you have my full support and can reach out at any time." She turned onto a side road, crept to a stop in front of the sober house and cut the engine. "Even if you don't reach out, I'll be sure to check in on you periodically to ensure you stay moving in the right direction."

Avery exited the vehicle and slung a bag over his shoulder. He clutched his plant to his chest and waited for Lauren to meet him on the curb.

"Need a hand?"

He adjusted his grip. "I think I can take it from here."

"Must be nice to travel light, huh?" Lauren started to smile but stopped. "Good luck with the job hunt. If you need any references or run into trouble, let me know." She reached out and hugged him.

"I'm pretty sure that's our first hug ever."

"Not to make it any less special, but everyone gets a hug. Good luck, Avery."

He waited to see her off before starting up the driveway, but something changed her mind as soon as she hopped into the driver's seat.

"It would be like me to forget," she said, hustling around the Jeep with a crudely wrapped gift.

Avery set his things down and took the present. "Can I open it now?"

"Only if you want."

He peeled away the newspaper and unearthed a raku flowerpot with a shimmering patina. "It's beautiful. Did you make this?"

"A friend of mine is into ceramics, so she did the heavy lifting, but I glazed it. Also, she mentioned something about raku being porous so it may or may not leak. Not sure if that's a good or bad thing."

Avery felt the weight in his hands and blushed. "It's perfect, though now I feel like a klutz for not having something for you."

"Actually, believe it or not, you do."

He looked up from the pot as Lauren whipped out her phone. "May I?"

Avery stiffened and smiled for the picture as Lauren counted down. "Does this mean I made it onto your photo wall?"

Lauren nodded as she inspected the picture. "Unless you'd rather not, but I can't think of a better way to offer hope for everyone following in your footsteps. You sure you don't need a hand?"

Avery declined again, said a second goodbye as he waved her off and took his time reaching the front door. He put his things down, knocked on the screen door and waited for someone to answer.

A shadow approached from the inside. "You said it was Avery, right?"

"Technically it still is."

"Funny," Gil said. "Come on in, and you don't have to knock since *technically* you pay rent here."

"Fair enough, but I wasn't sure if there's a check in process or something." Avery removed his shoes, picked up his items and stepped inside. "Thanks again for holding the bed for me. It means a lot."

"Don't thank me, thank Uncle Earl. Besides, if you have the means to pay a month's rent in advance and not move in, be my guest. Personally, I think it's crazy, but I guess there's worse things out there to spend your money on."

"Well, between you and me, I didn't have much of a choice. I'm required to secure an address and provide a thirty-day move-out notification to law enforcement before leaving the hospital."

"Hmm. Still crazy, if you ask me, even though it was nice having our whole room to myself." Gil peeked at his wristwatch. "Since my show isn't on yet, how about a house tour? Might as well get to know each other since we'll be living on top of one another."

"If you don't mind, sure."

"Not at all, but you go ahead and leave your stuff here for now so you don't have to lug it around with you." Gil turned around and started through the living room but didn't linger long since Avery knew it well.

The back of the living room led to a dining room with a table surrounded by several mismatched chairs. The table's finish was scratched and marred with water rings, despite more coasters on the table than chairs in the room.

Avery followed Gil into a dated kitchen with rusting appliances, peeling cabinets and cheap laminate flooring. He looked around as if it were his first time there and pointed at one of two fridges.

"Since we're roomies now, I'll let you in on a little secret; in the event you ever decide you want to leave this place, the fastest way out of here is to eat someone else's food or not do your dishes."

Avery opened the first fridge and poked his nose inside. Reminiscent of the hospital, most of the food had passive-aggressive labels in Sharpie, such as "Kapu" and "Eat at your own risk."

He closed the fridge and caught up with Gil in the adjacent nook. A large window loomed over a padded bench that butted to a built-in bookcase.

"Take a book, leave a book," Gil said. "If reading's your thing, that is. Just don't expect to find any peace and quiet down here since someone's always coming or going."

Gil knocked on a closed door and apologized to whoever responded. "That's the downstairs guest bathroom, but you're welcome to use it in a pinch." As they worked their way into the family room, Gil took a passing glance and kept moving. "Nothing special to see here."

Avery picked up his belongings and tailed Gil up carpeted steps that creaked underfoot. Gil took his time and paused to catch his breath at the first landing. When they reached the top, he pointed down a long hallway lined with three closed doors on each side.

"The first door on the left is us. Nani and Tino are our neighbors and at the end of the hall is a bathroom we all share. On the other side is Nigel and Berto, then Terrance and Rod along with their bathroom they share." Gil spun around and pointed at two doors behind them. "That one's Uncle Earl and that's Kātisu; because of their seniority, they each have their own room. Just so you know, no one's allowed inside anyone else's room without their permission."

Avery followed Gil into their room and placed his bag on the unmade bed. The room was more rectangular than square with a flaking popcorn ceiling and drab uneven walls that felt a bit defeated. The two steel-framed twin beds were tucked into opposing corners of the room with as much distance between them as space would allow. Avery glanced at the mismatched wooden dressers and approached the one closest to him to test the slide of the drawer. It slid out easily enough, and after closing it, he tilted the dresser back just to confirm that none of the furniture was bolted down.

"I take it this is mine?" he asked, turning back to Gil.

"Sure is, as long as you pay the rent." Gil closed the door behind him. "That's Otto's old bed. Remember him?"

Avery stared at the mattress. "I take it he's the one who relapsed?"

Gil nodded. "Better him than me." He stepped forward and nudged the frame of the bed with his foot. "I know it doesn't look like much, but this bed will take you places as long as you let it. Just remember though, there are no second chances beyond this point. Don't be one of those people who asks for help after it's too late and there's nothing any of us can do for you. That's probably the biggest mistake I see people make; they don't know how or when to ask for help and believe they can talk their way out of anything."

Avery nodded. "I can relate."

"We all can. That's why I'll commit to having your back, but only if you do the right thing."

"I appreciate that, thanks." Avery watched Gil leave the room and stood there staring at the empty door for a moment. Then, not knowing what to do with himself, he turned around and began making his bed.

10

NOVEMBER 25TH

One Week Later

Despite Avery's willingness to work anywhere for any pay and for anyone, his lack of resume or work history proved to be a much larger red flag to potential employers than he ever would have suspected. By leaving the door open for an interviewer's imagination to run wild, he learned over a futile week of job hunting that the worst was always assumed. This left him little choice: either continue with an inexplicable seven-year employment gap that seemed to pigeonhole him as a convict or draft a resume to include his time spent at the hospital where at least he maintained a steady job.

Based on the lack of results he had seen, Avery started toward the bus stop to return home and draft a resume. He passed a farm supply store and pawnshop, neither of which was currently hiring, then noticed the plant nursery closed earlier in the day had opened its doors for business.

Avery paused and debated his next steps, then decided to stretch his luck and crossed the street. A breeze pushed him from behind and a hand-painted plywood sign banged against the rusty chain-link fence. The sign read "Back to Eden," a fitting name in Avery's opinion for any bustling nursery that calls paradise home.

Keiki tropical fruit trees in nursery pots lined the fence next to pallets brimming with bags of black cinder, forest bark, chicken manure and soil conditioner. Two stone statues of Buddha propped the front doors open, allowing the unmistakable fragrance of puakenikeni to travel on the wind and dissipate into the parking lot.

Avery walked an aisle to get a feel for the place, then jumped in line and waited for the cashier to finish ringing up a customer. On the wall behind her, specialty garden tools dangled on pegboard hooks next to dusty packages of alphabetized seeds. He waited patiently while the cashier boxed up garden trays with micro greens and seedlings, then stepped forward when she waved at him.

"Good morning. I was hoping to speak to a manager or the owner. Would that be you by chance?"

The woman shook her head. "The owner is here, but she's doing payroll. Is something wrong?"

"No, not at all. I was in the area and wanted to see about getting an application or perhaps even an interview. But if she's busy, I'm happy to try again another time."

"We're talking about an employment application, right?" The woman paused, then frowned. "Sorry, I don't think we have those. We're old-fashioned and save paper where we can, but you can leave a resume with me if you want."

Avery made a show of tapping his pockets. "Actually, I'm all out, but I can drop one off tomorrow if that's okay?"

"Sure. We'll be here." The woman extended a ringless hand. "I'm Emi, but Jas is who you really want to talk to. Back to Eden is a third-generation family business, and she's the owner."

"Avery." He couldn't take her hand fast enough. Emi looked about his age though he wasn't quite sure and knew enough not to ask. Her hand was slick with the high humidity of the late morning, and her hair, a deep black with strings of early gray, was pulled back into a low, messy bun to showcase soft eyes. She wore a forest green Back to Eden work shirt, beige hiking shorts and matching boots. A sunrise shell rimmed in yellow gold dangled from her neck, and she wore little to no makeup. "You're a surfer?" Avery said, tapping his left eye.

Emi released his hand and mirrored him. She nodded as she touched her right eye, the one with a pterygium growth that streaked across it and disappeared into the crater of her pupil. "More of a bodysurfer, though I longboard from time to time to mix it up. What about you?"

"It's been a while, but I've always preferred to be under the surface. Things are quieter down there."

"And less risk of UV damage. The sun is so strong out here, especially on the water. I should have protected my eyes when I was younger." Emi shrugged and looked past Avery. "Live and learn, I guess."

He glanced over his shoulder and noticed a customer standing in line. "I'll be out of your hair and stop by tomorrow if that's okay. Thanks again."

Avery went to leave, but a rack of orchids near the door caught his eye. He studied the flowers, then lingered until the customer at the counter finished paying for a few pounds of dragon fruit.

"Hey Emi, can I show you something? I think you have an issue with this Dendrobium Anosmum."

She closed the register and circled the counter. "An issue with what?"

"This Honohono Orchid. Here. Look at this." Avery angled the pot to show her the underside of the flower. "You see this lip fringe and crippling on the petal? You may want to consider culling these diseased flowers since there's no cure for the virus."

Emi leaned in close and Avery caught a subtle scent of green apple shampoo. "I'm not sure what I'm looking at, but I'll bring it up to Jas. Mahalo."

"Anytime." Avery saw himself out and cut through the parking lot on his way to the sidewalk. He slapped the button on the crosswalk, took a step back as a city bus roared by and thought he heard his name being called.

Someone whistled and he turned around to see Emi leaning halfway out of the door. She motioned for him to return and then dipped back inside.

When he reentered the store, Emi was nowhere to be seen but reappeared a few seconds later with a prim woman in a floral romper.

The woman wore heavy boots caked with mud as if she had managed to sneak in a sunrise hike before work. She had a deep nut-brown tan, sharp eyes and a strong face that seemed conditioned to getting what she wanted. Between her hands she opened and closed a pair of horn-rimmed reading glasses. Avery noticed that despite her nails being clipped short, they were jagged and stained with dirt.

"Avery, thanks for sticking around. This is Jas, the owner."

Jas reached out and shook his hand. "Nice to meet you," she said in a pleasant voice. "Emi mentioned you had something to show me?"

"Of course." He turned around and motioned toward the diseased plant. "Granted, I'm no orchidologist, but I noticed on my way out what looks to be telltale signs of Botrytis."

Jas put on her glasses and hovered over the orchid bloom. She ran her finger over tiny, brown necrotic spots on the petals. "Good eye. I'm impressed."

"He's looking for a job," Emi whispered.

Jas removed her glasses and studied his face. "Out of curiosity, do you have any idea what may have caused this?"

Avery pressed a finger to his lips. "Honestly, it's hard to tell just by looking at it because Botrytis can be chemically induced or start as a genetic anomaly. But if I had to guess, I'd lean toward environmental factors and suggest that whoever is watering them should be mindful to keep moisture off the flowers." He reached out and flicked the stem which sent droplets of water flying through the air.

Behind Jas, Emi crossed her arms and shifted her weight.

"Though there's no way to know definitively that watering has anything to do with it," Avery added. "We all know fungal infections are common, especially when plants bloom."

"And out of curiosity, say this was your plant, how would you treat it?" asked Jas.

"I would cull the damaged blooms, water the plants earlier in the day and keep an eye out for similar signs in the future."

Jas smiled and motioned to Emi. "May I see his resume?"

"Actually, I'm fresh out," Avery said, "but I'm more than happy to drop one off tomorrow if you'd like?"

"I have a better idea—when can you start?"

Avery let out a deep breath. "I mean, I can start now if you need me to."

Jas chuckled. "You don't need to put in your two-weeks notice with your current employer?"

"No, not really."

"In that case, let's have you start on Monday. We open at ten."

"Wow. Thank you," Avery said. "So really that's all it takes? Just like that, I'm hired?"

"You seem qualified, so yes, unless there's anything else I need to know?"

Avery stood there for a moment, then pointed at Emi's work shirt. "Assuming I get a shirt, I'm an XL but can squeeze into a large if need be."

Jas smiled. "It's good to know you're adaptable. Emi will take care of you tomorrow. See you then."

11

NOVEMBER 28TH

As he waited for the signal to change, Avery stared at Back to Eden from across the street and couldn't help but second-guess himself. Having isolated himself most of the previous night, he had stewed in his room thinking of all the ways he could ruin a good thing if allowed to. It had been years since he had worked for someone else, and the idea of joining a team meant others would come to depend on him.

The light changed and he spotted Emi across the street approaching the gate. Something about her drew him in and before he could talk himself out of it, he hustled across the road and did his best to put on a smile.

"Hi, Emi. I want to thank you for believing in me last week," Avery said. "It means a lot and I don't know how to repay you."

She smiled and unlocked the chain on the front gate. "You don't owe me a thing, but if you insist you can pay me back by making my life easier any way you can. You can start by helping me get ready to open for the day."

"I'll do what I can." Avery closed the gate behind him and hung around long enough for her to secure it.

The two entered the nursery and began a feeling-out period where Avery familiarized himself with the intricacies of their operation while Emi sought to better understand his experience. They both tossed their belongings in the lunchroom, and on their way out, Avery noticed the orchids near the door were no longer for sale.

Emi led Avery down an overgrown gravel pathway that skirted the building. They made a pit stop at a garden shed where she introduced Avery to Kevin, a towering, gangly student from the local community college who worked when he could to chip away at his tuition. Avery tried to make small talk, but Kevin averted eye contact and kept the conversation brief.

"Did I say something wrong?" Avery whispered once Kevin was out of earshot.

Emi shook her head. "Don't think anything of it; he's like that with everybody."

She started walking again and Avery followed suit. Further down the path, they encountered a storeroom but Emi breezed past it until they reached the back of the building.

"Well, this is it. What do you think?" she asked once Avery caught up.

He did a double take and let out a low whistle. The sprawling outdoor space was split down the middle, with one side shaded for the species that would wilt away in the full sun. Plants hung from the fence line, bursting with bright reds, blues and the deepest of purples. Emi pointed out a rolling seeding table in the far corner, then a compost alley and plant library in the back. In the foreground, a sea of black garden tables ran parallel to one another, buried by trays of plants and the occasional garden gnome in a miniature Aloha shirt.

Everything was potted, and Avery surveyed the baking asphalt where striped yellow lines crisscrossed the walkways. "Joni Mitchell would be proud," he said.

"As in the singer?"

He nodded and scraped his shoe across the ground. "For once, someone paved a parking lot and put up a paradise."

Emi smiled. "We definitely have something special going on here. I hope neither of us ends up taking this job for granted."

"Trust me, I won't. Where I used to work, I could only dream of having a setup like this."

Emi motioned for them to head back inside. "Sorry, but where did you say you used to work again?"

"Too many places to recall." He held the door open and followed her inside. "Between here and Maui, I've worked at every type of nursery you can dream of, from big box stores to co-opts to community garden centers."

"I've always loved Maui." Emi bent down and picked up a bucket of flowers. "What brought you here?"

"I guess you could say a change of scenery. I left Maui behind shortly after high school and tried my hand at college, but someone has to pay the bills."

Emi shook a flower dry and began trimming the stem. "I've always admired those who always knew what they wanted to be, especially as someone who's had every job under the sun. While I enjoy this job, I'm just not sold on whether I want to do this forever." She slid a roll of brown paper in front of Avery and then passed him a pair of scissors. "How did you know?"

"Know what?"

"How did you know when you found your calling and knew what you wanted to be?"

Avery cut a piece of paper and laid it on the table. "It's a sad story, but when I was a kid—maybe twelve or thirteen—my childhood dog ran away and never came home. I searched for him every day after school, posted fliers, checked the shelters, but he just upped and vanished on me." Avery cut another piece of paper and placed his hand on it. "I was just a kid and couldn't help but take it hard, and after a few months my parents suggested we rescue another dog, but I begged them not to. I waited outside each night for so long that I began gardening to pass the time. I suppose I was drawn to plants because I realized they'll always stay put."

Emi cut a length of raffia and handed it to Avery. "Can I ask his name?"

"Mochi."

"Cute." She grabbed another bunch of flowers and began perfecting the arrangement. "You can tell me it's none of my business, but have you ever asked yourself if something happened and maybe Mochi wanted to come home, but couldn't?"

"Like if a car hit him?" Avery shrugged. "I thought about everything, and none of it helped."

"Well, whatever happened, the one saving grace is that all dogs go to heaven." Emi placed her bouquet in front of Avery. "I'm still interested in knowing where you worked once you moved here because I can't help but feel like we know some of the same faces."

"I highly doubt it. While I used to bounce around quite a bit, I've spent the last few years managing a small, private greenhouse."

Emi cocked a shoulder and leaned onto the table. "When you say 'private,' are we talking about a commercial operation?"

Avery thought for a moment, unsure how to answer. "Sure, I guess you could call it that."

She reached for her shears. "I think that helps explain why you've been so cryptic with me."

Avery avoided making eye contact. "What do you mean?"

"Come on, Avery, think about it; you don't have a resume, yet somehow you have all this experience and you've bounced around from 'job' to 'job' but can't say where? None of it adds up, though I get where you're coming from since you probably want nothing more than a reliable job and an honest day's work."

He cleared his throat but didn't respond.

Emi pushed off the table. "Look, if you're not comfortable opening up to me, that's totally fine. I know we just met and we don't have to speak of this again. But before we move on, I just want you to know something; we don't choose the gifts we are handed and if you have a green thumb, who are you not to use it? I'm not here to judge you and even if I were, I have to say there are so many worse things to be in this world than a little ol' pakalolo grower."

Avery cracked a smile, looked away and wished it could be so simple.

After circling the block, Bri lucked out and found street parking across from Leo's famous malasada truck.

"Malasadas?" Avery asked, popping his seat belt. "Malasadas for lunch?"

"Yeah. Why not? We're all adults here."

"Right, but aren't they straight sugar?"

Bri nodded. "They're also filling. Besides, can you think of a better way to celebrate your first day at work?"

"You do realize the day's not quite over?"

She opened her door and watched him study the long line. "Don't worry, it'll go by fast."

"If you say so." Avery lowered himself from her lifted Tacoma and the two jumped in line. "What are you getting?"

"My usual. Cinnamon sugar with haupia filling . . . unless they're sold out. Otherwise, their macadamia nut is just as ono."

He took a step forward. "Either of those sound good to me."

"Order number sixty-eight!"

"So, what's new?" asked Bri as they moved forward in line. "How have you been and how good does it feel to be out?"

Over his shoulder, Avery noticed a small group of tourists join the line behind him. "I'm doing fine," he said in a hushed tone. "It's been a change, but I think I'm hanging in there."

"I bet. It must be nice to have so much more freedom than you're used to."

"One would think, but I'm juggling a litany of added responsibilities so they offset each other."

Bri took another step forward and Avery followed suit. "Such as?"

"The basics. Calling in med refills and scheduling appointments to start, then there's keeping up with my laundry, shopping and cooking and blah, blah, blah."

"But that's great, Dad. You're living life on life's terms."

"*Order number seventy-two!*"

"I am and hope it doesn't sound like I'm complaining. I'm just telling you how it is." Avery watched the woman at the front of the line pay for her order and skimp on tipping. "It's all a process but once I work out my routine, it'll all be second nature."

Bri smiled. "I like the sound of that. Take it one step at a time, and don't overwhelm yourself. If I can help, promise me you'll let me know."

"You have my word."

The last couple in front of them took their receipt and moved aside to wait for their number to be called. Bri stepped forward, placed their order and dug into her purse.

"I'll get it," Avery said. He reached for his money clip, but Bri cut him off.

"Nice try, but we're celebrating your big day, not mine."

"If you don't mind, I'd like to get it."

Bri brushed his hand away and passed the cashier her Mastercard. "Really, Dad . . . you're fine."

Avery stared at the twenty in his hand for a moment, then reached over her shoulder and slipped it into the tip jar. Bri signed her receipt and joined him along with the rest of the crowd waiting for their orders.

"We're seventy-six," she said.

Avery nodded but otherwise stood there in silence. His hands took on a mind of their own and gently worked against one another. "Thanks for lunch, but next time I'd like to get it. I have money."

"I know you do, but you're also getting back on your feet and

I want to be supportive." She pulled out her phone and checked the time.

"You've always been supportive and I love that about you, but I've worked hard to get to where I am today and want to enjoy it."

"I understand." Bri tucked her phone away, stepped up to the window and grabbed their order.

"How are we looking on time?" Avery asked, taking his box from her. He picked up his pace as they returned to her truck. "I probably shouldn't be late returning from lunch on my first day."

"Trust me, I won't let that happen."

The two climbed back into the truck and Bri placed her box in the backseat. "Feel free to eat; no sense going back hungry."

Avery drummed his fingers on his box. "I can wait. The last thing I want to do is make a mess and get sugar everywhere."

Bri smirked and pointed to her backseat. "Please. Have you checked the seat behind you? I have a five-year-old, remember?"

He thought about it a moment, flipped the lid back and flooded the cab with a spicy-sweet aroma. "You sure you don't want me to wait for you?"

Bri smiled. "I'm sure."

He picked up the sugary fried donut and sunk his teeth into it, using the box as a catchall for the morsels that rained down.

"Good, huh?" Bri asked.

Avery nodded, took another bite and stared at his sugar-covered fingers while he chewed. "Better than I remember."

By the time they returned to Back to Eden, Avery had cleaned up and was fending off a sugar high. Bri pulled into a customer's only stall and cut the engine.

"Back on time as promised," she said.

"Thanks again for meeting me today," Avery said. "No matter how much or how little time we have together, it's always nice to see you." With his box in hand, he hugged her and lowered himself out of the truck.

"Oh, and one more thing," Bri said. She hopped out of her seat, opened the door behind her and removed the lid from a banker's box packed with housewarming gifts and toiletries. "Me and Micah wanted to do something nice for you." She pushed a pair of rubber slippers aside and stood a package of linens on end. "He wanted to get you a SpongeBob set, but I told him not to be silly and we compromised on the more age-appropriate Spiderman set instead. Also, in case the sheets are the wrong size, there's a gift receipt inside if you need to exchange them."

Avery took the box in his arms and smiled. "This is so sweet and please be sure to thank Micah for me."

"Of course." Bri looked up from the box and turned as a woman approached.

"Everyone have a good lunch?" Emi asked.

Avery turned around and nodded. "Emi, I'd like you to meet my daughter Brianna."

"Bri is fine."

"So nice to meet you." Emi shook Bri's hand and broke into a grin. "I wish I could say I heard nice things about you, but someone didn't mention he had a daughter." She stepped forward and peeked into Avery's gift box. "He also didn't mention it was his birthday."

Avery started to respond, but Bri beat him to it. "Oh, it's not. This is just a little care package to help out with the transition into his new place."

"Are those shower slippers?"

Bri shrugged. "It might be overkill, but we figured since the sober house has communal showers, it's better to be safe than sorry."

Avery cleared his throat and glanced at the entrance. "Thanks again for lunch, Bri. I should probably get back to work."

Emi pressed her lips flat and turned to Bri. "Same. It was a pleasure to meet you."

. . .

"Come on! Let's go already!" Uncle Earl called out, placing his foot on the first rung of the staircase. "Everyone's waiting on you."

Berto popped around the railing and scrambled down the staircase. "Hey, don't blame me! Blame whoever forgot to refill the toilet paper and left me stranded."

Uncle Earl put his hand on Berto's back. "When will you start taking responsibility for your life? We even go out of our way to make it easy for you; the house meeting is at the same time and place every week."

"Fine. Next time I won't be late, but don't blame me if I stink up the place."

"Don't be a smart ass." Uncle Earl gave him a nudge toward the crowded dining room.

As the sun set outside, long slivers of light speared through the window and ricocheted off the dining table, illuminating a rolling torrent of dust motes suspended in time. Ignoring the annoyed looks from his housemates, Berto snagged a seat in the corner of the room next to Avery.

"Apologies for the wait everyone. I'm calling this meeting to order at . . ."—Uncle Earl checked the time and side-eyed Berto —"6:34 pm. Secretary, kindly make the roll call."

Kātisu donned a round pair of reading glasses and went around the room checking off names. "All present."

"Mahalo," Uncle Earl said. "Would someone mind leading us in the Serenity Prayer?"

Tino clasped his hands and hung his head. "God . . ."

Avery closed his eyes and mumbled along with the rest of the group.

"And who would like to read one of the sober house traditions? How about you, Berto?"

Berto leaned back in his chair. "I read it last week. Can't you pick someone else?"

"I could, but I won't." Uncle Earl picked up the house manual and hand-delivered it to Berto.

Berto snatched the manual and flipped to a random page. "Number four—we are not affiliated with Alcoholics or Narcotics Anonymous, neither organizationally or financially, but we realize that active participation in either organization offers the assurance of continued sobriety." He leaned forward and lobbed the manual onto the table.

"That wasn't so hard now, was it?" Uncle Earl asked, turning to Nani. "How's that treasury report looking?"

Nani ran through a detailed report recounting receipts and expenses, then presented a motion to allocate funds to replace a broken coffee maker. All present were in favor except for Gil, who took the opportunity to remind the house that not only was he a tea purist, but if they knew what was good for them, they would be too.

The meeting transitioned from previously unfinished business to new matters, then Uncle Earl shared some highlights from his week and asked Rod to keep the momentum going. Rod mentioned a recent promotion at work and Nani upped him by announcing her new role as assistant manager at her hole-in-the-wall Poke shop. Avery recounted his first day of work and though drained, had no complaints to speak of.

One by one, the housemates shared small wins, struggles and updates. With the finish line in sight, Uncle Earl shifted gears and asked if anyone had issues with each other.

Berto pulled his chair forward. "Yeah, I do. I have an issue with someone though I don't know who. It could be Terrance, Rod or Nigel for all I know, but how hard is it to replace the toilet paper when you're done? I'm sick of finding out I need toilet paper when it's too late."

Terrance turned to Nigel and they both shrugged at each other.

"That reminds me," Gil said, dropping his elbows onto the table. "I have an issue as well, and I *do* know who to address. Berto, you need to lay off my laundry detergent. I've told you before and I'm not going to tell you again."

Berto turned to Uncle Earl. "This guy is crazy. Always accusing people of stealing."

"It's not an accusation; I *know* it's you. I can smell it on your clothes."

"So you're creepy too? Stop sniffing my clothes, you dead-headed weirdo."

"I wouldn't have to if you stopped stealing my stuff, you trifling thief."

Berto stood up. "Why don't you keep your stuff in your room where it belongs instead of leaving it up for grabs in the common areas? That way, you won't have to go around accusing people of stealing and come off like an ass."

"This is ridiculous." Gil jumped out of his chair and pounded the table. "Maybe I wouldn't have to accuse people of stealing if thieves like *you* didn't *steal* in the first place."

"Call me a thief again and see what happens, you gizzard."

"Nuff already!" Uncle Earl shouted. "Both of you need to calm down. Remember, the point of bringing up issues isn't to make matters worse but to address them and come to a *peaceful* resolution." Uncle Earl turned to Berto. "I'm not saying you are or aren't using Gil's detergent, just that you can't. This should go without saying." He turned to Gil. "Berto is right; personal belongings should be stored in your room to avoid mix ups like this, and that goes for everyone."

"So we're saying stealing is a 'mix up' now?" Gil asked, shaking his head. "I make a motion to vote this piece of shit thief out of this house once and for all. All in favor?"

Berto lunged forward, but Kātisu cut him off.

"That's it," Uncle Earl said, stepping between them. "I want you both to grow up, shake hands and settle this like men."

Neither one of them budged.

"Then put it this way; no one is leaving until you two put this behind you. And if that's something you two grown men are incapable of doing, then you can both find a new place to live."

The stare-down continued until Berto stepped forward and reached an arm out.

Uncle Earl bit his tongue until Gil finally shook Berto's hand. "Good decision. This meeting is now adjourned and I want everyone to give each other space for the rest of the night."

"With pleasure," Gil said.

Berto sneered and turned to Avery. "Just so you know, your roommate over there was the only person in this room who voted against letting you move in." Berto smirked at Gil. "Isn't that right, Mister '*I can't trust crazy people*?'"

Avery glanced at Gil, who looked away. "Seriously?"

Uncle Earl stepped forward and clapped his hands. "Like I said, this meeting is adjourned! Everybody out, now!"

12

NOVEMBER 29TH

Avery moistened a plug tray and used a narrow trowel and choice words to coax a seedling from its container. He rolled the cube of soil in his palm, then turned to Emi. "I know we just met," he said, "but you seem unusually quiet this morning. Something bothering you?"

Emi focused on teasing two tangled seedlings apart, mindful not to tear their wisp-like roots. "'Bothered' might not be the right word, but I have some questions."

He placed the plug in front of her. "Questions about me?"

She nodded.

"Like what?"

"I'm not sure since I only know what I've found online and what you've told me, which isn't much." She looked at Avery, who averted eye contact. "Can I ask, when someone takes the insanity defense, what exactly does that mean?"

"It means a lot of people think you took the easy way out despite there being nothing easy about it." Avery bit his tongue as a customer approached and asked where to find worm juice. He pointed her in the right direction and waited until she was out of sight before turning back to Emi. "About eight years ago, I was officially diagnosed as schizoaffective, though I had suspected it for some time."

She squared her shoulders to face him. "Schizoaffective? What exactly does that mean?"

"You've heard of schizophrenia before, right?"

"Of course."

"So you probably know that schizophrenia is what's known as a thought disorder, but in my case, it's only half the battle. I also suffer from debilitating depression, which is classified as a mood disorder. The combination makes me schizoaffective, though the mood component could be mania, bipolar type one or so on. It's also partially why I've struggled with alcoholism and the all-too-common trap of self-medicating." He opened his mouth to say more but thought better of it.

Emi finished untangling the roots and reached for another plug flat. "You seem nervous. Is this something you're comfortable talking about?"

He shook his head. "Not really, but I understand people have questions and sometimes not having answers can be more unsettling than the truth."

She pried another plug from the tray. "You know, I can relate in my own way. I fought off bouts of depression when I was younger but can't imagine what it must be like to suffer from schizophrenia. Does that mean you hear voices?"

"I've heard voices in the past, along with other aural hallucinations, but not a word or peep in years, and not since I've been officially diagnosed." He reached for the watering can and soaked a freshly homed seedling.

"And when you heard voices, what did they say?"

Avery flashed a wavering smile. "Mostly that I was worthless and didn't deserve to be happy."

"Did they tell you to harm yourself or others?"

"Are you asking if I'm a violent person?" He shook his head. "Besides my one assault charge and my drinking, I've never been a danger to myself or others."

She teased out another plug with her butter knife and caught it squarely in her palm. "But you assaulted a police officer?"

"Yes, in a fit of mania, but that was one incident and me at my worst. And not to change the subject, but it's important to mention that statistically speaking, people with mental health disorders are far more likely to be the victims of violence rather than the aggressor. I only say this because it's something most people—as in, people like my roommate—overlook when crafting their narrow and one-sided opinions."

Emi wrinkled her nose. "I take it we're talking about your roommate at the sober house?"

He nodded. "His name is Gil. To my face, he acted like he wanted the best for me—even promised to have my back—but it was all a façade and he never wanted me around."

"I'm sorry to hear that. Did he say why?"

"Not to me he didn't. Someone else tipped me off, but this isn't anything new to me. Maybe he fears me which may explain why he came off so nice. He probably figures if he puts up a front and gets on my good side, I wouldn't come after him if I snapped."

She shrugged and turned back to her work. "I like to think I'm good at reading people, and you don't give off the vibe of being dangerous." She placed her butter knife down between them. "You mentioned being medicated. Do you mind me asking if you find these drugs helpful?"

"They're more than helpful; they gave me my life back. I'm on Zyprexa—an antipsychotic medication, and Lamotrigine—a mood stabilizer that doesn't murder my kidneys like Lithium." Avery tamped dirt into a pot around a seedling, then picked up a watering can and gave it a healthy soaking. "Ever since my doses have been dialed in, my symptoms have been nearly nonexistent."

"That's good, but do you have to take these medications forever?"

"No, not forever. Just until I die."

She cracked a smile. "Funny, but doesn't that mean you're only being treated and not cured?"

"Perhaps, but how does one cure something without knowing what causes it?"

"All I'm saying is if they don't know what causes it, how can they treat it?"

"They have ideas," he said stiffly. "But you have a point and ideas can change. Back in the day, premature dementia, atonement for sin, supernatural or demonic possessions, even bad parenting have all been thought to turn people schizophrenic. Mostly, it's been a long, troubled history of scientific wandering, but the current consensus seems to have settled on what's known as the dopamine hypothesis. I suppose this explanation works for me, though it'll probably change since the mind is largely unknown and unmapped." He pushed a seedling aside and took a break. "Look, whatever the cause and whatever the treatment, all I know is that I haven't had a severe episode in ages, so something's working."

Emi transferred another seedling to a pot. "But isn't it hard on your body to take these medications forever?"

"There are downsides, sure, but the downsides are nothing compared to sitting through electric shock therapy or a lobotomy."

". . . They didn't."

"No, not on me or anyone I know, but want to hear something creepy? They still have the old lobotomy room down in the basement, or so I've heard."

She shuddered and went quiet for a moment. "There have to be holistic remedies or naturopathic alternatives that can help if not cure you. Have you ever tried essential oils, vitamins or supplements?"

"No, because the way I see it, if there were truly a cure for schizophrenia, someone would have capitalized on it ages ago."

"I'm not so certain because what incentive is there for them to release a cure? If anything, Big Pharma would rather profit off your 'treatment' for the rest of your life."

Avery grimaced at the thought. "You know, despite my condition, I've never been one for conspiracies."

"I'm not saying that's what this is, just asking questions." She rubbed her brow as if to force out a thought. "What about side effects?"

"What about them?"

"Do you have any?"

"I experienced headaches at first, but the med team adjusted my dosages accordingly. Otherwise, the occasional stomach upset and weight gain were off-putting, but I'll take those minor inconveniences over my symptoms any day of the week."

Emi stacked a handful of empty plastic trays together and pushed them aside, then looked up at Avery. "When you experienced those side effects, did you stop to wonder if you were stuck in a prescription cascade cycle?"

He cocked his head. "A what?"

"You take medications and don't know what a prescription cascade is?" She lifted a single eyebrow. "It's when the side effects of one prescription are diagnosed as symptoms of another condition, leading to more and more prescriptions. I'm not a doctor, but if there's even the possibility of a natural alternative, I'd look into it. Take Ocean Therapy, for example. It's done wonders for my life ever since I started trying to get into the ocean at least once a day."

"But you're not schizophrenic."

She turned to face him. "No, but the point is salt water heals, and so does fresh air and the sun." She peeled off her gloves and stacked them on the table. "Any chance you're an early bird?"

"I can be if there's a reason."

"In that case, why don't you meet me for dawn patrol tomorrow? I body surf every morning before work, either at Makapu'u or Sandys. It's a great way to start the day and helps clear my head, not to mention my sinuses."

"I think I can make that happen."

"Perfect. Do you have a pair of fins?"

"No, but I'm sure one of the guys I live with has a pair lying around."

Emi glanced down. "What size are you? Eleven?"

Avery nodded.

"Okay, I'll bring a pair. See you tomorrow?"

"Sure. What time?"

She cracked a smile. "The whole point of dawn patrol is to be in the water by sunrise, so I'll see you then."

13

NOVEMBER 30TH

Alone in the dark, Avery gripped a beach towel around his neck and sidestepped down a steep, crumbly path. Having almost tripped a few steps back, he carefully worked his way down the sandy hillside, mindful not to get hung up on any other rocks buried beneath the surface like forgotten land mines.

Far below, the rumble of breaking waves reverberated through the cove of Makapu'u Bay. A light wind billowed Avery's board shorts and carried with it remnants of conversations and excitement from the shoreline below. He did what he could to collect himself, then poked his heel into the sand to take the next step.

When he reached the bottom, the pinprick glinting on the horizon had exploded into a roiling fire in the sky. Shadows with a golden tinge lapped on the water's surface and flashed behind every forming wave that stood tall before curling into an endless barrel.

With slippers in hand, Avery made his way to the water's edge where the compressed sand became easier to trudge and navigate. He searched the silhouettes dotting the shore and made out Emi in the distance, sitting cross-legged on a towel.

"You made it," she said as he approached, sounding somewhat surprised. Emi patted an empty towel spread out next to hers. As Avery got comfortable, she reached for a soft cooler and pulled out two vegan wraps.

He took the wrap and turned it in his hands. "Thank you, though I'm embarrassed to say I didn't think to bring you anything. Maybe next time we do this, you'll let me make it up?"

Facing the water, the two ate in silence and studied the breaking waves. Between bites, Emi pointed to a small group of bodyboarders who formed the makings of a lineup.

"That same group is here every day without fail. They paddle out before first light to beat the crowd and get their fix in before work."

Avery watched one of them drop into a set wave. Bright lights mounted to the back of his board illuminated him from behind as the barrel closed out on him.

Emi took her last bite and passed Avery a set of mismatched fins. "I hope these fit, because you're going to want them out there."

He crammed his feet inside and flexed his toes. "Like a glove."

She rose, tied her hair back, then replaced her shirt with a white rash guard covering a Jolyn bikini top. Avery tossed his shirt over hers and traced her footsteps into the water.

The onshore breeze didn't do the shape of the waves any favors, but the moment Avery ducked under the first wave and felt the power course through him, something inside him woke up. He was at home in the water, and no amount of landlocked years could ever take that away from him. When he popped to the surface, he continued his pursuit of Emi, kicking and keeping his head above water as he chased her glowing silhouette into the sun.

A new set rolled in and Emi spun in place and launched into a dolphin kick. With both arms outstretched, she arched her back and pulsed her hips on the surface until the wave broke and embraced her, propelling her down the face and curling behind her to hold her in the pocket. He dove at the last minute and spun underwater to make out her blurry form gracefully rocketing toward shore.

The two caught their fair share of waves as latecomers encroached on their fun and competed for the best rides. After a half hour, Avery sensed he was tiring and had no choice but to slow down, eventually treading water through entire sets to catch his breath before heading into shore. He had gone over the falls twice, and not wanting to risk slamming into the bottom harder than he had already, he tracked down Emi. As they crossed paths, he let her know where to find him and not to come in until she was ready.

After returning to the beach, Avery shook some water out of his ears and dried himself off. Sitting on his towel, he watched Emi from afar and realized he couldn't take his eyes off her. He admired her gracefulness and strength, but as the morning sun warmed his skin, a familiar darkness coursed through him, and he couldn't help but resent where life had taken him.

Avery laid back and closed his eyes.

He wondered whether he was attracted to Emi or her energy and realized the answer was yes to both. He considered whether her refusal to push him away was the same as inviting him into her world. He wondered if she was single, and if so, was she single on purpose or damaged by a previous partner? Was she healing or hurt, and would he ever find out?

A darker shadow came over him, and Avery felt drips of water falling onto his feet. He opened his eyes and raised his palm to his brow.

"How are you feeling?" Emi asked.

Avery sat up and smiled. "Exhausted, but good."

"That's Ocean Therapy for you." She removed her rash guard and reached for a towel. "Normally, I'd take a breather and head back out for round two, but you look to be done for the day. Why don't we rinse off and grab a cup of coffee before work?"

Avery couldn't get up fast enough.

· · ·

Shortly after lunch, a gray-haired woman on her phone approached the cash register and placed a potted plant on the counter. Then, with her free hand, she reached out and handed Avery a crumpled receipt.

"I'd like to return this please."

He flattened the faded receipt and inspected the plant. "I'm sorry, but I can't accept this return."

The woman held up a finger. "Jenny, can I call you right back? Thanks." She ended her call and slipped her phone into her purse. "Sorry about that. What did you say?"

"I said, 'I'm sorry, but I can't accept this return.'" He scratched the bark and showed the woman the cambium layer. "See how this is brown and not green? This plant is *dead* dead, which is almost impressive because breadfruit trees are hearty by nature." He slid the plant back to her and held out her receipt.

The woman refused. "I know the plant is dead. Why else would I be returning it?"

"But you can't return a plant you've obviously neglected." Avery tapped the rock-hard soil. "The soil is bone dry."

"Are you suggesting I should water a plant after it dies?"

"I think the general idea is to keep the plant watered to prevent that from happening."

The woman stiffened and removed her sunglasses. "I don't understand why you're making this so difficult; all the big box stores offer full refunds."

"They also over-fertilize their plants so they grow unnaturally fast, which means a higher likelihood of them getting diseases or dying."

The woman's posture stiffened. "I don't care what they do. I paid good money for a tree that's obviously a dud and I demand a refund."

"I don't know what else to tell you, other than plants don't lie. I'm just doing my job, a job I'll probably lose if I accept this return."

The woman's eyes narrowed. "Lose your job? So, you're not a manager?"

Avery shook his head.

"Then why in the world am I wasting my time with you? Where's your boss?"

"In her office. Would you like me to see if she's available?"

The woman rolled her eyes. "I think that's a lovely idea."

Avery disappeared and returned a moment later with Jas in tow, who politely asked the customer to step aside so Avery could ring up the next customer.

"Good afternoon," Jas said. "I'm the owner. What can I do for you today?"

"I don't understand why this man is saying I'm unable to return this plant. I've been a customer here for years and don't see what the problem is."

Jas glanced at the plant and smiled. "There's no problem. Would you like an exchange or a refund?"

"I wouldn't say no to an exchange, as long as the replacement isn't another dud as well."

"Wonderful," Jas said. "I'll tell you what, why don't I grab you two plants? That way, if one of them gives you a hard time, you'll have a backup on hand."

"Actually, if you don't mind, I'd rather grab it myself."

"Help yourself," Jas said. "Do you know where they are?"

"I think you missed the part where I said I've been shopping here for years." The woman smiled and headed for the back door.

When she was out of earshot, Jas turned to Avery. "I know what you're thinking, but don't take it personally. Whatever those plants cost, they're not worth a bad review online."

"From what I just saw, I'm willing to bet she still leaves one, except now she has two more plants to kill."

"Maybe you're right," Jas said. "Or maybe you're wrong, but

what else can you do when dealing with a disturbed customer who exists in their own reality? We both know there's no point trying to talk sense into her, so why not give her what she wants and hope she walks out of here happy?"

Avery's tone went flat. "Somehow, I doubt she'll be happy either way."

The woman returned, clutching two new plants to her chest. "These two look like the best of the bunch and I'll take these if you don't mind. Do you need to ring them up?"

Jas waved her off. "You're all set. Have a great day."

"You too." The woman started for the exit and turned around. "Also, I know it's not my business, but if I ran this place, I'd take a good long look at the people working for me and do some much needed pruning."

Avery stared at the woman and smiled with tension in his jaw. On the inside, he was shaking but refused to give her the satisfaction of knowing as much.

14

DECEMBER 1ST

"Pretty sweet digs they got you set up with." Lauren stepped into Avery's room and knocked on the wall with her knuckle.

"For what it's worth, it's not too bad."

"No, not bad at all. Trust me, I've seen much worse." Lauren pointed at the bed in the corner. "Is your roommate at work?"

"You mean Gil?" Avery rubbed his chin. "No idea. We don't talk much."

"That's too bad. Any particular reason?"

"I have nothing to say to him, not since I found out he voted against me moving in."

"Oof." Lauren winced. "I'm sorry to hear that, but maybe once you two get to know each other, things will fall into place."

Avery narrowed his eyes and stared at her. "I think you're giving him a little too much credit."

"Perhaps, but people change, and not always for the worse." Lauren pulled out her phone and checked the time. "Anyway, we've got a busy morning and should get a move on, but since I'm here, how about a quick med check for shits and giggles?"

Avery crouched down and removed a lockbox from under his bed. He fumbled with the code, then forked over a half-empty pill organizer.

She did a quick count and returned his case to him. "Have you already put in your refill order for next month?"

"No, but I will today."

"Good, and how are the meds working? Any new side effects or breakthrough symptoms to speak of?"

Avery stashed his meds away, reached for a clean set of socks and sat on the edge of his bed. "Everything seems to be working as intended. I have noticed I've been a bit more drained lately, but I've also been on my feet all day at work."

Lauren smiled. "That's a good problem to have. And how's the family?"

"Doing well. I haven't been able to see them as much as I'd like to since moving out, but hopefully that will all turn around as I adapt to a full schedule."

"It should. So it sounds like the new job is working out for you?"

The idea of mentioning Emi crossed his mind, but Avery thought better of it. "It's growing on me. The job is second nature, I work with decent people and my boss is pretty hands off, which is appreciated." He slipped on his socks and rose. "Only complaint so far is a handful of customers who think the world owes them something."

"But you'll find those kinds anywhere you go."

Avery smiled and grabbed his wallet. "Hopefully not wherever we're off to next."

"No promises, but I think you'll be in good hands."

Avery followed Lauren out of the house and stepped into his shoes. She beat him down the driveway and he hustled to join her in the Jeep.

"First stop is to meet Ava McKinley, your new community case manager." She buckled her seat belt and turned to him. "I think you'll like her. She's young but passionate, and her heart's in the right place."

Avery raised an eyebrow. "I'm confused. Why do I need a case manager if I have you?"

"Because the law says so. In order to see the psychiatrist at the mental health clinic, you're required to have a community case manager there as well." Lauren started the engine, then checked over her shoulder and pulled onto the road. "By the way, I forgot to ask if you're still drawing."

"Here and there, but like I said earlier, I have less and less energy these days."

"Once you get adjusted, I'm sure you'll get back into it. It's important to keep up with your hobbies and passions."

Lauren went quiet and drove in silence for some time.

"Speaking of passions, how's Kalani holding up in the greenhouse?"

"Kalani? He seems to be doing fine as far as I can tell, but what do I know about gardening?"

"Is the greenhouse still standing at least?"

Lauren slapped her blinker and pulled over in front of a weathered red-brick building stained by runoff from the roof. "As far as I can tell he's doing his best, and things look to be in order. Then again, you only just moved out so give him some time. He's human and will no doubt make mistakes along the way, but eventually he'll find his stride and figure out the lessons he's supposed to learn. Then, once he finally has it all figured out, it'll be his time to move out, and he'll stress over whether his replacement can hold it all together." She popped her seatbelt and killed the engine. "I hope that makes you feel better."

A thin smile formed on Avery's lips as he exited the vehicle. "A little."

They entered the building through automatic doors and approached a receptionist's desk littered with pamphlets. Avery traded his ID and insurance card for a clipboard stacked with intake paperwork and made himself comfortable in the waiting area next to Lauren. When he finished, he returned his paperwork, kicked back in his chair and rested his eyes.

"Mr. West?"

Avery tilted his head back to see a short-haired woman with a boyish face flipping through his documents. She smiled and waved for them to join her.

"How are you? I'm Ava, your case manager." She shook Avery's hand and turned to Lauren. "Good to see you again. How have you been?"

"Hanging in there for now, but ready for the weekend."

"I feel the same." Ava used the clipboard to motion down the hall. "Well, shall we get started?"

"Actually, I'll hang back if you don't mind," Lauren said. "One of my guys is on the verge of having a crisis and I need to clear the air with his employer before it's too late."

"Not a problem, and if I can help, please let me know."

"Will do." Lauren waved goodbye to Avery and turned back to her phone.

Avery walked in Ava's footsteps as she weaved through the clinic on their way to her office. She apologized for her chilly office and explained it was beyond her control. Her desk faced the door, and a large sliding window looked out onto the main drag. A picture of twin boys building a sandcastle hung on the wall, and a fake monstera plant sat in the corner.

"Please, have a seat." Ava motioned to a chair and circled her desk.

Avery helped himself and watched a steady stream of cars pass back and forth through her window.

"Did Lauren explain the purpose of our meeting today?"

Avery shook his head. "Only that the law requires me to be here."

Ava smirked. "True, but between us, that's the last thing I care about. My job—much like Lauren's and Dr. Nagasaki's, who you'll see next—is to help you succeed, whatever success looks like to you and the courts. I am here to support you in any way I can now that you've transitioned to community living. But more importantly, I want to see you meet your mental health care goals as you navigate this next exciting chapter of your life. How's that sound?"

"I'll take all the help I can get."

"That's wonderful. And where are you with your goals? Do you have any you'd like to share or need help achieving?"

He leaned back in his chair. "Off the top of my head? Not really. I've never been a goal-oriented person."

"That's fine, but maybe I can help. Why don't we start with the basics? I think a good goal we can agree on is for you to remain med-compliant and clean and sober. Then we can focus on any issues arising from your housing or employment situations. Do you have concerns regarding your medications or recovery?"

Avery shook his head. "Not at the moment. I think I'm in a good spot with both."

"Perfect. Then let's do a quick assessment before I hand you off to Dr. Nagasaki. He's a wonderful psychiatrist and I think between me, him and Lauren, you're going to be in great hands."

"Sorry to make you wait so long," Dr. Nagasaki said, showing Avery into his office. "I never quite know when a patient is going to have a breakthrough and I have to make the most of it when they do. I'm sure you can understand."

Rather than respond, Avery pulled back a chair and sat at the young doctor's desk. Having waited for over an hour, he had no time for niceties or interest in making small talk with the man.

Dr. Nagasaki took a seat across from Avery and began sorting folders. He appeared to be in his thirties and his dark hair was moussed and parted to one side, revealing a thin strip of scalp. He sported prescription glasses and a designer aloha shirt and smelled of herbaceous clary sage.

He removed a blue folder with Avery's name on the tag and pushed the slush pile aside. "I only work with one or two forensic patients a year," he said, "so this will be a real treat." He licked his finger and flipped a page. "This says you were first hospitalized seven years ago?" He glanced at Avery. "That's a long time. Why so long?"

Avery shrugged. "You'd have to ask the judge on that one."

"It just doesn't make sense to me. I'll never understand the logic in hospitalizing someone any longer than necessary, especially once they've been stabilized."

Avery shrugged again. "I don't know what to tell you. I don't make the rules."

Dr. Nagasaki flipped a page. "Speaking of stabilization, twenty milligrams of Olanzapine seems a bit overkill, don't you think?"

"I'm not a doctor."

"Well, I am. How's that dosage working out for you?"

"Fine."

Dr. Nagasaki leaned forward. "You do know that's the maximum daily dose according to prescribing guidelines, right?"

"What's your point?"

"My point is that it seems high to me."

"Well, even if I'm maxed out, that's the dose we found to be therapeutic. We tried lower doses before but I experienced breakthrough symptoms."

"And how long ago was that?"

Avery shrugged. "Don't know off the top of my head but it should all be right there in my chart."

"I'll have to look into it but it's something to think about." Dr. Nagasaki flipped the pages back and closed the folder. "I'll never understand why people coming out of long-term hospitalizations are always so overprescribed. Next time we meet, we should discuss titrating you down slowly over the course of a couple of months. Maybe drop you down to seventeen and a half milligrams a day, then fifteen, then twelve and a half and hopefully ten. In my opinion, that's a much more reasonable dose than what they have you on now."

"I don't know how I feel about that. Like I said, the meds are working fine."

"I know it can be scary any time you adjust your meds, but I'm telling you what they have you on isn't sustainable." He closed the folder and rocked back in his chair. "I'm curious to know about your side effects."

"What about them?"

"Do you have any?"

Avery shook his head.

Dr. Nagasaki cocked an eyebrow. "None?"

"No."

"What about suicidal ideations?"

"No."

"Any thoughts of hurting yourself or others?"

Avery kept a poker face as he thought about his hour-long wait in the waiting room. "No, none at all."

"Are you just going to say no to all of my questions?"

Avery shrugged. "No."

Dr. Nagasaki chuckled and glanced at his watch. "In that case, I think that's a good start for now. Why don't we call it a day and schedule a follow up in a month or two or whenever you're ready to open up?"

Avery sat there in silence before patting his armrests and rising to make his exit. When he reached the door, the doctor called out something about looking forward to their next meeting. Without a word, Avery slipped out of the room and casually slapped the door shut behind him.

15

DECEMBER 2ND

Emi placed her swim fins next to her towel, dropped to her knees and reached for her coffee. "Did you have a good day off yesterday?"

Avery, huffing with labored breath, patted his face with his beach towel. "I don't want to talk about it."

"You mean to say you ruined a perfectly good day off?"

Avery finished drying his ears and tossed his towel by his feet. "It sure didn't feel like a day off, not when I spent most of the morning waiting to meet my new psychiatrist."

Emi stuck her coffee cup back into the sand. "That sounds annoying."

"You have no idea. I don't see why I have to explain my hospitalization to someone who has unfettered access to my charts."

She pointed to a body surfer pulling into a set wave. "Maybe he had his hands full or figured it was best to hear it from the source?"

"Or maybe he wants me to do his job for him?" Avery reached up and massaged his temples. "What really bothered me though was how he kept going on about tapering back my meds because he thinks my dosage is too high."

"I don't get it. Wouldn't you be excited about reducing your meds?"

"It doesn't work like that. It took a lot of work to get me to where I need to be and I'm happy where I'm at. Not to mention, he doesn't understand that it's normal for people leaving the hospital to be on higher doses than the average Joe."

Emi scratched her jaw. "So you're saying the hospital over medicates everyone?"

"I'm saying people coming out of the hospital are at higher doses than those in the community because we're sicker going in, hence the required hospitalization. It makes sense, right? If someone gets to a point where they're that far gone, why wouldn't it take more effort to bring them back?"

"Something doesn't add up. Even if your goal isn't to get off meds entirely—which, in my mind, it should be—wouldn't you want to work your way down to a lower dose? You mentioned being stable for some time, so why not experiment and see what happens, especially if your doctor is pushing for it?"

"Experiment?" Avery pinched his lips together and turned to Emi. "Do you know what happens if I taper down and become symptomatic?"

Emi didn't respond.

"I will go right back to the hospital."

"Yeah, but if you never taper down and—"

He raised a hand to cut her off. "If you don't mind, I'd rather change the subject. You're not a doctor, and neither am I, but at least I know I'm headed in the right direction. The last thing I want to do is get in my way. And if that doesn't work for you, why don't you take down my therapist's phone number? Lauren can't get into the specifics of my case, but I'm sure she'll be more than happy to field these questions of yours."

Emi shrugged and handed Avery her phone, then turned her attention to her coffee and buried her feet in the sand. Her eyes were drawn to a lighthouse pulsing in the distance where the cliffs curled around the bay, marking the island's easternmost point. In the foreground, a gutsy paraglider who earlier had stepped off the twelve-hundred-foot ridge was swaying through the heavens with a bit of help from invisible thermal columns.

Avery apologized and studied the otherwise perfect morning. On their way in from their session, the high tide was rolling out, making an already shallow shore break much more dangerous. Now, Makapuʻu was firing on all cylinders with a northeast swell that rocked the bay with devastating waves.

"You don't have to apologize," Emi said. "You're right. I'm not a doctor, but I want the best for you. I care about you, Avery."

"You do?" He smiled and collected his things. "I care about you, too, so much so that we should get a move on. We don't want to be late for work."

Avery picked up his shirt and revealed a Moleskin journal beneath it. In the few seconds it took him to get dressed, Emi picked up the notebook and turned it over in her hands.

"I'll take that," he said.

Emi handed it over. "Is there a reason you bring this with you wherever you go?"

He shrugged. "I've always found drawing and poetry to be somewhat therapeutic. It's not like I just take meds, sit back and hope for the best."

She held a hand out. "Can I see?"

Avery stared at his notebook. "Most of this doesn't have context and would be hard to explain."

"But that's the beauty of being an artist; you never have to explain yourself." She shifted closer to him. "Of course, you don't have to share if you don't feel comfortable."

Avery didn't look up. Instead, he slid his thumb under the elastic band on the cover, flipped through a few pages, then turned the book around to show off a sketch.

"It's beautiful. May I?" Emi reached for the book and nestled it on her lap. She hovered her fingers over a pencil drawing of a wilted tomato plant dying on the vine. Then, without asking, she turned the page.

As she stared at the following sketch, Avery resisted every urge to snatch his book back.

"Is this me?"

He took a deep breath. "That was the idea. I look for inspiration where I can find it."

"You drew me body surfing? When?"

"You're always the last one out of the water, so I find time to add a little each day. But as you can see, it's not finished. I still have to redo this and turn that inwards, then shade the—"

Emi turned to look at Avery. "It's perfect. Can I have it? Or a signed copy?"

His mouth parted. "But it's still a work in progress."

"Aren't we all?" She pulled out her phone and unlocked it. "Can I at least take a picture for now?"

He thought for a moment, then handed her back the notebook.

"Thank you. It means a lot." She placed the notebook on her towel and tapped her screen to focus when a breath of wind caught the page and flipped it.

Instead of taking the photo, she went silent as her fingers dropped to a verse. Her lips moved silently as all tension escaped her body. "Avery? Is this poem about me?"

He stood there for a moment, lost in his head. Then, without a word, he leaned forward and pulled the journal from her hands.

She looked at her empty palms and then up at him. "Sorry, I didn't mean to—"

"It's fine," he said as he began packing his things. "Come on. We should really get to work."

"Good evening," Emi said to the hostess. "Long time no see. How long is the wait for a table for two?"

"Without a reservation?" The hostess ran her finger down a list and checked her watch. "Right now, maybe somewhere around forty-five minutes."

"That long, huh?" Emi stepped back and turned to Avery. "Sorry I didn't think ahead to make a reservation. Do we want to hang out or try our luck elsewhere?"

Though hungry, Avery preferred to be easygoing. "Up to you. I'm good either way."

Emi thought for a moment, then returned to the counter. "I think we'll try again some other time. Mahalo."

"I don't blame you." The hostess smiled and clapped her book closed.

Together, the pair stepped out of line and wandered down the sidewalk so slowly that the night seemed to sweep them away.

"I need to apologize for this morning at the beach," Emi said, bumping into Avery with her shoulder. "I didn't mean to over-step and read your poetry without permission, but when I saw what you wrote and realized it was about me, I couldn't look away. I don't know about you, but I've spent most of today wondering if there's something here."

Avery scratched the back of his neck and smiled.

She reached up and took hold of his hand. "I don't know why you entered my life or why I entered yours, but I have to say that I enjoy having you around. I just wish I knew what you were looking for."

He thought for a moment and stopped walking. "Honestly, I wish I knew myself. For years, the only thing I've been chasing is a sense of stability in life, but now that I'm nearly there, I'm not sure what the next stop is."

She stepped forward, gripped the bottom of his shirt and pulled him towards her. "Then let's take it one step at a time, just you and me. You're growing on me, Avery. Do you feel the same way?"

He took a deep breath and nodded as the faint scent of salt water in her hair brought him down to earth.

She tugged on his arm. "Come on. There aren't many vegan options in this neighborhood, but I have everything at home to throw together a decent meal."

Emi's house was within walking distance, and by the time the couple arrived, she was nestled comfortably under Avery's arm. A motion sensor clicked on and illuminated an uneven brick pathway overgrown by dandelions.

"I wasn't expecting guests, so please forgive the mess." She approached the modest two-bedroom house and unlocked the front door.

Avery removed his shoes and felt something brush up against his leg.

"Sorry, I should have thought to ask. You're not allergic, are you?"

He shook his head, bent down and scratched the Burmese cat behind her ears. "What a sweetheart."

"That's a rescue animal for you. Meet Yuki, my roommate's cat. Nora is a nurse and works nights so you'll have to meet her some other time." She reached around him and locked the door.

Avery scanned the room and noticed the place was eerily free of clutter. Decorative throw pillows lined the couch, and a built-in bookshelf was brimming with books, organized by color and trim size. "Nice place you got here."

"You think? I know it's not much, but that's the Hawai'i housing market for you. Why don't you make yourself comfortable and I'll see what's on the menu."

He made his way to the couch as she lit a candle and opened the windows to let traces of a cross breeze flow into the room. In the kitchen, she placed an onion on a cutting board along with carrots, ginger and a few cloves of garlic. Behind him, a sizable Bohemian tapestry rippled on the wall as Yuki purred at his feet, shamelessly vying for attention.

"I can make tofu katsu curry if you don't mind having left-over rice?"

He lifted Yuki and set her on his lap. "No, not at all. Do you need any help?"

She picked up a carrot and pointed it at the cat. "Thanks for offering, but I don't think Yuki will be too happy if I steal you away."

When she finished cooking, she dished out their meals and grabbed a wine glass from the cupboard. "I know you don't drink, but do you mind if I have a glass with dinner, or would you prefer I didn't?"

He brushed the cat away and got up to help set the table. "Doesn't make a difference to me. Help yourself."

She poured herself a glass and sat across from him, loosening up over dinner. Then she pulled her seat close enough to steal a kiss when they finished.

"Why don't you stay with me tonight?" she asked, rubbing her hand down the inseam of his pants.

He nuzzled her neck and inhaled her breath. "I would love to, but I have to be back by curfew."

"What time is that?"

"Midnight."

"And it's what, only a quarter to eight?" She stood up and pulled him toward her bedroom. "In that case, come with me. We have plenty of time, but not a minute to waste."

16

DECEMBER 3RD

The following day, Avery returned to the hospital for advice or at least something close to it. He opened the door to his former room and stuck his head inside. "Knock, knock. Anybody home?" He let the door close behind him and averted his gaze as Marv squeezed into his boxers.

"You came crawling back so soon? Let me guess, you couldn't hack it in the real world?"

Avery made a show of scratching his cheek with his middle finger. "I just finished a treatment conference with the treatment team, smartass. But before I take off for work, I figured I'd come and check in on you since it's about time you had your first visitor."

"But I enjoy having no visitors. Far fewer people to impress."

Avery walked up and hugged him. "I can't believe I'm going to say this, but it's good to see you. How have you been?"

"Same old, same old." Marv let go and motioned to Avery's old bed. "Kalani filled your shoes, but other than that, no complaints."

"Is he not a good roommate?"

"He has his moments but I've had worse." Marv smiled and

sat down on the edge of the bed. "Have you visited the green-house yet?"

Avery shook his head. "That was my next stop right after here."

"In that case, don't panic, but I think he needs a little help. He's trying his best, but from what I've gathered, some plants might be on their way out."

Avery glanced at the door. "Maybe I should head there now?"

"Before you go, I'm curious to know how it's going out there. Is it everything it's chalked up to be?"

Avery leaned against the wall. "You know, it's not as bad as you make it sound. Maybe you should try it out sometime? You'd probably get a kick out of it, and who knows, it could be good for you?"

"What makes you say that?"

Avery motioned for Marv to look around. "You know the concept of fish only growing to the size of their tank? Why stunt your growth here when there's an entire ocean out there? Sure, you'll survive as long as you stay put, but is that really our purpose here?"

"I thought I warned you about the dangers of philosophiz-ing, and since when did surviving become a dirty word?" Marv leaned forward. "I know what I'm capable of, and it's in every-one's best interest that I stay put."

"But you've changed, Marv. Same as me. Did you not enjoy your last pass?"

"What about me going to a funeral sounds enjoyable to you?"

"At the very least, the food is normally good, but you're missing the point. You *went*. That's the first step, and now you just have to keep it going. Tell you what; why don't we go on pass some time, just me and you? We can catch a movie or hang at the beach? Or, I know a great—"

Marv crossed his arms over his chest. "Is that why you're

here? To guilt trip me into following in your footsteps? Because you know me better than that."

"No, that's not why I came. Like I said, I was in the area and wanted to say hi."

"Then say what you came to say and remember, if I ever ask for your opinion, remind me to check with the med team and see about getting my doses adjusted."

"Hardy har."

Marv picked up his teeth and broke into a smile. "All joking aside, I think that's enough about me. What's new with you?"

"Not much. I got hired at a little plant nursery and am still settling into that sober house."

"I'm happy for you. Do you have a new roommate?"

Avery's eyes shined as he looked at Marv. "I do, and I can't believe I'm about to say this, but he actually makes me miss having you around."

"Well, they say one never knows what they have until it's gone. What about relationships? Any prospects on the horizon?"

"Believe it or not, I'm kind of seeing someone."

Marv rolled his eyes and suppressed a laugh. "Already? Where the hell did you find someone as crazy as you? Wait, let me guess, online?"

Avery shook his head. "Wrong as usual. She's a coworker."

"A coworker? Is that a good idea? What if it doesn't end well?"

"Whatever happens, we're both adults, so we'll act like it. But speaking of ending well, I have something that's been bothering me. I don't really know how to say this, but last night we hooked up for the first time, and I kinda couldn't perform to save my life."

"What do you mean you 'kinda couldn't perform?'" Marv cocked an eyebrow. "You couldn't stay hard? Or you couldn't finish?"

"Both, and I've never had that issue before. I don't know what's wrong with me."

"Well, are you attracted to her? Because if you're desperate and looking to hookup with the first woman who has no standards, maybe you—"

"She's beautiful, Marv. Inside and out."

Marv went quiet for a moment. "In that case, there's only one other thing it can be. But if it's what I think it is, it's out of your control."

"How so?"

"You're still on Olanzapine, right?"

Avery nodded.

"Has anyone ever told you that ED is a common side effect? Same goes for having a reduced libido."

"To be fair, they very well may have, but since I've been out of the game for years it would have gone over my head." He rubbed his forehead while staring at Marv. "You seem to know what you're talking about; what options do I have?"

"Like I mentioned, not much. Your hands are tied because you need your pills, and while the shrink can always cut you a script for boner meds, that's only half the battle. Viagra may help you get it up and keep it there, but if you're also struggling with ejaculatory dysfunction, you're on your own."

"Just what I need, another prescription when this woman is riding me to cut back."

"Cut back on what? Your meds?" Marv went quiet for a moment. "I'm confused. You said she was a coworker, but is that code for your psychiatrist?"

Avery frowned. "No, of course not."

"Okay, good. I only ask because your shrink's the only one who should be telling you what to take and when."

"I understand, but this woman cares about me and wants me to get healthy. But back to the ED; do you know of any natural alternatives that can set me straight?"

"Were I you, I'd start with the standard lifestyle changes: diet, exercise, getting good sleep and whatnot. Only then would

I try my hand at ginseng or maybe a Voodoo doll, but what do I know?"

"More than me, apparently."

"Which isn't saying much," Marv said. "Seriously though, be careful out there with anyone who thinks they know what's best for you, especially if they don't have a clue on what they're talking about. Have you ever gone off your meds before?"

"I have, and it didn't end well, but at least I learned my lesson."

"And you remember the definition of the word 'insanity,' right?"

Avery nodded. "To do the same thing again and again while expecting different results."

"Bingo, so whatever you do, be careful out there and don't play with fire. You've come too far to throw it all away for something as overrated as love."

"Hey Avery, do you have a minute?" Emi joined him behind the cash register and rubbed the small of his back. "How are you feeling today?"

"I'm good, just hanging in there." Avery turned to face her, causing her hand to drop. "About last night, I wanted to apologize for—"

"You don't owe me an apology." Emi scanned the store to ensure no eyes were on them, then grabbed his hand and squeezed it. "As you said, it's been years since you've been intimate, so it's understandable if you're a little rusty."

He studied her hand, hoping she didn't hold last night against him. "As long as you know it has nothing to do with you. In fact, I just learned it's likely not anxiety but a side effect from the meds I'm on."

Emi dropped Avery's hand and waved at Kevin.

Kevin waved back and approached the counter. "Hey guys.

Before I went to Jas, I wanted to ask if it's cool with you two if I take off early to study for finals."

"Of course," Emi said. "And like I said before, you never have to ask."

She waited until he was out of earshot, then turned to Avery. "I can't tell you what to do, but what I can say is this—if I were the one taking meds and the side effects were more than I bargained for, I'd think long and hard about looking into alternative options. Our bodies are amazing, and there have to be healthier means out there to heal and manage whatever chemical imbalances you have going on."

Avery stood in silence as her words sank in. "Being chemical free sounds good in theory, but I've been on meds for so long it's hard to picture a life without them."

"Even if you're over medicated?"

"Trust me, it beats being under medicated."

"Then let me ask you this—do you like the way you physically and mentally feel about yourself?"

He shook his head. "Meds or no meds, I've never liked the way I felt."

"So now that you're free, what are you going to do about it?"

A customer approached with three bags of fertilizer in a cart. Avery rang him up and pitched the receipt in the trash since the customer wanted nothing to do with it.

He turned back to Emi. "You make it sound like I have a choice, but titrating or discontinuing my meds altogether without having a game plan in place is in no one's best interest. It's irresponsible and definitely not something Lauren or my case manager would ever approve of."

Emi moved closer and dropped her voice. "Of course they won't give you their approval, because they're only interested in avoiding culpability and protecting themselves. All they know is Western Medicine which over prescribes everything from antidepressants to opioids. Most of these drugs are barely biologically useful, and all of them are Band-Aids that don't actually address the underlying issues."

"I hear what you're saying, but I can't help but wonder how you can be so sure?"

"You said it yourself, Avery. If you stop taking your meds, what happens? The problem resurfaces, right? And aren't you the one who said, 'I'm not on meds forever, just until I die.' I know you were making a joke, but a lot of truth is said in jest."

Avery's face soured. "You know I never asked for this."

"Of course you didn't, but until you dig deep and attack the roots, the best you'll ever have is the appearance of order. Coming from someone who cares about you, I hope you address this problem head on so you can finally heal and move on with your life."

"It's not that easy, Emi."

"I know it's not, but take a step back and at least consider the alternative. You owe yourself that much."

Avery nodded and turned his focus back to his work.

"Wait, you're moving out?" Avery asked, darkening the doorway to their room. His words hung in the air as though he was speaking to himself.

Keeping his back to Avery, Gil finished folding a shirt and nodded. "Kātisu's been approved to move home with his wife, and as next in line, I called dibs on his old room." He placed the shirt in a pile on his bed and removed a pair of slacks from an open dresser drawer. "Hope it makes you happy."

"Why would it make me happy? I have nothing against you."

Gil looked over his shoulder. "You sure about that?"

Avery nodded. "These past few weeks have been trying for sure, but don't forget you were the one who didn't want me here, not the other way around."

Gil placed his pants on the stack of clothes and patted them flat with his palm. "Like I said before, it was nothing personal. I didn't vote against letting *you* move in, so to speak; I voted against the idea of living with someone who was found to be clinically insane and doped up on psych meds. It's not what I signed up for."

"What does that even mean?" Avery asked, frowning.

Gil turned around. "It means that once a danger to society, always a danger, and you can't argue with that. Don't get me wrong, I'm glad you seem to be doing well for now, but we both know there's no cure for schizophrenia, just like there's no cure for pedophilia. No matter what you do or say, you, my friend, will always be a ticking time-bomb."

Avery took a step forward and felt his nails dig into his palms. "Fuck you, Gil."

"Yeah, sure, fuck me." Gil picked up his clothes and clutched them to his chest. "*Fuck me* for wanting a good night's sleep without worrying that my psycho roommate will gut me alive."

Avery bit into his lip as Gil brushed past him.

"Oh, and one more thing," Gil said, turning around. "I may have been the lone vote against you, but don't be fooled into believing I'm alone in my thinking. Truth is, everyone else feels the same, but I'm just the only one here who doesn't have a problem speaking my mind."

Avery stood there shaking as Gil pulled the door shut behind him, then he turned and collapsed into his bed.

As he lay there and wrestled with making his way under the sheets, Avery did his best to keep his thoughts from being clouded by anger and pain. He couldn't remember the last time he saw red, but he knew Gil wasn't wrong about there being no known cure for schizophrenia. But lacking a cure and not knowing the cause are two very different things, and Gil couldn't fathom how much of a struggle it had been to remain hopeful in the presence or absence of both.

Avery knew that no one in their right mind ever asked for mental illness or a chemical imbalance in their gray matter, not even those with drug-induced schizophrenia. He also suspected

Gil likely fell victim to the same trap that too often pits society against one another. People like Gil tend to fear what they don't understand or can't comprehend. Still, regardless of what causes schizophrenia, if faulty brain chemistry precedes mental illness, then it's reasonable that every person out there with a mind of their own can become disturbed under the right or wrong circumstances.

Deep down, Avery suspected this subconscious fear could explain Gil's outward hostility, but he wasn't in the business of changing people's minds. If Gil wanted nothing to do with him, Avery would give him what he wanted and accept that Gil's flawed thinking was as prevalent in this life as it was perverse.

He rested his head on his pillow and closed his eyes, turning his thoughts inward as he often did. Avery recognized he had long accepted his schizophrenia following his arrest, but a younger self fought and resisted the label at every turn. This refusal of treatment proved far worse than the actual diagnosis since he'd stumbled through an existence where his alcoholism and depression fed off one another.

He looked down the length of his torso, crossed his legs and covered his eyes with his forearms. Then, despite a clear understanding of Anosognosia—a condition where one is unaware of their psychiatric disorder—Avery reverted to a familiar thought experiment he had performed more times than he could remember.

The question was whether he was better off being a prisoner to his prescriptions or his disorders. The problem he faced was not knowing what quality of life would better serve him, having no recent reference for functionality in the absence of meds. While he could never forget his life before his diagnosis, he couldn't help but wonder what progress he may have made in the years since.

He rolled onto his side and clutched his pillow with sweaty palms. Avery knew that if he temporarily cut his meds and discovered he desperately needed them to function, he may never feel comfortable stopping them again down the road. But Emi had a point; if there were alternatives out there that could bolster the stability of the mind and recalibrate peace and harmony within—especially without known side effects—he owed it to himself to roll the bones and see what happened.

As he turned in place and further kicked the idea around, a third option invaded his mind, though admittedly, it was always lingering in the ether. Avery considered cutting his meds altogether and becoming unassisted. It was by far the riskiest and most extreme move he could make, but potentially the most rewarding if things worked out and proved manageable. He reasoned that if the idea proved fateful, he could always soften the blow with a step back toward a holistic approach that addressed the physiological embodiments of his illness. Then he could and would gravitate toward Emi's ocean and talk therapies, along with vitamins, minerals, extracts and the like. In the end, if those treatments failed him and he needed more support, he could revert to his meds as a failsafe and know once and for all where he stood.

With his mind made up, Avery unlocked his lockbox and grabbed his case of meds. He removed the next day's pills from his organizer, took one last look at them and headed to the bathroom.

17

DECEMBER 12TH

One Week Later

Emi approached the cash register with an older woman in tow. "Avery, can we borrow your muscles for a second?" she asked. "Mrs. Yap has a will call order for a few bags of topsoil and we could use a little help loading them into her truck."

"It would be an honor." He locked the register and hurried around the counter. "Good morning, Mrs. Yap? How are you doing on this beautiful day in Hawai'i nei?"

She hiked up her floral mu'umu'u and slowly turned around. "No complaints here."

He took his time leading Mrs. Yap to the parking lot where Emi had parked a pallet loaded with soil.

"We got it from here," Avery said, opening Mrs. Yap's door for her. Once she was safely inside, he closed the door like a gentleman and approached Emi. "That's a lot more than a few," he said, counting the stack.

"But nothing a workhorse like yourself can't handle." Emi patted his butt, maneuvered the pallet jack in place and then pulled the lever to drop the forty bags with a thump. She slipped around Avery, popped the tailgate and hopped into the truck's bed.

After donning a pair of work gloves, Avery hoisted the first twenty-pound bag into the bed. "Why do I feel you just tricked me into doing all the heavy lifting?" He slid the bag toward her boots with a smirk.

"Well, you've spent all week telling me how good you feel, so I figured why not make the most of it?" She grabbed the bag and slid it into the corner. "By the way, I wanted to thank you again for last night. I don't know what's gotten into you lately, but that was incredible."

Avery tossed the next bag into the bed, then peeked over the rail to see if the driver's window was down.

"Don't worry," Emi whispered, not looking back. "She can't hear us even if she wanted to. So, how about a repeat tonight? Same time, same place?"

He reached for the next bag. "I'd love to, but we have a house meeting tonight and attendance is mandatory."

"Even if you're working?"

Avery lugged the next bag onto the tailgate. "I really can't. The guys know my schedule, plus my sleep has been all over the place so I'm hoping to squeeze in a nap before the meeting."

"You don't seem to be exhausted. But even if you are, if you come over tonight, I'm happy to do all the heavy lifting."

Avery flipped a bag into the bed. "I'm sorry, but what part of 'I really can't' don't you understand?" Despite a flurry of thoughts running through his head, he realized he wasn't getting anywhere. "Are you trying to get me kicked out of the sober house?"

"*Kicked out*? What are you talking about?"

He turned back to the pile and grabbed another bag.

"Avery?" Emi squatted in the truck's bed. "What the hell are you talking about?"

With the crook of his elbow, he wiped his brow and started over. "I'm talking about how I can't afford to miss this meeting or any other. Why don't we take a rain check for tomorrow night and I'll make it up to you."

Emi took the load from his hands and placed it onto the stack. "I'll tell you what," she said, sounding hurt. "Do what you need to do and let me know when you're free. Because while I can't wait to see you again, I also don't want to impede you from doing whatever it is you have to do."

A raucous uproar rang through the family room as the sober house residents joked and shouted over one another. Opting not to participate, Avery sank further into the couch and did his best to ignore the commotion.

"Alright everyone, let's get this party started." Uncle Earl snapped his fingers to get the group's attention and turned to the man he was leading into the room. "Everyone, I'd like you to meet Mr. Austin Wilder. Austin, meet everyone."

Clean cut and in his early twenties, Austin removed his phone from his back pocket, placed it on the scuffed wooden coffee table and sat stiffly in his chair. He fluffed his clean white tee to cool down in the cramped room. When he dropped his shirt, he wrung his hands, showcasing forearms sporting traditional American tattoos with bold lines that would hold fast in any season, including a panther, a ribbon-wrapped coffin and a compass pointing to true north.

"How are we all doing today?" Austin made it a point to make eye contact with each person in the room.

Nani sized him up, turned to Avery and whispered, "I vote hell to the yes."

Avery stayed quiet and drew his eyes away from Austin's phone. He leaned back on the couch and watched from a distance.

"As always, thank you all for making it today. It makes my job a hell of a lot easier." Uncle Earl turned to the group. "Austin, it's my pleasure to introduce Tino, Gil, Nigel and Berto, and that's Rod, Avery and Nani. Unfortunately, Terrence is at work so he doesn't get a say in today's vote, but you just have to take my word that he's a good guy."

"Oh, I'm sure he is."

Uncle Earl smiled at Austin. "As House Prez, I want to ensure that new applicants are a good fit for us, but before we take the time to get to know you, I think it's best you get to know us a bit."

Austin rubbed his palms together and nodded. "I'm just along for the ride. Whatever works for you, works for me."

"Perfect." Uncle Earl began introductions by rambling about himself and cracking jokes that missed the mark. He passed the torch to Tino, who let the warmth spread throughout the room. The fire smoldered a bit with Berto, but Rod was quick to breathe oxygen into the chamber. As he spoke, Avery's downcast eyes tuned out the world around him.

"Avery?" Rod said again, glancing back at Uncle Earl.

Nani nudged him with her elbow, forcing Avery's crossed arms to disengage. A bit shook, he looked up from Austin's phone and pulled himself forward on the couch.

"Is everything okay?" Austin asked.

"I don't know. Is it?"

Austin laughed nervously and leaned forward in his chair. "What's that supposed to mean?"

Avery didn't respond. Instead, his gaze fell to the carpet, and he rubbed his eyelids as if he had something stuck in them. The room fell silent, and Avery sensed his every move being watched. "It's nothing," he finally muttered, tapping Nani's thigh. "Come back to me."

She placed her hand on his back and changed the subject to her favorite beaches, hikes and hole-in-the-wall restaurants within walking distance. Once Nani noticed Avery's breathing had settled, she wrapped it up and sunk back into the couch.

"Sorry about that," Avery said. "I'm not sure what's gotten

into me." He puffed his cheeks and released his breath. "As they mentioned, I'm Avery. I'm new here and I like plants."

"And don't forget," Tino said, "assuming Austin moves in, the two of you will be roommates." He wagged his stubby finger between the two men.

Austin donned a playful grin. "Sounds like a blast."

"I like that attitude," Uncle Earl said. "So that's us in a nutshell. We may not be much to look at, but we share a lot in common and that's always a good start. Now, why don't you tell us a bit about yourself?"

Austin ran his fingers through his hair. "For the sake of making a long story short, let's just say I started down the wrong path but saw where it was taking me and decided I didn't want to end up like most of my friends. Thankfully, I turned back while I still could, which means I've not only learned my lesson, but this journey has turned out to be a blessing in disguise. I'm fortunate to be figuring this whole 'recovery' thing out while I'm still relatively young and have my whole life ahead of me."

"And you've been clean for how long?"

He counted backward on his fingers. "Going on nine months, thanks to Hina Makai."

"Oh, you went to Hina Makai?" Tino asked, turning to Berto. "Didn't you go there too?"

"I've been to every treatment center on this rock," Berto said, chuckling. "At least once. Are you on paper?"

Austin shook his head. "Nope, thank God. I didn't want it to get that far. I was a walk-in and checked myself into residential treatment once I realized I couldn't quit on my own. Then I did the legwork and now I'm here."

Rod raised a finger. "What I don't understand is why make the move to a sober house after graduating from Hina Makai? Isn't their goal to reintegrate each client back into the community straight out of treatment?"

"It is, but like I said, I want to proceed with caution. The last thing I'm trying to do is get ahead of myself and end up back where I started."

"Smart kid," Gil said. "Makes me wish I had a head like yours on my shoulders thirty years ago. Would've saved me a world of hurt and heartbreak."

"Same here." Uncle Earl checked his wristwatch and motioned for Austin to rise. "I think we're good here. Why don't you step outside while we take a vote? I'll come get you when we're done."

Austin reached for his phone. "Sounds like a plan. Take as long as you need, and thank you again for the opportunity."

"As if we even need to vote," Nani said, staring into the empty hallway. "I no can imagine an easier decision."

"Either way, policy is policy, even if we know where you stand." Uncle Earl dropped his hands. "So I take it that's a yes from Nani. Who else is with her?"

Berto, Tino, Rod and Gil all raised their hands simultaneously.

"Good, and I vote yes, too." Uncle Earl turned to Avery. "What's your vote?"

Avery stayed quiet for a moment.

"Earth to Avery, are you still with us?" Uncle Earl asked again.

Avery remained fixated on the coffee table but knew he couldn't stay quiet. He first turned to Uncle Earl, then to the rest of the room. "Am I the only one bothered that Austin just recorded the entire interview?"

"Is that a joke?" Uncle Earl asked. "What makes you think that?"

"Come on, you all saw his phone, right? He didn't even bother trying to hide it." Avery looked around the room in disbelief.

"Avery, wats your point?" Nani asked, holding her phone up. "We all get phones."

"My point is I don't trust him. So I vote no and think the rest of you should reconsider."

"And look who's the lone vote now," Gil said to no one in particular.

"That's enough, Gil." Uncle Earl took a step forward. "Not to say he did, but even if Austin recorded us . . . who cares? It's not like we have something to hide here, do we?"

"I don't," Rod said.

"Me neither," Tino added.

"Exactly, but either way, this is why everyone gets a vote. Now, if you don't mind, I'm going to adjourn this meeting and share the good news with Austin." Uncle Earl headed for the door and disappeared out of sight.

With vacant eyes, Avery scanned the rest of the room. He no longer had questions about where Uncle Earl and Rod stood. Instead, he wondered when exactly everyone had turned against him.

18

DECEMBER 13TH

"Avery, I hope you know you can talk to me about anything." Emi nudged him with her hip and leaned against the counter's edge. "I can tell something's not right with you, especially when you try to hide it."

He twisted the key to open the cash register, cracked open a roll of dimes and dumped them in the till.

"You can ignore me all you want, but I'm not going anywhere until my shift is over."

Avery closed the drawer with both hands. "I'm not ignoring you. Or, if it seems that way, please know it's not my intention. My mind's just elsewhere right now."

"'Your mind's elsewhere?'" Emi lowered her voice. "And where exactly would that be?"

He placed a hand on the counter. "If I tell you what's going on with me, will you promise not to think I'm crazy?"

She took his hand in hers. "Of course."

"They're ganging up on me," he said.

"Who is?" she asked, squeezing his hand. "Who's ganging up on you?"

"As far as I can tell, all of them are."

"Excuse me," Jas said, approaching the counter. "Avery, could I have a word?"

He felt Emi pull her hand away but ignored her. "Sure. What's going on?"

"I'd prefer we speak in private, if you don't mind."

"Yes, of course."

Emi leaned against the counter and made way for Avery as he brushed past her. He followed Jas into her office and shut the door behind him.

"Have a seat," Jas said.

He pulled the chair back but kept his hands on the seat back. "Is this about me and Emi?"

"Emi?" Jas shook her head. "I don't know anything about that, and as long as you both get your work done, it's none of my business. But there is something we need to discuss, and I meant to have this talk with you sooner, but the work never stops." She sat herself down and brushed a mountain of paperwork aside. "Please, make yourself comfortable."

He did the best he could and felt the chair wobble beneath him.

"Look, I don't want this to be awkward," Jas said, sagging a bit in her chair, "but since you're part of the BTE 'ohana now, I think it's time we clear the air and get a fresh start."

His eyes dropped to her bony fingers, adorned by vintage jewelry and precious stones passed down through the ages. "I'm not sure I understand."

"I don't remember the name of the facility, but I heard you're from the psych hospital." As her words left her lips, Jas flashed a knowing smile. "And that's all fine by me, though I have to ask, is there any chance you pose a danger to yourself or others?"

Avery bit his tongue and shook his head.

"Good, and sorry to be so blunt, but I feel like I have to address it even though I'm the last one to judge. I understand we all need help now and then, and I want you to know my main concern is your wellbeing and success."

Avery rocked back in his chair. "The facility is called Hale Maluhia, and while I appreciate the thought, you giving me a job is far more than someone could ask for." He smiled at the ground and hoped she couldn't read his mind. If she could, she'd see his thoughts spiraling over who tipped her off. Someone obviously wanted him fired, but for the life of him, he couldn't imagine why.

"If you can tell me how best to support you, I'll do the best I can," Jas promised.

Avery ignored her sentiment and rubbed his hands down his pant legs. "If you don't mind me asking, who told you I came from the hospital?"

Jas cocked her head. "It's all public knowledge. You know that."

"It's only 'public knowledge' to those who seek it out."

"It's nothing to be ashamed of, Avery. It's really not." She rested her clasped hands on the edge of her desk. "No one asks to be schizophrenic."

"You don't understand, Jas; that's beside the point." Avery crossed his arms tightly over his chest. "You said you *heard* I was from the hospital. All I want to know is . . . how?"

"Avery, you know how it goes; it's a small island and an even smaller town. Everyone knows everyone and everyone talks, and you know firsthand how many people walk through our doors each day."

"Was it a customer?" He thought for a moment. "Was it that woman who returned the dead plant and wanted to see me fired?"

"No, and I haven't spoken to or seen her since."

"Then was it a coworker?"

Jas rose from her chair. "Again, it doesn't matter who said what because I don't hold it against you. On the contrary, I want to help. I want you to succeed."

His eyes searched hers. "Why do you care so much about someone like me?"

"Because I know how hard schizophrenia can be on someone, and while I don't have firsthand experience, someone very close to me does. Or did." Her eyes started to well, but she blinked the tears away.

Avery stayed quiet and took it all in. Her performance nearly moved him, but he knew better than that. It was a skill to recall overwhelming emotions at a moment's notice, but a skill nonetheless. Had he thought about losing his daughter or his childhood dog never returning home, he could also cry on demand.

"Please, Jas, I know you think you're protecting me, but you're not. I need to know who has it out for me."

She wiped her face, and when she removed her hands, her face was slack. "What are you talking about? No one's out for anyone."

Avery scouted for the nearest exit. He thought, not her too.

Avery raised his fist and debated knocking on Emi's door when the porch light flicked on, casting a long shadow beneath his brow. The front door flung inward, and a petite Thai woman in chambray blue scrubs lingered in the doorway.

"Holy shit, you scared me," she said, pressing a palm against her chest.

"Sorry, I didn't mean to. I was just about to knock."

She dropped her hand and straightened out her collar. "I take it you're here for Emi?"

He nodded.

"You must be Avery? I've heard so much about you."

"You have? Like what?"

"Just the usual." She cocked an eyebrow and smiled. "I'm curious to know, do you always move in silence and appear unannounced?"

He returned her smile. "Those days are long gone. Emi invited me over for dinner."

"Ah, so that explains why she's cooking for once." The

woman extended her hand. "Nice to finally meet you. I'm Nora, Emi's roommate. I had a feeling we'd cross paths at some point, but it's just my luck I'm running late for work. Have a good night and I'll see you around."

"You bet." He stepped aside to let her brush past him, then caught the door with the heel of his fist before it closed on him.

"You made it," Emi said as she placed a steaming cast iron pan on the counter. She removed an oven mitt and wiped her hands on a towel. "I've been thinking about you all day and hope you're feeling better."

He bent down to scratch Yuki, but his hand stopped inches from her head. He felt lightheaded as a chill coursed through him.

"Everything okay?" Emi asked.

Dropping to a knee, Avery combed his fingers through the cat's wiry hair. "How should I know?"

Emi tossed her towel on the counter. "Avery, please don't do this again."

He stroked the cat's tail. "Don't do what?"

"Don't scare me. Not after what happened earlier."

"I scared you?" He pressed off his knees and stood up. "How?"

"Let's just not go there again. It's bad déjà vu."

He wrapped his hands around the cat's belly and hoisted her up. "Speaking of déjà vu, do you ever experience it?"

She eyed him with suspicion. "Not really, no."

"Must be nice," Avery said, scratching Yuki behind her ears. He looked up. "It's an odd feeling, really; to second-guess everything you think you know. It's almost like being lost in a thick fog where you can't see your hand in front of your face, yet somehow you feel it in your bones that you've been there before."

Emi leaned into the counter. "Avery? What's going on with you?"

"Did you know they say there's a correlation between déjà vu and schizophrenia? Or active schizophrenia, I should say."

"Why are you telling me this?"

"Take a guess," he said, absently staring at Yuki. "Or on second thought, I'll just let the cat out of the bag. I did it, Emi, just like we talked about."

"Did what?"

"I cut my meds. About a week ago or so, if memory serves me correctly."

"Why? That's not what we talked about. The plan was to work together to wean you off your meds and manage your withdrawals holistically, not to quit cold turkey." She went quiet for a moment. "I can't believe you didn't think to involve me."

"Don't take it personally, Emi; I didn't think to tell anyone." He fiddled with the cat's whiskers before setting her down. "Please don't hold it against me. My intention was never to hurt you."

"I'm not the one I'm worried about getting hurt here." She paused in thought, then moved a step closer. "So?"

"So what?"

"Well, how do you feel?"

"I'm not sure. On one hand, I've had a flood of energy, but I'm also working through a wash of despair that my entire life has been pointless."

"Come on, you know that's not true. Just look at Bri and Micah, and you'll see more meaning than you know what to do with."

"Thanks, but you're missing the point; none of that matters." He took a deep breath and tilted his head from side to side as if to dislodge a thought. "It's almost as if it doesn't matter who I am or what I've done, as if this life of mine isn't mine to experience, if that makes sense."

"You should have told me," Emi said. She approached him and opened up for a hug. "But better late than never. Now, tell me how I can support you."

He accepted her hug and didn't hold back. "I'm not looking for support," he said. "My idea was to test the waters on my own and see if I sink or swim."

"And if you sink?"

"Then I sink, but at least I know."

She looked deep into his eyes. "You really should have told me."

"Well, I'm telling you now, and the good news is that despite the undertow, my head's still above water."

"If you say so." Emi smiled and turned her attention to the table. "Why don't you have a seat and let's talk about it over dinner? I don't know about you, but I'm starving, and the food's not getting any warmer."

Avery started to serve himself and seemed lost in the vibrant colors.

"Is something wrong?" Emi asked.

He reached for his fork and began picking apart the dish. "What is this?"

"You've never had Ratatouille before? Or rather, vegan Ratatouille I should say." She served herself and dug in. "It's my favorite, which reminds me, I've been missing my favorite body-surfer lately. It's kind of hard to pull off the whole buddy system thing when you're all alone out there."

"But you're never really alone, right?" He watched her take a bite and loaded his fork.

"The lifeguards don't start until nine, and I'm always out of the water by then."

"I know that," Avery said. "But there's always someone else in the water."

"Almost always, but that doesn't mean I trust them with my life. The ocean may be many things, but she's not known to be forgiving." Emi watched him take his first bite and waited for his reaction.

"It's good." He smiled and rested his fork against his plate with a clink. "You know, there's something that's been bothering me. About work."

"No surprise there, not after how you stormed out of Jas' office this afternoon."

"Yeah, about that." Avery took a long drink of water and dabbed the corner of his mouth. "You understand that if I lose my job, I don't just lose my job, right?"

"You think you're going to lose your job?"

He shook his head. "You're missing the point. If I lose my job, I lose my housing, and without housing, I'm nothing, as in they'll send me right back to the hospital to start over from scratch."

"I'm still confused. What makes you think you're going to lose your job?"

"You're confused? What's there to be confused about?" Avery pushed his plate forward. "What made you think you could share my business with Jas?"

"Are you serious right now?" Her eyes narrowed as her smile faded. "I'm going to do my best to forget you just said that."

"How convenient."

"Just stop."

"Stop? I'll stop once you explain to me how she knew."

"How she knew *what*?"

"About my plea? About the hospital?"

"Here's a bright idea; did you ever think to ask her?"

"I did, but she beat around the bush."

Emi gripped the table and leaned forward. "You need to understand something about me, Avery—I'm not one to gossip. You know me better than that."

"I thought I knew you better than that, the same way I thought you cared about me."

"Of *course* I care about you. So much so that I'm worried about you."

"Somehow I don't believe you."

"Fine. If this is how you're going to act and there's no trust here, then you might as well leave."

Avery pushed back his chair and stood up.

"But before you go, I want you to ask yourself something." Emi leaned back in her chair. "I know Jas well, and if anyone's an ally to you—other than me—it's going to be her. You should be grateful she found out."

Avery chose his following words carefully. "Jas may want the best for me, but anyone who takes it upon themself to put my business out there isn't a friend of mine. I don't care what they say." He nudged Yuki away from the door and pulled it open. "Thanks for dinner. Please give my compliments to the chef."

"You're wrong about this, Avery." Emi followed him onto the porch and cupped her hands around her lips as he started down the sidewalk. "I didn't speak to her about you. Not a single word."

Avery resisted the urge to look back and jammed his hands in his pockets as he sauntered down the sidewalk. He couldn't believe Emi thought so little of him or would be one to insult his intelligence, yet there he was, forced to admit he had her all wrong. Lauren had taught him that the simplest explanation tended to be the fastest pathway to the truth, and the lesson had served him well. Although he wanted to give Emi the benefit of the doubt, he couldn't think of anyone else who would go behind his back to betray him and have the means to do so. And so he walked on, refusing to dignify her with a response.

CHAPTER 19: PT. ONE
DECEMBER 14TH

Avery jammed the tips of his dive fins into the rocky sand and watched the sun crest over the darkened silhouette of Mokoliʻi. As legend has it, the iconic islet was formed when a monster Moʻo attacked the goddess Hiʻiaka—the first of her kind to dance the Hula in its purest form.

Mokoliʻi was at most a leisurely thirty-minute swim from where he sat, though twice a day, when the tides receded from Kāneʻohe Bay, the daring could make the trip on foot, wading through the waist or chest-deep water, depending on their height. But the island was deceptively close, timing the tide was tricky—if not a skill—and many kicked back to shore holding their phones and keys sky high above their heads.

Risk-averse beachgoers cracked open their wallets and launched rented kayaks from the shoreline. Avery leaned back onto his hands and wished the best for a heavyset couple wrestling a two-person kayak into the water. Once finally under-way, he considered calling out to let them know they were holding their paddles upside down and backward, but he thought better of it and watched as they zigzagged their way toward the island.

Once they were out of earshot, he brushed his feet clean of sand and stretched the straps of his fins over his heels. Leaving his shirt and slippers in a pile on the shore, Avery slung a weighted dive belt around his waist and used it like a sheath to hold onto a long stick he had found near the bus stop. Then he spat into his dive mask to prevent it from fogging and set the strap around his forehead.

While waddling into the shallows, he thought back to how he had stormed out of Emi's house the night before and wondered whether she would hold it against him. Jas, on the other hand, made it clear where she stood, having allowed him to take a mental health day off from work. When he attempted to explain himself, she added that no explanation was necessary and left it at that.

Avery pulled his mask down over his eyes and splayed out on the water's surface like a jellyfish surfing the wind. His hands hugged his hips as he kicked to propel himself, but as soon as he started, he sat upright in the water and removed his right fin. A few grains of sand had wedged themselves in his fin and were digging into the top of his foot, and as he brushed them away, he recalled a quote along the lines of: "It isn't the mountains ahead that will wear you out; it's the pebble in your shoe."

Starting up again, he floated past a waterlogged honey bee and reminded himself that some trips were taken not for the destination but the journey. Slipping his fin back on, he decided to keep a safe distance from Mokoliʻi and let the current guide him.

The water was murkier than he would like, spiked with a tinge of green. The visibility was low thanks to recent rains that stirred up the shoreline. A trickle of water leaked through the skirt of his mask, pooled in the lens, and washed away the creeping formations of fog. He pressed on the upper frame of his dive mask and blew out forcefully through his nose, clearing most of the water away.

The rocky terrain beneath him continued as far as he could see, disappearing into the deep blue yonder where coralline algae and prickly seaweed rollicked forever in the shifting currents. He kicked again and watched the bleached whites, muted purples and dull greens all meld into one, then tuned out the outside world.

It wasn't so much a hunt as it was a game that brought him back to his youth when he needed it most. Water seeped into his ears as he scanned the seabed in search of holes surrounded by tiny mounds of sand and fragments of cowrie shells. When he finally spotted one, he withdrew the stick from his belt, took a deep breath and went to see if anybody was home.

The dive was less than ten feet, but by the time he sank to the bottom, the pressure forced him to clear his ears and equalize. His lungs pulsed, and with time against him, he wiggled his stick into the hole until he hit resistance, confirming what he had suspected. The tunnel was unoccupied, and though it appeared collapsed or caved in, he could read the rock and knew the complete story; some diver had beaten him to it, ripped open the roof to capture the inhabitant and replaced the stones out of respect.

Avery pressed his feet into the seabed and propelled himself upward, breaking the water's surface first with his hand and then with the crown of his head. As a stream of water ran down his face, he expelled a stale breath and spun in place in search of kayakers or boats. Confident he was alone, he returned his face to the water when out of the corner of his eye, something watching him nervously slunk into a crevice.

He kept his eyes trained on the hole, knowing how easy it was to lose sight of objects underwater. Not wanting to open the door for escape, he was quick to dive again, and the creature, upon seeing him coming, retreated further into the shelter of its lair. With a few gentle prods with his stick, Avery coaxed it out of hiding, one dexterous tentacle at a time. A series of arms crept up the stick and spiraled up his hand, to which Avery responded by giving the stick a firm tug. The Heʻe held fast, emerging from the hole with unseeing eyes and a territorial response to its reflection in the mirrored mask. Without warning, a thick, inky bloom engulfed Avery but quickly dissipated in the currents as fast as it came.

Despite the stinging accumulation of carbon dioxide invading his every cell, Avery twisted his arm and admired his familial ʻaumākua manifested in the flesh. Honored in lore and Hawaiian legend, ʻaumākua were guardian spirits known to embody animals, plants—even elemental forms like rain-bearing winds or the pounding surf. Respected as protectors or ancestors returned, these guardians often came in time of need, offering guidance or warning of misfortune—depending on one's luck.

Part of him wanted to rise with the Heʻe and witness the mesmerizing color change in the sunlight on the surface. But a better part of him realized he had already caused enough disturbance, and in his final few seconds on the seabed, he peeled back the tentacles and brushed the boneless Heʻe from his hand. It slurped itself back into the hole, and in the fleeting moments before the surrounding deep blue closed in on him, Avery flattened the sand around the opening and brushed away the bits of cowrie shells littered near the entrance.

Avery surfaced and took his time kicking his way back to shore. He rolled onto his back, shifted his mask to his forehead and squinted as the sun bore down on him. Sea water lapped over his face, and embracing the feeling, he closed his eyes and focused on his breath.

Back on land, Avery thumbed water out of his ear and while still wet, he tossed on his shirt. He had yet to determine if he got what he came for and didn't know what to make of it. With a tense smile, he tied a towel around his waist and started for the bus stop. He had yet to determine where his next stop would be, only that the last place he wanted to find himself was back home dealing with Austin.

After flashing his bus pass to the driver, Avery took a seat in the rear and leaned his head against a vandalized window. He rested his eyes, opening them every so often to check his progress. Then, when the time was right, he yanked the cord to request a stop and followed two others out of the bus's back door.

He first passed a local bakery, then entered the Urgent Care Clinic and a wash of frigid air came over him. He adjusted his towel and returned a smile to a paunchy man sitting with pain behind his eyes. On the other side of the waiting room, a young mother helped her daughter ice her ankle while comforting her the best way she knew how.

Avery approached the counter and clutched his dive fins under his arm.

The receptionist motioned for him to hang tight while she scheduled a follow-up appointment with a caller. Once done, she set her phone in the cradle and rocked back in her chair. "I was wondering when I'd see you here," she said, crossing her arms. "But aren't you supposed to be at work today?"

He nodded. "I took a mental health day."

"Is everything okay with you?"

He pressed his lips together. "Why does everyone keep asking me that?"

She smiled and turned to her coworker. "Darlene, can you cover the phone for a few minutes? I need to have a word with my dad."

Darlene nodded and struck a stapler with the heel of her palm as Bri and Avery stepped outside.

"I'm not sure what's going on," Bri said as Avery leaned against a guardrail, "but it's always good to see you." She hugged her father and stepped back to leave the sidewalk clear. "How were the waves?"

"Flat where I went, which worked out because I needed to clear my head."

"And why would you need to do a thing like that?"

His expression darkened as he considered opening up to her. The last thing he wanted was to worry her, but she of all people could wrap her head around the truth. "I know how this is going to sound," he said, "but promise me you'll hear me out."

"I promise." She took a step closer. "What's going on?"

He pinched the bridge of his nose. "I think my roommate has it out for me and is working to turn the whole house against me."

"What roommate? You mean Gil?"

Avery shook his head. "Well, him too, but there's a new guy at the sober house who took Gil's place. He goes by Austin."

"Goes by?" Bri rubbed her eyes and shook her head. "What makes you think he has something against you?"

"I think the question should be, why wouldn't I think that? All the signs are there. It's the timing. It's the person. It's the fact that he replaced Gil, who hasn't exactly made it a secret that he wants me gone." Avery paused for a moment, then clasped his face. "I'm such an idiot; how could I not see it?"

"Dad?" Bri grabbed his wrist. "See what?"

"I'm willing to bet that Gil was behind Austin moving in. It makes so much sense."

Bri went silent for a moment. "Dad? Can I ask you a question?"

"Of course."

"Don't take this the wrong way, but do you hear yourself right now?"

"What's that supposed to mean?"

"It means what it sounds like. Do you hear yourself? Do you hear what you're saying?"

"You think I'm making this all up?"

"No, I'm not saying that, though it sounds odd to me." She took a deep breath and shook her head. "I think you need to be kinder to yourself. Remember, you're living in a high-stress environment with a bunch of people who all have their own issues."

Avery stared at the sidewalk. "You don't understand."

"You're right, I don't. Have you talked to Lauren about this? I'm sure she'll have a better idea of where this is coming from."

He dismissed the idea. "I haven't had the time. Austin just moved in a couple of days ago."

"Then how about this; let me take you home and if Austin's there, maybe I can meet him and judge for myself. How's that sound?"

Avery tightened his grip around the railing and forced the blood out of his fingers. "I can't have you do that."

"Seriously? Why not?"

He looked up. "You shouldn't get involved."

"I'm your daughter, remember? I'll always be involved. Just gimme a sec to grab my keys and ask Darlene to cover for me."

He reached out and caught her arm. "Bri, please. I can't have you coming around right now. Not until I figure out if these guys are dangerous or not."

"Dangerous? You can't be serious."

He squeezed her arm tighter and stared at her in a way that told her everything she needed to know.

After testing the temperature of the water with his foot, Avery slipped into the shower with a newfound appreciation for his shower shoes. The curtain snapped closed, and he avoided letting the clear plastic liner brush his body. Perpetually damp from whoever showered last, the liner showed signs of mildew and who knows what else. But it was the outer curtain that caught his eye as a once vibrant cacophony of colors nicked straight from Pollock's playbook now reflected the dullest of sheens.

He welcomed the steady stream of water cascading down his face, ridding his body of the sticky sea salt that had baked into his pores over the day. For reasons unknown to even him, he skipped the showers when leaving the beach and lived to regret his decision ever since.

Despite the unpleasant sensation of salt clashing with sweat, Avery discharged the rest of the day after leaving Bri's workplace by exploring his lazy town on foot. At times, he strolled by a building that caught his eye, then backpedaled a bit to admire the landscape out front and how the plants played off one another. He challenged himself to identify the plants by their genus and soon found his test of skills became a distraction from the reality that the further he traveled, the further he was followed.

Followed not by someone, per se—though he checked over his shoulder just to be sure—but by an almost forgotten feeling he couldn't shake. It was a sensation that no words could quite define, like a splitting of sorts, but even that picture missed the mark.

Feeling drained, Avery stretched his jaw and let hot water collect and puddle on his tongue until it spewed from the corners of his mouth. He swallowed what he could, spat out the rest with a squirt and knew he couldn't lie to himself. A dark depression burrowing into his bones and a fleeting dizziness that came and left at will were not normal. As much as he detested the idea, the signs showed face, bubbling to the surface like some mythic leviathan coming up for air.

Avery closed his eyes and focused on the falling rain. He imagined the cascading water washing incomplete thoughts away through him and around him, spiraling down the drain. He pumped a palmful of shampoo into his hand and massaged it into his scalp, allowing the shampoo to work its magic while he leaned into the tile and watched his breath swell in his chest. He focused on the rise and fall, hoping to regain a semblance of control when a crack of thunder sounded in the distance. The noise clapped again, closer now, and hearing his name called, Avery clutched his ears, wishing it all away.

"Avery? Can you hear me?" the voice called out, penetrating through the door, the curtain, the liner and his skull.

Avery asked himself if he was imagining things, and as his insides churned, he wondered if he was becoming sick again. He gripped the edge of the curtain and peeled it back a crack. "Is someone there?" he asked, his pupils darting high and low, avoiding the mirror, fearing what they might see.

"It's me," Austin said from behind the door.

Avery clung to the curtain as his mind ran wild, then steeled his voice. "What do you want?"

"I just want to know how much longer you're going to be?"

He's lying.

"Go away!" Avery shouted. He released the curtain and withdrew into the shower.

"I'm not going anywhere. You've been in there a long time, and I need to get ready for work." He knocked on the door again. "Can I at least grab my things so I can ask to use the other shower?"

Avery attempted to read between the lines but couldn't decipher Austin's true intentions.

"Avery? I know you can hear me." Austin jiggled the doorknob. "I don't get it; are you trying to make me late for work on purpose?"

Again, Avery considered responding but bit his tongue.

"Fuck it, then. Stay in there all day for all I care. But just so you know, I need to start a load of laundry before I leave. What do you want me to do with your clothes in the washer?"

Avery snapped the curtain open. "Don't touch my stuff."

"Or what?" Austin asked. "I may be new, but I pay my rent the same as you. Tell you what, I'll toss them in the dryer and you can thank me later."

Avery stood limply in the shower and stared at the closed door with growing fury. To purge himself of the pressure, he closed the curtain and focused singly on one thought and nothing more until the surety of time escaped him. Slinging both palms against the wall, he bowed his forehead into the sharp stream of water, hung his head and listened carefully.

Some time had passed when a voice called his name once again. It was not distant but upon him, smothering him as if breathing down his neck.

"Avery? I need you to get out of the shower and get dressed. We need to talk."

Avery's turquoise bath towel flopped over the shower rod and hung in his face. He took the cue, cut the water, tugged on the towel, then blotted his torso dry before cinching the towel around his waist. When he was done, he pulled back the shower curtain to reveal Uncle Earl standing before him with Austin and Tino looming in the doorway. "Talk about what? And what do they want?"

"Never mind them," Uncle Earl said. "This is about you. What's going on here?"

"Exactly what it looks like." Avery patted his towel. "I'm showering. Or was trying to before Austin interrupted me and you barged in."

"No one barged in on anyone."

Avery reached for his shirt on the toilet seat and stretched it over his head. "Then explain to me how you got in here."

Uncle Earl stuck a thumb under his collar and jerked on a stainless steel ball chain necklace. A key and a pair of dog tags flopped onto his chest. "No explanation necessary; it's my house, remember?"

"That doesn't give you the right to invade my privacy."

"True, but you bringing drugs into the house does."

"Drugs?" Avery's face slowly drained of color. "What drugs?"

Uncle Earl reached into his pocket and removed a tiny Ziploc baggie. He held it up high to show off the foamy white residue inside.

"What's that?" Avery leaned forward to steal a better look.

"Why don't you come clean and tell me?"

"How? I've never seen that before and I don't know where it came from."

"Somehow I doubt that. This was found in your belongings, so you can play that game if you want, but you will lose. Possession is nine-tenths of the law."

"'Found in my belongings?' By who? And where?"

"Doesn't matter, and on second thought, I'm not playing games with you. Now let's go; you have thirty minutes to pack out and time is not on your side." Uncle Earl tossed the baggie into the toilet and flushed it.

Avery watched the baggie spiral out of sight. "I have a right to face my accuser."

Austin stepped into the bathroom. "I found it," he said over Uncle Earl's shoulder. "I found it when I pulled your clothes from the washer."

"Bullshit." Avery turned to Uncle Earl. "You're telling me you don't find that suspicious? Isn't it obvious he planted that bag to set me up?"

"Set you up?" Austin laughed at the mention of the idea. "I don't know what's going on in that head of yours, but leave it to you to say some crazy shit."

"That's enough. We're not doing this." Uncle Earl pressed Austin out of the room. "Austin, I think it's time you hele to work."

"No, don't leave just yet." Avery stepped out of the shower and approached Uncle Earl. "You can't kick me out."

"That's where you're confused. I'm not the one kicking yourself out of here; you are."

Avery shook his head. "Please don't do this to me. We both know those machines run all night and day. Isn't it possible that the baggie belonged to whoever used the machine before me?"

"If you think I haven't thought of that, then you haven't seen yourself recently." He took Avery by his shoulder and spun him around to face the mirror. "You can avoid looking at yourself all you want, but you're obviously tweaking on something."

Avery refused to open his eyes until he turned around. "Fine, but before you kick me out, I want to be drug tested. Or, better yet, I want you to drug test everyone, especially Austin."

Uncle Earl crossed his arms. "Why not just be honest and save us all the hassle? Those tests don't lie."

Avery turned around and opened his eyes. "I know. Why do you think I'm asking?"

CHAPTER 19: PT. TWO
THAT NIGHT

Emi cinched a handcrafted Terry-Cloth robe around her torso and nudged Yuki from the doorway with her shin. She stepped onto her front porch and into the humid night, one hand rubbing her eyes, the other pulling the front door shut behind her with an audible click.

"Avery? What are you doing here?" she asked.

He glanced over his shoulder, then moved to greet her. "If you don't mind, can we take this inside?"

She sidestepped to cut him off and stared down the dimly lit sidewalk. "Why don't you tell me what's going on first?"

He dropped his hands and took a step back. "It's complicated."

"What is?"

"Honestly, I'm not sure."

She studied him with a tinge of distrust in her eyes. "If you don't know what's wrong, how can you ever expect to fix it?"

He began to shake his head and caught himself. "Today's been rough, but that's not why I'm here. I came to apologize for the way I stormed out last night. That, and for doubting you."

She leaned against the siding. "I appreciate you thinking of me, but like I said, I'll be fine. It's you I'm worried about."

"I don't blame you." He squeezed his forehead and closed his eyes. "I took to the water this morning to clear my head, but realized that there was no use. Then I saw Bri and thought the day was looking up, until my roommate set me up and planted drugs in my clothes."

As a haze came over him, Avery described the lengths Austin had taken to see him return to the hospital. He didn't know why, nor did he want to find out. Emi listened intently, finding herself caught in a messy web of conspiracies, starting with Gil and ending with Uncle Earl. As he rambled along, she kept waiting to make out a sensible motive but nothing came to mind, not even after stretching her imagination.

"Let me get this straight—Austin found a bag of meth in your clothes and—"

"Claims to have found a bag of meth in my clothes."

"Right. So he claims to have found this baggie thing in your clothes, but if everyone in the house tested clean for drugs, yourself and Austin included, then where did the drugs come from?"

"Good question. Unfortunately, I'm not sure anyone cares about the answer."

"How so?"

"I think their logic is that since the drugs had to come from somewhere, it doesn't matter that no one popped dirty— someone has to take the fall."

"So right now you're in a he said, she said thing?"

"I guess so, but I think this is only the beginning. Who knows what else Austin will do to set me up."

Emi went quiet for a moment. "I don't know. I get why you're upset, but something doesn't add up. And I'm aware that I haven't met Austin, but I can't imagine anyone coming after you, at least not the way you put it." She took a deep breath, then clutched his hand. "What is clear to me, though, is that none of this started until you cut your meds, so I have to ask—is there any chance that all of this is in your head?"

He retracted his hand from Emi's grasp and fought against

the thought. He knew himself well enough to know he could go there or be taken to that dark place, but he knew he wasn't there yet. A more rational thought was she wanted him to believe he was delusional, perhaps to protect him from being hurt by the truth. People protect those they care about, don't they? Of course they do, sometimes even at all costs. But what did she stand to gain and what did he stand to lose? He clutched his eyes and saw himself returning to the hospital just in time to prove everyone right. No, he couldn't go back. Not for Austin. Not for her. Not for anyone.

"Hey. Don't do that." Emi reached out and took his hand tenderly. "Don't shut down on me. I want you to stay present with me, and here's what I propose; we're going to go back in time, okay? Just me and you. Let's rewind the clock nine days ago when you were last on your meds. Is that something we can do?"

Avery squared his shoulders and stared into her eyes. "Weren't you the one who wanted me to come off the meds?"

"I was, but not the way you discontinued them. If you recall, the idea was to wean you off them responsibly and replace them with something better, but forget about all of that for now. We can cross that bridge down the road. Right now, we need to bring you back online before things get any worse. So let's get you back on your meds and set you straight."

Avery shook his head. "I'm afraid that's not possible."

"And why not?"

"Because I don't have them."

"Okay, no problem. Give me a sec to grab my keys and I can take you back to the sober house and you can get them."

"Can't do that either." He sighed and rubbed his lips. "I flushed them a few days ago—all of them—back when things seemed to be going great. I should have known better, but leave it to me to go and ruin a good thing."

Emi let go of the doorknob. "In that case, let's call Lauren and tell her you need a refill. I'm not sure if the pharmacy is twenty-four hours, but I'm happy to keep you company until they open."

"No, that won't work. If I ask for an early refill, they'll know something's up."

"So tell them you lost them."

"Lost them how? From my lock box that lives in my room? That's even more suspicious."

"Then lie if you have to. Say they got stolen."

"By who exactly? My roommate? That's not a light accusation to make, and they'd want an investigation." He paused and pressed his lips together. "No, that wouldn't fly. It's not like we're talking about pain meds here. Remember, we're talking about drugs where even the people prescribing them don't want to take them."

"Then what about finding someone who's on the same meds as you?"

"Anyone who's on the same drugs I'm on can't afford to share."

"Ugh," Emi cried, running her hands through her hair. "I need you to think, Avery. There has to be a way to fight yourself out of this bag."

He paused, then dismissed the idea with a wave. "The only option I can think of is to stick it out and wait for my refill."

"Which is when?"

"The end of the month."

"Do you really think you can make it another week like this? Let alone two?"

"No, but technically I'd only have to make it nine days since we're allowed to pick up our script early to avoid any lapse in medication." Avery heard himself speak and laughed at the idea. Every last muscle in his face tightened as he searched for another answer.

Emi took notice and traced his gaze to her window. "Avery? What's wr—" A sharp crash rang out behind her, startling her and disturbing the dead of night. She spun around to see Avery had backed himself into a corner of her porch, his bloodless knuckles gripping the edge of her plantation-style railing. On the lawn behind him lay her peace lily plant, knocked free from the railing and writhing in a pool of its own soil.

"Someone's inside," Avery whispered, eyes transfixed on the empty window.

"Inside where? Inside my house?" Emi's eyes naturally drifted to the window, but she snapped her attention back to Avery. "What are you talking about? It's just me and Yuki in there."

"No." He rubbed his eyes and stepped forward. "Someone's inside. I just glimpsed him through the window."

"I don't think so, Avery. I've been home all night, alone."

He took another step forward with an outstretched hand. "I know what I just saw."

She brushed his hand away. "Listen to me. I promise you there's no one inside. Why would I lie to you?"

He turned to face her with the coldest eyes. "I don't know. Why does anyone lie?"

"Fine." She reached for the doorknob and pressed the door open. "If you refuse to believe me and won't take my word for it, then feel free to see for yourself. Do whatever it is you need to do to be at peace."

He hesitated for a moment as though balancing on a precipice. Then, once he had gathered himself, he brushed past her and entered the front door with a determined look. Yuki paced at the entrance and he closed the door to prevent her escape.

You're a damned fool.

Avery ignored the voice and leaned back against the door. He asked himself more than once why he was doing this, then told himself there was still time to turn back. *There's no one here*, he thought, but against his better judgment, he stepped forth into the room. He spun in place and looked out the window, expecting to find Emi watching his every move. Instead, he saw she had turned her back on him through his reflection bearing down on him.

The bathroom was empty, including the shower and the closet no one but a contortionist could squeeze into. It was a similar story in the two bedrooms and having checked under each bed to ensure no monsters were lying in wait, he returned to the front door while compiling an apology in his head.

"I swear I saw someone but there was no one inside but me and Yuki." He stepped onto the porch and closed the door behind him. "Sorry for putting you through that. I hope you don't hold it against me."

Emi didn't immediately respond. Instead, facing away from him, she muttered something hurriedly and fumbled with her pockets. When she turned around, she pursed her lips in a knowing smile. "You don't owe me an apology," she said. "The main thing is that you're going to be okay."

His smile faded as his eyes narrowed and darted to her pockets. "Were you just on the phone?"

Emi held her palms out. "Come on, Avery. What else am I supposed to do here?"

"Who were you speaking to?" He took a step forward. "You didn't call the police on me, did you?"

Her mouth parted, and she placed her hands on his shoulders. "No, of course not, but I need you to ask yourself, what kind of support person would I be if I did nothing here?"

"Emi? Who'd you call?"

She took a deep breath. "Lauren, because you gave me her number for a reason."

"Is she on her way?"

"Listen to me, Avery; you're not in trouble. We're all on the same team here and you're going to be okay."

He couldn't stand to look at her. "Do you have any idea what you've just done?" He began to backpedal, but Emi took his hand and refused to let him go without a fight.

"Don't do this," she pleaded. "Running will only make it worse."

"Make it worse for who?" Then, without another word, he yanked his arm free, made a break for the steps and took off straight into the shadows.

Gripping his slippers in hand, the smell of a far-off rain came to him, but Avery had bigger things on his mind than a measly squall headed his way. He continued working his way down the beach through the swash zone where the sea lapped the shoreline and teased of her tremendous power. Distantly, the lighthouse appeared to float in the dead of night, spraying light from its fresnel lens onto the ocean as it has for over a century.

Avery walked at a slight tilt in an endless struggle to stay upright. With each step, wet sand oozed between his toes and a heavy breeze toyed with his shirt. He tasted salt on his tongue between lulls and thought little of the hissy waves breaking in the distance.

With his vision still adjusting to the dead of night and no desire to see what life had in store for him, Avery admired the far-flung stars blinking behind the moon as they slipped through the clouds above. For a moment, his mind went away as he hoped to make out a constellation, despite not knowing where or what to look for. He thought back to a long-since-donated refractor telescope that collected dust in his childhood closet, then to the only time he put it to good use. He remembered camping out in his backyard and braving the night long into the wee early hours, only to be disappointed after discovering the cosmos lacked the suddenness of color he had come to expect from space propaganda. Years later, he came to learn that black-and-white imagery from space is artificially colorized, but by then, any interest in backyard astronomy or expanding his horizons had long since fizzled out.

A surge of water washed over his feet and Avery entertained the growing part of him that wished to be swept away to a world unknown. Convinced of his imminent return to the hospital, he went over in his mind a scene of Bri informing Micah that visitations were no longer a thing of the past. It almost broke him when he wondered how the poor boy would take it. Switching gears, he rubbed his eyes, only to see Emi's face forming in the sightless night. Knowing the two of them were over, he questioned how long it would take for her to become a distant memory and move on. He thought of Lauren—the last woman in his life—and wondered how disappointed she must be and whether she would ever take him at his word again. Determined to move on, he wondered whether all efforts to recover were in vain, based on how rapidly the voices had returned after lying dormant for so many years. The thought alone was maddening and confirmed what he had always suspected and feared, but Avery put it past him and let his mind wander to the one string of questions that would push him to the brink: who was Austin, what did he want and where did he come from?

Despite his aching mind and senses rearing up, he doubled down on his plan of going nowhere fast, hoping he would find some answers. Back to combing his way down the beach, he sidestepped skittering crabs and fought to dispel the barrage of sweeping thoughts when out of the corner of his eye, he caught the fading flash of what he imagined to be a shooting star unzipping the moonless night.

Back on earth, he never saw it coming. From beyond the confines of his psyche, familiar voices that once haunted his daydreams shook free from the shadows and swooped around his head like a murder of crows. He fought them off in a panic, his face wide with fear, but they had long known his weaknesses and easily broke through his defenses. They beat him into the ground, accosting him with words too brutal and personal to be repeated or remembered.

Collapsing to his knees, Avery clamped his ears and fought against the swirling assault by shifting his focus to anything other than the scattered voices: the caw of wedge-tailed shear-waters circling overhead, the pops and fizz of seawater perme-ating the hard-packed sand underfoot, the sporadic thrum of traffic on the bending road behind him. He latched onto anything able to bind him to reality, not wanting to feed the madness and play into its hands.

At last, something gave, and as fast as the auditory hallucina-tions had appeared, the voices broke and scurried their separate ways, retreating into the night. With no time to catch his breath, Avery knew he had to be on his way and rocked forward, leaning onto his wrists to regain his composure. Seawater washed over his hands, knees, shins and feet, but he ignored the sensation and other distorted senses, focusing instead on a throbbing pinpoint of light pining for him in the distance. Entranced, he sat back on his heels and knuckled his eyelids. Then, with his mouth agape, he wondered what was real and what wasn't while massaging his radiocarpal joints until the feeling returned to his hands.

He propped himself up on one knee, then rose to his feet and scraped sand from his palms before walking toward the light. Saltwater trickled down his legs, and with each passing step, his pants grated against the gritty sand stuck to his skin. Yet he slogged on, leaning into the wind and ignoring the chafing pain, focusing instead on that perfect orb of energy winking in the distance.

The blood-orange light pulsed and appeared to die out before snapping back to life. But he stayed the path, trudging down the beach, sweat prickling the back of his neck. He knew he was getting closer as the light grew, then slowed and leaned into the wind. A gust carrying casual voices blended with the faint persistence of a solo ukulele strumming Island music. Then came the smell of scorched earth choking out the night, and Avery was suddenly a teenager again in a better place at a better time.

He stopped walking and clung to the shadows, not daring to set foot into a ring of light that circled the bonfire. The light cut across the shore and spilled out into the ocean. A party unfolded before his very eyes and a darkened silhouette passed in front of the pyre. Some of them sat cross-legged on the sand, nursing drinks and enjoying good company. Something in the fire burned blue and a bundled couple laying on a blanket wafted smoke from their faces when the offshore breeze shifted and came right for them. Behind them, a man playing his ukulele sat perched on a cooler with either a cigarette or a spliff dangling from his lips. As for the rest of the herd, they danced around the fire, bathing both bodies and hair in smoke.

Avery tried to name the song when he heard voices approaching from behind. He spun around in time to make out the outline of two young men lugging a Coleman cooler between them. He stood his ground with nowhere to run to except into the ocean or into the light. Though they were headed straight toward him, both men existed in a world of their own until one of them spotted Avery and halted in his tracks. His unwitting friend walked on, tearing the handle from his hand and plunging the cooler into the sand with a rattle of glass.

The one who stopped first peered through the dimness at Avery then whipped out his phone's flashlight. He shined it in Avery's face and immediately flicked it off. "Sorry about that," he said with a slur. "I thought you were one of us."

Though appearing as little more than a silhouette in the dim light of his phone, Avery noticed the University of Hawai'i logo on his shirt as the student's friend set some distance between himself and the cooler.

"We're not in any trouble, are we?" the friend wondered aloud.

"Trouble? Why would you think that?" Avery asked. "Oh, because you're underage?"

"Not all of us," the student said, nudging his friend.

Avery turned around and studied the group. "No one here is driving anywhere tonight, right?"

The student shook his head. "We just came to catch the

meteor shower, and perhaps sunrise too, assuming we all don't sleep in."

Avery's eyes turned to the heavens. He felt the winds shift and sniffed the air as a thin slick of smoke passed overhead. "Those aren't pallets I'm smelling, are they?"

"No, never. Maybe a bit of Keawe mixed with some driftwood, but we would never leave a bunch of nails in the sand." He burped and wiped his mouth with the back of his fist.

Avery turned to the voice. "Whatever you pack in, you pack out."

"Automatic."

"Then I don't see any issues here. Besides, even if I did, you're not my kids, I'm not the cops and frankly, I have my own problems to worry about."

"Problems like what?"

Avery waved the question away. "It's complicated."

"Hold on," the friend said. "If you're not the cops, who are you? Someone's dad or uncle?"

"I am, but not to anyone here."

"Well, I can tell you're not a fisherman, and they're the only ones who ever make it out this far at this hour."

Avery turned to face the ocean and admired the wheeling stars overhead. He considered looking away as a bead of water struck his brow, followed by another and another still. "I'm just a nobody taking a stroll and trying to collect my thoughts."

The student turned on his phone's flashlight again and aimed it at Avery. Silver spikes of rain cut through the dead space between them. "You're soaked. Are you sure you didn't go for a swim? Or wash up on shore?"

His friend laughed. "Or maybe you pissed yourself?"

"Are those my only options?"

The light went away. "No," said the student to Avery, "but if you really don't want to tell us what you're doing out here, that's your right. This is America, after all."

"Is it?" the friend asked. "Depends who you ask."

Avery wiped his face dry. "I already told you who I am."

"You said you're a nobody. What does that even mean?"

"It means my story isn't worth telling and you should learn to take a hint."

"Why's that? You think we can't handle it?"

Avery rubbed his face against his sleeve. "I don't know what to think," he said in a strange voice. "That's the problem. But enough about me. You're both here to have a good time so have at it. Have a good one."

"Before you go," the friend said, "I think you're forgetting something."

Avery stopped walking, tapped his pockets and turned around. "Before you offer me a drink, just know that I—"

A bright flash popped as the friend stole a sliver of Avery's soul and tucked his phone away. "Just in case someone comes up missing on the news or something. You're acting fishy and one can never be too safe these days."

Avery stood there in silence, then muttered a low response.

"Don't worry, I won't post it anywhere," the friend said.

Avery shook his head. "I don't even know what that means, but I do know I'm no danger."

The friend held up his hands. "'Hey, 'I don't know what to think,' remember? But I know this—there's more to your story than what you're letting on."

Avery considered the ramifications of opening up to his new friends and the various ways it could come back to haunt him before deciding it wouldn't change a thing. "Fine. You want to know who I am? My name is Avery West and I'm a patient—or former patient, I should say—of Hale Maluhia. Ever heard of it?" His eyes passed between the two friends as they shook their heads. "That's our state psychiatric hospital for the mentally ill. Oh, and since you asked, I'm also off my meds and have been for some time, which explains the episode."

"What do you mean, 'The episode?'"

"You know, the reason I'm hearing and seeing things that aren't really there."

The student scoffed at his friend, then turned to Avery. "Is this like your shtick or something?"

"How so?"

"Like, some sick joke you play on unsuspecting people to get your kicks off?"

"No, not at all. And trust me, even if it were a joke, the joke's on me."

"I don't get it," the friend said, taking a step back. "So you're saying you're psycho? That's what you're saying?"

"My actual diagnosis isn't important, but as for being 'psycho,' I'm not convinced I'm floridly psychotic yet. But am I on the cusp of psychosis?" He shrugged. "Only time will tell, but all signs point to yes."

"What does that mean?" the student asked, turning to his friend and back to Avery. "Are you going to go on an axe-murdering spree or something? Because that ain't cool, man."

Avery stared at his empty hands. "I'm not violent, and this isn't a scary movie. Besides, my dumbass left my axe behind at the last crime scene."

The friend took a step back.

"Relax, it's a joke . . . I never leave home without my axe. '*It's better to have it and not need it than to need it and not have it,*' right?" Avery dropped his guard and turned to the party. "All joking aside, I imagine tonight ends with me crawling into a dank, dark hole. From there, I might watch the meteor shower, might not, but either way I'll be praying to the heavens for it all to end. That's the problem; psychosis is a tricky thing. It can last days, weeks, months—some never come back from it. It all depends on the help one gets and the meds they're on. Now if you don't mind, I'll be on my way. I'd rather not outstay my welcome." Avery turned to take off but didn't make it very far. He knew the voices were out there and sensed them watching his every move, lying in wait.

Behind him, the friend quietly opened a web browser on his phone and hurriedly typed in the name Avery had given him. Then, he swiped back to the photo he had taken and compared the picture in his library to Avery's public mugshot. "Holy shit," he whispered to the student. "He's not lying."

"Why would I?" Avery asked with his back to the students. "I have nothing to hide other than being on the run."

"Hold up. Are you saying you're an *escapee*?"

Avery turned around. "Not an escapee, no. I'd just rather not go back."

The friend stood there stiffly. "You know, there's not much to see past this point, and even if there were, I don't like the idea of letting you out of our sight." He kicked his cooler, rattling the slurry of beer and melting ice. "You sound like you're having a rough night. Why don't you take it easy and join us for a bit? We've got more than enough to go around, and that way we can keep tabs on you and make sure you don't do something you regret."

"I appreciate the offer but think I'll pass; I gave up drinking long ago."

"Then hang with us and at least have something to eat."

Avery peered into the dead of night. "If you don't mind, I'd rather be on my way."

The friend pulled out his phone, tapped three numbers and showed his screen to Avery. "You sure you want to go that route?"

CHAPTER 20
DECEMBER 15TH

"Yo! Let's go. Time to get up." Lauren shook Avery's foot for a second time and twisted to face Uncle Earl. "Thanks again for understanding and not making this any worse for him than it has to be."

"No need to thank me, I'm just doing my job." Uncle Earl leaned over her shoulder and looked down at Avery. "I've said it before and I'll say it again; if someone wants to ruin their life, that's their right. He isn't the first and we both know he won't be the last. But once someone's decisions threaten the rest of us and our sobriety, that's when we have to take a stand."

"I completely understand where you're coming from." Lauren turned to Avery and placed a cup of coffee near his shoulder. "Did you hear that?" she asked, jiggling his arm. "It's time to go. This isn't your home anymore."

Avery's eyelids flickered open to reveal glimpses of bloodshot scleras that strained to register their surroundings. In his peripheral vision, he made out Lauren squatting next to him but avoided eye contact. He tucked his chin to his chest and peeked under the sheet draped over his torso. He had no recollection of making his way home to the sober house last night or why he crashed out on the cold floor of the carport of all places. All he knew was that he hurt everywhere and rather than stare at his naked body for another second, he released the sheet and covered his eyes with his palm.

"Come on, there's no time for that." Lauren shook his wrist and worked his hand away from his face. "I need you to get up. Don't make me ask again."

Avery tensed for a moment, then caved and curled onto his side with a guttural moan. With his free hand clutching his forehead, he muttered something wordless.

Lauren leaned over him. "Sorry, I missed that. What did you say?"

"I just want to be left alone."

"We both know I can't do that."

"Who said I was talking about you?"

Lauren heard the footfall of Uncle Earl approaching from behind and motioned for him to hold him off. "Avery? Who are you talking about?"

He forced a bent smile, distracted by the acrid taste of smoke lingering in his throat and a vision of meteoroids streaking through his memory.

"You're hearing voices again, aren't you?"

He groggily propped himself up on an elbow and nodded.

"Can you tell me what they're saying? Are they telling you to do anything?"

He thought for a moment and shook his head. "No, and none of it's clear anyway, at least not yet. It's more of a cacophony of noise that needs to go away."

"You know what you need to do if you want it to stop. Come on, let's get you up and dressed. Your coffee isn't going to drink itself."

Lauren helped him sit up and began to search for his clothes when Uncle Earl tapped her shoulder and pointed to the corner of the carport. She walked over and stared at a pile of soaked, sandy clothes.

She turned to Uncle Earl. "If it's not too much to ask, could I trouble you for one more favor?"

He read her mind and disappeared. Lauren turned back to the pile of soiled clothes and crouched over them. "Do I even want to know the story here?" She turned around at the sound of Avery retching, surprised to see he not only made it to his feet but had his head buried halfway into a trash can. "I guess better there than in my Jeep," she said as he adjusted his grip on the lip of the bin. "Hopefully that helps you feel a little better."

He cursed himself, cinched the sheet around his waist and used the trash can like a spittoon. "I can't believe this happened," he said, craning his neck to look at her.

"Seriously? Did you expect something good to come from cutting your meds and getting yourself drunk?"

His only response was a far-off stare.

"Well, regardless of what you thought, don't beat yourself up over this. The reality is relapses happen, but it's where you go from here that matters. Remember, if recovery was easy, everybody would do it."

Avery swiped the back of his hand across his mouth and spat into the bin.

"How much did you have to drink last night?"

"No idea. I lost count after one."

"I guess it doesn't really make a difference. 'One drink is too many . . .'" Lauren paused to observe his distress. "How are you feeling now? Still intoxicated?"

He shook his head. "Despite being a lightweight these days, I think I slept most of it off. I still feel like shit, but even worse, I feel like an idiot."

"Avery, you're not an—"

"You say that, but look at me! All that work, and for what? What a waste. It's almost like I . . ." His words trailed off and silence invaded the void. He cocked his head as something behind him commanded his attention. His eyes turned slightly, but he refused to look.

"Hey, look at me," Lauren said, tapping the corner of her eyes. "Obviously, this isn't what either of us wanted, but this situation is fixable, and we're going to get through this together. Just you and me. That's what I'm here for. You have to trust me on this."

"And how long will that take? Another seven years?"

"No, of course not, but now more than ever, your future is up to you, not me and not anyone else. And if you can't see that, look around. Clearly, this situation isn't working for you, and you're not doing well or making good choices. You also didn't turn yourself in or tell on yourself when you had the chance, which is unfortunate. The good news though is that as of this moment, all of that's in the past. So let's work on getting you back on your meds and back in the right headspace, then we can figure out your next steps."

"I'm glad one of us is optimistic," Avery said, then laughed bitterly. He hiked up his bedsheet as something came over him. "I still can't believe Emi called you."

"She did you a favor, Avery. It's obvious she cares about you."

He went quiet for a moment. "Cares about me? How? Ever since she learned I was on meds, she's been on me to get off them."

Lauren paused. "I didn't know about that since you didn't tell me, but what made you think to listen to her over your support people? Remember, there are lots of Emi's out there, and while most of them won't mean you any harm, you can't count on others to make the right decisions for you. Your recovery is in your hands, and that's just the way of the world."

"Easy for you to say."

"Nothing about this is easy for me. If anything, it gets harder every time."

"Here we go and sorry for the wait," Uncle Earl said. He entered the carport with a bulging contractor's trash bag slung over each shoulder. He set them on the ground and turned to

Avery. "Normally, I'd give you thirty minutes to pack out, but because of the current situation, I figured it's best for everyone that we bag up your belongings for you. Feel free to go through the bags and let us know if we forgot anything."

Avery stared blankly at his world belongings. "When you say 'we,' I hope you're not talking about who I think you're talking about."

"You mean Austin? He's a good kid, Avery, not to mention your roommate. He did you a favor by making sure we didn't forget anything."

"Who the fuck said he could touch my stuff?"

Uncle Earl flexed his knuckles and stepped forward. "No talk heavy with me, brah. I may be old, but you don't make it this far in life by being a pushover." He glanced at Lauren, met her eyes and then breathed to calm himself. "Remember, you're in this situation because of your choices and yours alone." He nudged one of the bags with his foot. "I suggest you get dressed and be on your way. Oh, and don't forget to take that pisspoor attitude of yours when you leave."

Lauren thanked him as he backed out of the carport and shook her head when she heard the front door to the house slam shut. She picked up Avery's bags and dragged them over to him. "I know you're going through a lot right now, but I'd think twice about burning any more bridges if I were you. We both know how small this island is." She turned her back on him and waited for him to get dressed.

He kneeled, undid the drawstring and paused. "Can I ask you something? Do you not find any part of this suspicious?"

"How so? Getting booted from a sober house following a relapse is standard protocol pretty much anywhere you go."

"That's not what I meant. It's not at all suspicious to you that the same guy who's had it out for me is the same one who packed my stuff?"

"You think Austin has it out for you? Why Austin?" Lauren looked around, dumbfounded. "I'm going to need you to break that down for me and make it make sense because I find it hard to believe."

Avery yanked a shirt from the bag and gave it a good shake. "I don't want to get into specifics in case someone's listening, but I've thought about this a lot and there's only one explanation here."

". . . Go on."

Avery's voice hushed to a whisper. "Austin's been hired by someone from my past to seek revenge on me." He inverted the shirt and inspected the seams.

"Hired by who? And revenge for what?"

"I'm still trying to figure it out."

"And you know this how? Do you have any proof to support your claim?"

"He's good at what he does and covers his tracks well, so nothing yet, but let me finish going through these clothes." Avery stretched the shirt over his head and reached for a pair of boxers and shorts. "Knowing him, there has to be a tracking or listening device in here somewhere."

Lauren turned around to offer Avery some privacy. "Let me know when you're done."

"Just a sec." He finished inspecting his outfit and got dressed. "Okay, you can turn around now. Look, I know what you're thinking, but none of this is a coincidence. If you still don't believe me, I need you to ask yourself why Austin would want to help pack my things."

"Avery, please." She reached out and placed a hand on his shoulder. "While I hear what you're saying, frankly I'm concerned over your attachment to reality right now. So my question is how do you know any of this to be true? Has Austin told you these things himself?"

"No, of course not."

"And do you have any evidence or firsthand knowledge to back up this claim?"

"Lauren. Look at what's happening to my life. I'm about to lose everything I worked for, all because of him."

"Could it also be possible that when you quit taking your meds, you opened the door to invite the resurgence of delusions back into your life?" She picked up a pair of Avery's jeans from a pile he had started and began folding them.

"I'm sure because it's too perfect not to be true. Trust me, I would love to be wrong, but I have to go with my gut."

"Fine, then say my perfectly logical explanation makes little sense, ask yourself this: who are you, and what makes you so damn important that someone would spend the time, energy and possibly even their hard-earned money to send someone after you?"

Avery's hands dropped into his lap as he realized he couldn't count on Lauren anymore.

"Don't look at me like that. This isn't about me being tough on you. It's my job to ask the hard questions, especially when things aren't quite adding up. Remember Occam's razor? The simplest explanation is more often than not the right one." Lauren set the jeans on a stack of clothes and squatted beside him.

"I knew you wouldn't understand." He turned out another pocket and stared at crumbs and a ball of lint. "So where do we go from here?"

"Today we'll go back to the hospital, and since you don't appear to be floridly psychotic or a threat to yourself or others, I don't anticipate any problems returning you to the ward. I've already spoken with the psychiatrist, and she's expecting to give you a quick mental status exam this afternoon. My guess is she'll get you on something to help with any anxiety you're experiencing and then restart your meds, assuming you don't refuse."

"And what about the courts?"

"Good question. In this case, the law mandates I notify them about the return of any patient as well as the circumstances.

Beyond that, they'll look at the treatment team's recommendation as to where you go from there."

The thought made Avery give up on his search for the time being. "What exactly are we talking about?"

"Anything from revocation to being sent to rehab or even finding you another sober living environment with a different structure. Basically, it's all on the table, unless you decide to start removing options."

Avery scrubbed a hand over his face. "Can I make one request?"

"You can make it, but no guarantees."

"I don't want Bri to know what happened."

"Avery, you can't hide this from her. People just don't return to the hospital for no reason."

"I get it," he said, shoving the last of his clothes into his bag. "But I don't want her to know I relapsed. I can't imagine letting her down again."

"Because of HIPAA, my lips are sealed and I can't disclose anything without your permission, but that doesn't mean Emi, your coworkers or even your former roommates won't. The truth has a funny way of coming out and if you want my advice, I'd say it may be easier on her if you get in front of it and let her hear it from you."

"Maybe you're right, but I can't think about that right now." He tossed the last of his belongings into his bags and checked to ensure he wasn't leaving anything behind.

As the two of them exited the carport, Avery heard a faraway voice and turned to see Nani pacing on the porch.

"Sorry to see you go," Nani yelled out. She puffed on her cigarette and fanned a cloud of smoke away from her face. "I know some of da boys are pretty irraz with you right now, but nevahmind them. Jus take as long as you need and who knows, maybe we'll see you back here one day?"

Avery thought of warning her to watch out for Austin but

kept his thoughts to himself. Instead, he said the only reasonable thing that came to mind, waved goodbye and started for the car.

As they pulled away, Avery leaned forward to watch the house disappear in the side-view mirror. When they turned the corner, he slumped back in his seat and felt an overwhelming desire to break the silence.

"I want to apologize for being such a disappointment," he said. "I know you've worked really hard to get me to this point, and I can't believe I've let you down."

Lauren checked over her shoulder and switched lanes. "You're not a disappointment, Avery. You know me better than that."

"Somehow I don't believe you."

"You think I'm lying?"

"Not necessarily, but you know how it is; in your position, you can't always tell the truth because sometimes the truth hurts."

Lauren kept her eyes on the road and continued to drive.

"It's okay," Avery said after a moment. "If I had myself as a client, I'd see me as a disappointment, too."

"Again, you're not a disappointment," Lauren insisted. "No matter how many times you say it. But am I disappointed? A little. I'm disappointed that you didn't at least attempt to reach out for help, and I'm definitely disappointed that you have so many resources available to you and yet chose not to use them. But am I disappointed in you as a person?" She shook her head. "Of course not, because what kind of person would that make me?"

"Sorry I'm late. I got a flat on my way back from lunch and help took forever to arrive." Dr. Levin eased the door to the conference room shut and took a seat across from Avery and Lauren. "Be thankful you don't own a car yet, Avery. Those damn potholes get me every time and I don't care what your deductible is. New rims aren't cheap."

"If only this hospital was a tourist attraction, the State would be all over patching up that road," Lauren said.

Dr. Levin removed her sunglasses and cocked an eyebrow. Her silky hair was drawn back into a tight ponytail that ran the length of her back. She wore a collared royal blue blouse and enough makeup to be noticeable, but not so much that it overpowered her sharp cheekbones and other features.

"You know that used to be a thing?" Lauren asked with a smile. "Not here at Hale Maluhia, of course. But back in the day, asylum directors treated their sanitariums similar to zoos and sideshows. Just like a carnival, they'd hawk tickets to the public so tourists could tour the grounds, tap on the glass and marvel at the gravely disabled. Talk about dark days in our history."

Avery shook his head at the thought and continued to shuffle his feet on the floor.

"I have heard that," Dr. Levin said. "Though for what it's worth, those tours did evolve from a means to fetishize the mentally ill into a means to rebuild the public's confidence in hospitals as a place for treatment and healing."

"Fair enough, but don't you find it odd that the same people fascinated by psych wards have zero interest in touring places like cancer wards?"

"Not really, but to be fair, I haven't put much thought to it." Dr. Levin turned to Avery. "Avery, what do you think?"

"Me?" Avery looked up. "I wouldn't feel comfortable having strangers poke their heads in my room."

"Who would?" Lauren said. "This is your home, after all, at least while you're here."

Dr. Levin cracked Avery's patient file open and tucked her bangs behind her ears. She dragged a finger across the chart and paused. "Despite the circumstances, it's good to see you again. How are you holding up?"

"I'm angry at myself, but hanging in there," he said with a jerk.

"That's perfectly normal, especially at a time like this, but you should be proud of yourself for keeping your head in the game. And I'm glad to see you've made the first step in the right direction; you could have just as easily refused to come back."

"You mean like the patient who supposedly left for work, boarded a flight without an ID and absconded to Cali?"

"Ouch," Lauren whispered. "Too soon."

"Seriously? It's been years."

Dr. Levin pursed her lips. "I must say, I appreciate you not putting us in a similar situation, but at least you see my point."

A thin smile crossed Avery's lips. "Do you want to know why I didn't run? Not only do I have nowhere to run to, but from what I can remember, I could barely walk."

"You got that drunk, huh?" Dr. Levin dropped her elbows onto the table. "Was that your first relapse? Or have you been drinking for some time?"

Avery shook his head. "That was it."

"Can I ask what type of alcohol you had?"

"Mostly beer, but I remember some box wine being passed around too, which probably explains the splitting headache."

"Is that all? Wine and beer?"

"That's it."

"No drugs?"

"No, but you're more than welcome to check my pee if you want to."

"We will, and it's not so much that I want to, but I have to," Dr. Levin said. "Policy is policy, but we'll handle the UA later." She flipped a page in her binder and reached for a pen. "When exactly did you stop taking your meds?"

Avery turned to his fingers to do some dirty math. "Around a week ago, at least. Maybe nine? Ten days?"

"If you had to take your best guess."

"I'd say ten."

She made a quick note. "Any auditory, visual or olfactory hallucinations?"

"Just auditory."

"How so?"

"At first there was this static buzzing in the background, like a beehive rattling in the distance. I definitely hear music too at times, and then of course the voices."

Dr. Levin marked her paper and looked up. "And I take it you're still experiencing these hallucinations?"

Avery nodded.

"Okay. The good news is that as soon as we get you up and running, your mood should start to shift, but I would still plan on four or five days before you should expect to feel relief. Granted, I've seen it take up to a month or longer for some people, but those are exceptions to the norm. You may also want to do what you can to stay cool, calm and collected. Keeping your stress levels low should help not to exasperate the symptoms. Think you can do that?"

"No promises, but I'll try my best."

"And that's all you can do. Now you said you were hearing music as well, correct?"

"Yes."

"Can I ask what kind?"

"Depends. Usually, it's just some rendition of whatever I've been listening to lately."

"Was it loud? Quiet?"

"No, not loud. Sometimes it's barely perceptible and so quiet that I second-guess if I'm hearing anything at all."

"Does it play all day? Or do you ever get a break?"

"It's sporadic, but I noticed it's stronger in the mornings. I'm not sure why."

"Hmm." Dr. Levin scribbled a note and tapped her chin. "That's a first for me, but I wonder if it's a carryover from the night before? It's well documented that delusions appear stronger at night, so perhaps your abrupt discontinuation of meds is resulting in sleep dysfunction? Or maybe your coping skills aren't as accessible to engage when you first wake up? I'll have to look into it more and get back to you on that one, but for now, back to the voices . . . do you mind sharing with me what they say?"

"Mostly it's just a bunch of jumble, but nothing I haven't heard before."

Dr. Levin tapped the tip of her pen on the paper. "Any chance you could be a little more specific?"

"Again, they're not coming in loud and clear, but basically they remind me how hopeless and worthless I am, as if I somehow forgot."

"Hey, let's not do that." Lauren reached out and shook his knee. "You're none of those things, and anyone who tells you otherwise is not your friend."

"Lauren's right. You're a good man, Avery." Dr. Levin tapped her pen on the desk. "Back to the voices. Have they said anything about you hurting yourself or others?"

"No, not at all."

"And would you tell me if they were?"

Avery thought for a moment. "Of course."

"Good." Dr. Levin flipped a page. "What about sleeping and eating? Any issues there?"

"My sleep is all over the place, but I think we know why."

"Yeah, that will happen." Dr. Levin scratched out a question. "What about restarting your meds? Any resistance there?"

"No."

"Good answer, because I'd hate to see you placed back in the locked ward." Dr. Levin made a final note and closed Avery's file. "Here's what I'm thinking; I'm going to reissue your meds along with a PRN for Ativan to offset any anxiety that comes with reentering the ward. That's to be taken every eight hours as needed, so if at any time you're ever feeling overwhelmed or anxious, just mention it to a med nurse and they'll set you straight. Also, since you're a readmission, I have to put in new orders with the pharmacy so expect your first dose to be ready tonight for evening meds. And, as I'm sure you'll understand, all meds from here on out need to be administered at the med window."

"Makes sense," Avery said, his voice filling the dead space in the room.

Dr. Levin smiled. "Speaking of meds, there's something else I should mention; research tells us that psych meds are most effective the very first time someone takes them, meaning every time they're discontinued, they lose efficacy. I can't tell you how many people I've worked with who have gone on and off of their meds over the years. Those who do it enough find their neuro receptors become shot and they become quite the challenge to help. I'm not saying you may or may not notice a difference this time around, but just a heads up in case you take longer to respond to the meds."

"I understand," Avery said.

"Any questions?"

"Not about meds, but do you know if there's any chance I can get my old bunk back?"

Dr. Levin shrugged. "That's not exactly my wheelhouse, but I'm sure you and Lauren will work it out." She pushed back her chair and rose. "Please reach out if questions or concerns come up, and thanks again for being cooperative. I'll put these orders in and track down a PSA to come and administer your urine screening."

Lauren waved goodbye as Dr. Levin closed the door behind her.

"So I take it that's a no on my bed?" Avery asked.

"You know the drill; your seniority ends the moment you move out."

"I figured as much. I also figured it never hurts to ask."

"No, it doesn't."

"So who's Marv staying with?"

"Kalani, and you'll be proud to hear he seems to be doing a great job in the greenhouse."

"Good. I'd like to see what he's done with the place."

"You will, but do me a favor and give it a day. You're still on a Ward Hold until you're back on your meds."

Avery nodded and stared ahead at the wall.

Lauren pulled her chair closer to his. "You feeling alright?" she asked.

"I'm not sure. Right now, it's all sinking in." He turned to look at her. "Marv was right. I should have never left."

"Listen, between us, while I believe Marv means well, just like you, me or anyone else you'll meet in this lifetime, he has his own demons and fears holding him back. If I can speak to you as a friend for a moment, I'd say not to let him project his own insecurities on you for the sake of having common ground. Instead of dwelling in dread, I suggest focusing on what led to your relapse and what prevented you from reaching out for help."

Avery rubbed the back of his neck when a faint knocking from outside grabbed his attention.

"Come in," Lauren said, twisting in her seat.

The door cracked open and a hand reached into the room, dangling a bag with a specimen cup inside. "I heard we have a urine screening," Sam said. "Is now a good time, or should I circle back later?"

"Now is fine," Lauren said, nudging Avery. "Why don't we end here? You go with Sam and take care of business while I catch up with Gail on some reports we owe the courts. Let's reconvene after dinner and med pass."

"Sounds great." Avery rose from his seat, tucked in his chair and acknowledged Sam with the slightest of nods.

"After you," Sam said. He held the door open with the heel of his foot, and as Avery passed, he flashed a half-hearted smile at Lauren before the door shut in his face.

Both men worked their way through the corridor in silence.

As they approached the bathroom, Sam grabbed Avery's shoulder.

"Hey man. Mind if I share something with you?" he asked.

"Have at it."

Sam stopped walking and faced Avery. "I don't know all the details of your situation, but I've been doing this for a long time and can't tell you how many people I've seen come and go. To anyone fortunate enough to find their way back, I always tell them there are two days in any given week that there's no point in troubling yourself over. Any chance you know what days I'm talking about?"

Avery's mouth parted, then closed.

"Yesterday and tomorrow," Sam said. "You can't undo yesterday any more than you can control tomorrow, so whatever happens, don't let something beyond your control interfere with you making the changes when and where you can." With that, Sam handed Avery the bag with the cup inside.

Avery studied the door for a moment, then held it open for Sam. "After you."

"Go ahead. I'll wait right here."

Avery's expression went slack. "Don't you need to come inside to observe me?"

"Like I said, I've been doing this a long time. If I can't tell by now whether I can trust someone, I might as well pack it up and ship it out."

"Rusty, my ass," Marv muttered as he flicked his king over. He scanned the game room as if to buy him some time. "Best five out of seven?"

Avery shook his head. "Like I said two games ago, I've had a rough day. I'm not trying to drag it out."

"Come on. I'm just getting warmed up."

"Yeah you say that, but you're getting worse with each game."

Marv pretended not to hear him and began arranging Avery's pieces. "One more before you go to bed. You know you want to, and it's the least you can do for leaving me with Kalani."

Avery let a smile slip. "Fine, but last game."

"Does that mean it's winner takes all?"

"I don't care, Marv. Just move."

Marv scooted his chair forward and started the game. "Out of curiosity, what did you miss about this place? The food? The games? Or the fact that there's always someone around when you need something?"

Avery thought for a moment and brought out his knight. "I didn't miss anything."

"Nothing? Not even me or your plants?"

"I was just a caretaker," Avery said. "If they were really my plants, I would have taken them with me."

"You're really taking this hard, aren't you?"

Avery stared at the game board. "How else am I supposed to take it? I cut my meds and am symptomatic. I relapsed and feel like shit. I don't know what to tell Bri. I'm depressed. I'm alone. I lost my housing, my job and even lost a woman I was into." Avery brought his queen out and slammed it on the board. "Worst of all, I'm right back to where I started. Check."

"You speak like coming full circle is such a bad thing. Aren't you at least grateful you didn't offend again and wind up back in jail?" Marv pushed a pawn forward to defend his king. "I understand things may not have worked out the way you intended, but at least you made it back to the place where all of your needs are met."

"My needs?" Avery double-downed on his attack. "What do you know about needs?"

"I know we all have them, and I know I'm comfortable living in an environment where I'm not at risk of going off my meds. I'm well fed here and get good medical care. I'm safe and accepted for who and what I am."

"But you don't want more?"

"It doesn't matter what I want," Marv said, then pulled his king to safety. "That ship has sailed."

Avery's hand hovered over his piece. "I think you lost me."

"Come on, man. You of all people should know exactly where I'm coming from, and if you believe anyone with a NGRI plea will ever be accepted in the real world, you're lying to yourself."

"And how would you know? You rarely leave, and when you do, you can't hightail it back here fast enough." Avery infiltrated Marv's protective pawn cover with a knight and twisted the pawn in his fingers. "Check."

"How would I know? You'd be surprised how much you can pick up from watching and listening, mainly that society wants nothing to do with us. I know I don't go out much, but when I do, I pick up on how we're viewed."

"And how is that?"

"As evil monsters who don't deserve fresh air or sunlight. Just like in the movies. Just like in the books. It doesn't matter whether we've gotten better or turned our lives around because we can't change who or what we are." Marv paused to catch his breath and countered, attacking Avery's knight with his pawn. "You know what it is, Avery. Don't lie to yourself and act like you don't. The second someone learns of your past is the second they begin waiting for you to slip up. I hate to say it, but you are no longer a human anymore but a liability, because in this game, someone will always be watching from the sidelines, waiting for you to drop the ball."

Avery studied the board and rubbed his brow. "Don't go there," he said in a low voice, then tapped his bishop to reveal a discovery check. "And I hate to break it to you, but you're wrong. Not everyone is like that. I know for a fact there are people out there who want us to succeed."

"Of course there are, but only because they're terrified of what will happen if we fail." Marv returned Avery's knight to the board and leaned over his game pieces. "I think that's enough doom and gloom for now. Earlier you mentioned a girl? This doesn't happen to be the same coworker I warned you about?"

"And say it is, what difference does it make? Do you want to hear that you were right?"

"No, because I know I'm right." Marv leaned across the table and accidentally elbowed a rook onto the floor. "I only ask because I'm interested in if she has any friends."

"Of course she does, tons of them. But unfortunately for you, they're all plants." Avery handed the piece back to Marv. "By the way, her name is Emi, and yes, she has a roommate—a roommate that I barely know. But why would you care? I thought no one out there wants anything to do with us?"

"I guess it never hurts to ask, right?"

"Maybe not, but in this case, no one's asking anyone anything. Especially not after what happened, but I'd rather not get into it."

Marv leaned forward. "Avery. Don't do this to me. You can't walk me to the edge and leave me hanging. Can't you see I need closure here?"

Avery went to move a piece but reconsidered. He returned it to its square and cocked his head back. "Fine, but if I explain it once, do you promise you'll never bring her up again? I'm doing my best to forget about her and so far it's not working."

He raised three fingers to his forehead. "Scout's honor."

"Basically, Emi seemed to think I'd be better off without my meds until I quit taking them and things started getting dicey. Granted, I was the one who stopped taking them, but the moment things fell apart, she betrayed me and went behind my back to call Lauren and tell her everything."

"Wait. That's it?"

Avery cocked his head. "Were you even listening?"

"I did, but I don't see why you make it sound like a bad thing."

"Marv, look around. Do you not see where we're at?"

Marv leaned forward. "There's nothing wrong with her reaching out for help, and if anything, you probably scared the bejesus out of that poor girl. But look at the bright side; at least she called Lauren and not the cops. That means she cares about you, because if she didn't, she wouldn't have wasted her time." Marv thought for a moment. "Maybe I was wrong. Perhaps there are some good apples out there after all."

"You don't understand. From the moment I met Emi, she's encouraged me to move away from pharmaceuticals. Then, when I finally did and needed her the most, she turned her back on me."

"Probably because she's not equipped to help you. Has that thought ever crossed your mind?"

"You know what? I don't want to talk about this anymore."

"Fine. It's not like I came here to argue with you, anyway. I'm here to defend my—"

"Title? Hate to break it to you, but you've already lost. Two moves back." Avery pushed his chair back and extended his hand.

Marv, refusing Avery's handshake, gripped the table and leaned over the board, desperately hoping to keep his head in the game. "Hold on, give me a second to—"

"Good game," Avery said, then patted his old roommate on the back. "Now do yourself a favor and try to get some sleep, assuming you don't have nightmares of how badly you just got your ass handed to you."

CHAPTER 21
DECEMBER 16TH

Running off a rough night's sleep, Avery reached the greenhouse and contemplated knocking but instead, he paused to prepare himself for what may come. Pulling the door halfway open, he felt a sense of dread and released the handle, letting the door bounce closed.

A voice called out from inside the greenhouse. "Something a matter, or have you developed OCD since we last spoke?"

Avery entered the greenhouse and his eyes dropped to a book in Benny's hands.

"Local author and artist, both from Kailua," Benny said, using his knee as a bookmark. "Some people talk it up, but so far I don't see what the big deal is about this memoir. Not to belittle this man's journey or anything, but it's nothing compared to some of the stories I've heard here over the years."

"I can only imagine." Avery turned and pointed behind him at the door. "By the way, what happened to the squeak?"

Benny picked up his book and looked over his shoulder. "Don't ask me; ask your protégé."

Avery stepped onto the footbath mat and shook his shoes dry. The greenhouse was nothing like the ruins he envisioned. Instead, the plants he could see seemed more than happy to be alive. As Avery passed Benny, he noticed a garden hose coiled on the floor beneath plants dripping from a recent watering. Only then did the music hit him as a faint chorus of strings rippled through the air.

"What's up, Boss? Come to check on me?" Kalani asked, rising from his stool. He poked a label into a plug and slid the seedling tray aside.

"I was in the area and figured I'd drop by." Avery worked his hands into his pockets and nodded approvingly. "I like what you've done with the place. I'm impressed."

"You sound surprised. Let me guess, you thought I'd run it into the ground?"

Avery cocked his head and shrugged. "Nothing against you, but the thought had crossed my mind."

"I wonder whether that would say more about me or my teacher." Kalani wiped his hands on his apron and shook Avery's hand. "Either way, I don't blame you. Even with what little time I've had here, I'd be anxious about turning the keys over to someone else, regardless if they knew what they were doing. This might sound weird, but it's almost like these plants have become part of my 'ohana."

"Not weird," Avery said, able to relate. "At least, not as weird as the fact that you like classical music."

"I can't stand it to be honest, but I've heard the plants love it. Think there's anything to it?"

"Who knows? There's no conclusive scientific evidence that I'm aware of, but if plants can pick up on light, scent, touch and even wind, then I don't see why not. Have you ever thought to ask them?"

"Ask them how?"

"You know, talk to them."

"You want me to talk to the plants?" Kalani looked around to see if Benny was listening. "Something tells me it's a bad look to be talking to inanimate objects, especially here."

"They're not inanimate, but living, breathing organisms,"

Avery said with a smile. "But give it some time and see what happens. Until then, I'm glad to see they're doing so well, even if that tells me I'm no longer needed."

"I wouldn't go that far. There is something I could really use your help with."

"What's that?"

"Actually, it's probably best I show you." Kalani turned around and motioned for Avery to follow him.

The two headed to the furthest corner of the greenhouse and approached a sickly tomato plant with a browning stem and blotchy lesions on its leaves. Avery leaned in close and inspected some of the fruit. Though ripe, the skin had a series of black depressions as though rotting from the inside out.

"I'm stumped," Kalani said. "What do you think it is?"

"Not think. I know exactly what we're looking at." Avery pressed off of his knees and stood up. "Late blight."

Kalani sucked his upper lip and went quiet. "Is that from overwatering?"

"No, though improper watering can help spread it if you splash the soil. So I take it you've never heard of it?"

"Not that I know of," Kalani said, shrugging.

"What about the Great Hunger or Irish Potato Famine?"

Kalani shook his head.

"Well, in your defense, it was a bit before your time, but this is the same disease, caused by the water mold phytophthora infestans. Translation—plant destroyer."

"Where did you think it came from?"

"Originally? Central Mexico, before spreading to Europe in the mid-1800s, then the US and eventually, the rest of the world."

"No. I mean, how do you think it got into the greenhouse?"

Avery scratched his throat. "That's harder to say since we're talking about a pathogen."

"A what?"

"A pathogen. Similar to a germ. Think of it as something you can only see the effects of." Avery twisted the pot and checked the underside for a price tag. "Where'd this plant come from? I know I wasn't gone long enough for you to have grown this from seed."

Kalani thought for a moment. "I think this was a donation from Sam who picked it up at a plant sale if I'm not mistaken."

"Then there's your answer. Are there any others?"

"Just one more."

"Where?"

Kalani pointed to another tomato plant that appeared unaffected.

Avery grabbed it from a stand and placed both plants next to each other. "I take it you didn't isolate these to confirm they were disease or pest free prior to introducing them here?"

"No. I didn't know I was supposed to."

"To be fair," Avery said, "it's not something I ever thought you'd have to deal with since we've always grown from seed or cuttings."

"So how can we fix it?"

Avery hesitated before answering. "The simple answer is we can't. There's no cure for late blight and at this point, our best option is to destroy both plants and hope there's no cross contamination to deal with."

"And how do we do that?"

"Traditionally, we'd burn them," Avery said. "Though somehow I don't think that'll fly here."

Kalani stared at the plants. "There's really no other way to save them?"

"There are steps one can take for prevention, but by the time a plant exhibits symptoms, it's too late."

"Why not isolate them and hope for the best? Or at the very least, why not keep the healthy one?"

Avery stared at the diseased plants. "This is your greenhouse now, so I won't tell you what to do, but my recommendation is they both have to go."

"But this one doesn't even look sick."

"You know, a minute ago, you didn't even know what you were looking at, so why not listen to someone who does? We're talking about rapid spread here, and one of the reasons late blight is so contagious is that the spores can survive dormant inside of the soil for years. Just because you can't see the symptoms on this one plant doesn't mean it's not there. So in my opinion, the only responsible decision here is to get rid of the plant matter now, monitor what's left moving forward and learn from this experience."

Kalani stared at the plant, then turned around and walked away. A few moments later, he returned dragging a trash can behind him. "If you think this is the only way, so be it." He broke the stems of each plant in half and stuffed them into the bin.

"I love this job, but just like life, it can't be all sunshine and roses all the time."

Kalani snapped the lid onto the can and got to thinking. "Speaking of life, don't you find it strange that ours are a lot like these plants?"

"How so?"

"Well, according to you, they have an incurable disease no one can see that lies in wait to threaten their very existence. And because there's no cure, the only 'solution' is to shove them in a bin and send them away before they do any more damage. Out of sight, out of mind."

"I hear what you're saying, but your analogy doesn't quite work."

"And why is that?"

Avery pointed at the bin. "To start, what we have is treatable and we have access to the tools that can change our outcome. More importantly though, late blight is contagious. My schizophrenia and your bipolar disorder aren't."

"But our disorders are known to be hereditary, right? So I wonder what's worse?" Kalani waited for a response that didn't come. "Think about it like this; who would you rather pass your disease to? Someone you love dearly like Bri or

Micah, or to a perfect stranger you'll never cross paths with again?"

"We both know that's not how it works."

"But humor me. Say you had to pick one. Wouldn't you be ridden with guilt if someone you loved became symptomatic?"

"Humor you? There's nothing humorous about it. I would be devastated and gutted, and it's one of my worst fears." Avery started to walk away and turned around. "But that said, if I was somehow forced to choose, I imagine I would choose to remove myself from the equation. There's no way in hell I would willingly pass this on to anyone if I had a say in the matter."

Avery returned to his room to find his new roommate away at lunch. He collapsed onto his bed and buried his face in his pillow, sitting in the darkness for a moment before pressing up on his elbows to turn over. Then, slipping a hand under his pillow, he removed his Moleskin journal and began thumbing through the pages until he came to his unfinished sketch of Emi.

He sat up, stared at the drawing and traced the curvature of the wave with his finger, then touched the form of Emi and closed his eyes. Despite the chatter in the background, he could hear her laughter and see her smile. He thought she deserved to be happy, so much more than he did.

When he opened his eyes, he gripped the edge of the sheet and tore it free from its binding before second-guessing himself. It was a ragged tear, but the drawing remained intact. Knowing what he needed to do, Avery flipped the page over, grabbed his pencil and began putting his thoughts on paper:

> Dear Emi,
> I've never been one with words or goodbyes, but I intend to keep my word and give you this drawing as promised. I've gone back and forth over finishing it but

have decided against it for fear of ruining it. As for me, I'm back at the hospital for the foreseeable future and wanted to thank you for our time together. As for us, I can only say you deserve so much more.

All the best,

—Avery

P.S. Please thank Jas for the opportunity, and if it's not too much to ask, please tell her I'm sorry for letting her down.

There was a knock on the door. Avery tucked the drawing back into his journal and slipped it under his pillow.

"Come in," he called out.

Lauren stepped into the room and approached his bed.

"Let me guess, you came to check up on me?"

"I did. I noticed you weren't at lunch and figured it couldn't hurt. Everything okay?"

He shrugged. "Hard to say. I'm still coming to grips with the reality that I'm not destined to make it on my own out there."

"Do me a favor and hold that thought." Lauren walked over to Avery's desk and grabbed his chair. She dragged it across the room, plopped it next to his bed and sat down. "Are you just being down on yourself, or do you honestly believe that to be true?"

He wrestled with the idea as she settled in. "Maybe a bit of both," he said. "It's just hard to accept that after all these years I'm right back to where I started."

"Do you want to know what I think? I think you've come a lot further than you give yourself credit for. I also think you're not back at the starting line just because you hit a bump in the road."

"A bump?" He looked around his room. "You call this a

bump? This feels more like I've careened into a bottomless sinkhole."

"Well, I guess it's going to feel like whatever you allow it to be but you're back in the driver's seat now. The path you take from here is entirely on you."

He lowered himself back onto his pillow and stared at the ceiling. "I'm in no condition to be behind the wheel."

"Try not to be so hard on yourself. Just give yourself time and everything will fall into place." She drummed her fingers on the armrests and let out a deep breath. "There's something else I need to talk to you about. It's about Bri."

He lifted his head from his pillow and rolled onto his side. "Is something wrong?"

"No. She's fine, but she called just now and left me a voice-mail saying she needs to speak with you. But as we've already discussed, you know that's not my decision to make."

"Shit," he said, slumping back into his bed and staring at the ceiling.

"Did you want to come to my office and call her?"

He thought for a moment, then shook his head.

"That's fine, but if you decide to change your mind, just—"

"No, it's not that," he said. "I just don't feel like a phone call does her justice. The least I can do is speak with her face to face."

Lauren nodded. "I agree. She'd probably like that. When were you thinking?"

"Sooner rather than later. I don't want her worrying about me any more than I'm sure she already has."

"Then let's do this; why don't we see if she's free to come in for a family visit and you two can have some time together to get on the same page? How's that sound?"

He became quiet. "I don't know. Now that I think about it, I'm really nervous about seeing her, knowing how disappointed she'll be."

"I don't think that's the case, but if you think having support will help, we can do a family session tomorrow instead. I can facilitate and answer questions that come up."

Avery nodded. "If you don't mind, I think I'd like that."

"I don't mind at all. Did you want to stop by my office and call her?"

"Actually, if it's okay with you, could you make the call? I'd like to keep to myself for the rest of the day."

Lauren stood and returned his chair to his desk. "Of course I don't mind," she said. "As long as you sign a release for me to speak to her on your behalf."

"I'm confused. I thought you already had a HIPAA release on file?"

"I did, but it's no longer valid since technically you're a new admission. Let me run and get a release worked up and I'll be right back."

"Wait. Before you go"—Avery reached under his pillow and grabbed his journal—"I'd like to mail this to Emi, but I don't want to fold the drawing. Do you have a manilla envelope or something I can use?"

Lauren stared at the drawing and smiled. "Is this a good idea?"

Avery flipped the drawing over and placed it in her hands. "I think so, but I'm also going to grant you permission to read this letter and trust that you'll tell me if you think I'm making a mistake."

Shortly after breakfast, Avery made his way to the courtyard and found an empty table in a shaded corner where he could keep to himself. He watched clients mill about, some stretching their legs and recharging in the morning sun while others played cards and nursed their coffee.

High above, the Java Sparrows were at it again, zipping by and making the most of life. Leo, Avery's new roommate, completed another lap around the courtyard and gave Avery a slight nod as he jogged by.

Avery was the first to see her and stood up, waving from across the courtyard. Bri spotted him and waved back, then pointed him out to Lauren. Avery focused solely on Bri as the two women approached and spotted a hidden pain in her eyes. She circled the table and tied her arms around her dad.

Avery clutched the back of her head and pulled back first. "I take it no Micah today?"

Bri shook her head.

"That's too bad. I was looking forward to seeing him."

"He feels the same way. I just wasn't sure if the timing was right."

"I understand." Avery motioned to the bench and sat down

across from both women. "Thanks again for coming. I wish it was under better circumstances, but don't we all?"

Bri stared at her father. "Before we start, can I say something?"

"Of course."

"I want to apologize for my role in this. I can't help but—"

"Bri, this is not your—"

"Dad. Please, I need to get this out." Bri pinched a tear away and stiffened her back. "I can't help but feel like had I not been so busy, I could have been around more and seen this coming."

"Again, this is not your fault."

Lauren glanced at Avery. "Bri, I know this is going to sound harsh, but sometimes the truth hurts. I want you to understand that no one leaves here without access to the skills and tools they need to be successful. Your father is no exception and unfortunately, he chose not to access the support network he had in place during a time of crisis. That's on no one else but him."

Avery nodded. "You need to understand that I decided to go off my meds and keep it a secret from everyone. There's nothing you could have done to change that and I knew it was risky, but I still did it anyway, and now I have to live with the consequences."

Something inside of Bri changed. She leaned forward and pressed her palms against the table. "No, Dad. We have to live with the consequences. We're in this together. Always have been, always will be."

"You're right. I'm sorry. I didn't intend to put you through this again. The last thing I wanted to do is cause you or Micah or anyone more pain."

"I know." Bri went quiet for a moment. "So, is it too soon to ask what happens next?"

"Actually, no," said Lauren. "Not at all. In fact, we typically start discussing a client's discharge plan the moment they're first admitted."

"We do?" asked Avery.

"I mean 'we' as in the treatment team, but yes, it's a conversation we need to have."

"So in his case, what does that mean?"

"Good question," Lauren said to Bri, then turned to Avery. "There's a few ways forward, but they all depend on whether you're willing to do the work."

Avery hunched forward and felt his cheeks burn. "I'm not one to shy away from work."

"Then in that case," Lauren said, "what probably makes the most sense in this case is IOP."

"What's that?" Bri asked.

"Intensive outpatient," Avery said, leaning back. His eyes shifted from Bri to Lauren. "Do you think that's really necessary? I was sober for what, seven years before this ordeal?"

"I know, but this is an opportunity to revisit your relapse prevention plan and recommit to your recovery. You'll also get a refresher on the step work and build a network with others in the same boat as you who can hold you accountable."

"How long are we talking about?" Bri asked.

"Every case is different, but my guess is at least two weeks to get into any treatment center because they all require a new client intake evaluation."

"And after that?"

"Most programs run about ninety days, give or take."

Bri looked at her dad. "You can do that time with your eyes closed."

"It goes by fast," Lauren said, "but that's the sweet spot as far as mitigating the risk to public safety. Remember, not taking one's meds is considered non-compliance and a violation of conditions of their release. So three months is the minimum grace period to get someone back on track and by then, any symptoms should be long gone. It also gives a running start on a sustained period of sobriety which is always reassuring."

"I like that," Bri said. "So I take it while Dad's in this program, he's still living here?"

"He is, and I should clarify, we're only talking part time. Most of these programs are about three hours a day, three days a week at a local treatment center where they offer classes, counseling and AA meetings."

"And once he graduates—if that's the right word—is he then able to move back out?"

"As long as we secure a suitable housing situation by then, I don't see any issue there."

Avery sat up. "I like the sound of that."

"Me too. Any other questions?"

Bri smiled at Avery and scrunched her face. "Actually, there is one more. What can I do to support you not only now, but also when you get out again?"

"Honestly, I think you're doing a great job as it stands. You're here, you're present, you're asking all the right questions and listening to all the answers. Just keep offering your love and support and don't stop educating yourself. Maybe you both can catch a meeting sometime, but even that's going above and beyond." Lauren looked at Avery. "Did I miss anything?"

He shook his head. "Bri, you've been so supportive throughout all of this, I wouldn't want you to change a thing."

"I agree." Lauren checked the time. "If that's it, I've got a meeting to prepare for, but why don't you two take some time to catch up?"

Avery waved goodbye and waited for Lauren to make it out of earshot. "Can I tell you something? Whatever it is you're feeling right now, you don't have to hold it in for my sake. I don't want to be a bigger burden than I already have been."

Bri drew her head back. "What's that supposed to mean?"

"It means you have every right to be angry or disappointed with me and you don't have to bottle it up. It's not fair to you."

Bri sat there in silence. "You think I'm angry with you?"

"How could you not be?" Avery glanced up as Leo shuffled by their table. "Like you said earlier, this is bigger than me. This affects us all."

"But that doesn't mean I'm angry with you. And I'm not disappointed in you either. If anything, I really thought this would be the time that stuck since you've been doing good for so long . . . but maybe that's more on me than you."

"What do you mean?"

"I don't know. Maybe I need to come up with realistic expectations?"

Her words hung in the air as Avery looked away.

"Something wrong?" Bri asked. "Lauren mentioned it may take some time before you're symptom free. Does that mean you're still hearing voices?"

He shrugged. "I am, but they're toning down. The meds are kicking in and something about being somewhere familiar seems to bring me back to center, if that makes sense."

"I can see how that helps." Bri paused and grew still to observe him better. "Can I ask a question? Are you still of the mindset that people are out to get you?"

"You mean like my roommate?" He blew out a breath. "I think it's safe to say that most of that was a delusion, despite how real it feels . . . I mean felt."

"When you say 'most,' does that mean you're leaving the door open?"

"Maybe. Or maybe it means I'm working through this and it's a process." Avery stared down at his hands and rubbed his palms together. "My turn. I'm curious to know how you knew where to find me?"

"It's a small island, Dad. Everyone knows everyone."

"It's not that small."

"Maybe not, but I don't want to fuel the fire if you're still feeling on edge."

"It won't upset me because I trust you. If anything, it'll settle my mind and dispel any lingering suspicions."

Bri studied his face and caved. "I was looking for you and swung by the sober house. Nani was out front doing yard work and said you left with the same wahine that brought you there."

Avery furrowed his brow and shifted on the bench to move with the sun.

"You okay?"

He nodded and stared across the courtyard at a group of women sitting in a circle in the grass. The gray-haired woman in a floral sundress relished in teaching the next generation the ancient art of weaving pe'ahi lauhala. Another lady showed off her newest creation to the group, then batted her handheld fan near her cheek.

"Can I tell you something? Yesterday I was talking with another patient here and something came up. I've never brought it up before because maybe I don't want to know the answer, but one thing I do know is that ignorance isn't bliss when it comes to my loved ones." He stared deep into Bri's eyes, those obsidian stones that swallowed the light. "Have you ever seen anything out of the corner of your eye? Something you couldn't put a finger on?"

She blinked and shook her head. "No."

"What about voices or music that shouldn't be there?"

"No, can't say that I have."

"Good. That's good." Avery let out a deep breath. "What about paranoia?"

"Can you be a little more specific?"

Avery thought for a moment. "Have you ever felt like you were being watched? Maybe followed by someone or something?"

"No, nothing like that."

"What about believing in something that everyone else tells you isn't true?"

Bri scratched her throat. "I know where you're going with this."

"Is that a no?"

She nodded. "Is that it?"

"Almost. Have you ever felt like God chose you for a certain purpose?"

Bri looked up at the clouds being tossed around by the trade winds. "I believe that I'm blessed—just like you—but as for a God complex? No. We keep it simple, me and him. I pray. He listens." She dropped her hands to her lap and smiled.

"So you have no concerns about being schizophrenic?"

"I wouldn't necessarily say that. Why else do you think I don't drink?"

"Because you didn't like the taste of alcohol? That's what you've always said."

"I know, but I also don't like the idea that schizophrenia is hereditary and that external forces may trigger the onset of the disease."

"Do they really say that drinking triggers schizophrenia?"

"Some do, and as long as it's up for debate, I think I'll play it safe." Bri checked over her shoulder to make sure they were alone. "Speaking of drinking, there's something I really need to talk to you about."

Avery leaned forward. "What's going on?"

Bri took a cleansing breath. "Tristan stopped by my work two days ago. He says he's sober again and has a new sponsor who helped him do the whole ninety meetings in ninety days thing. Now he's working the steps and wants to make amends to me and Micah but I don't think we're ready yet." She paused and licked her lips. "I mean, I don't think I'm ready yet. I told him I had to think about it, but what I really needed was some advice."

Avery forced a smile. "I'm really glad to hear that it sounds like he's on the right track again. That said, in the grand scheme of things, ninety days isn't that long. It also seems pretty fast to be working on step nine so I have to ask, do you trust his intentions?"

"What do you mean?"

"I guess what I'm asking is, do you think he's really looking to make amends, or is he looking for a second chance?"

"I hope not because he's already had a second chance . . . and a third . . . and a fourth . . . but that doesn't stop me from wanting him to get his act together, at least for Micah's sake. So what do you recommend?"

Avery ran his hands through his hair and ignored Leo as he hustled by. "As you already know, whatever happens between you two, Micah always comes first. That said, I don't think it hurts to hear what he has to say, just remember that actions speak louder than words."

"So you think I should hear him out?"

"I would, because if he's serious about working the steps, it can really start the healing." Avery reached across the table and squeezed her wrist. "One of my biggest regrets as a father is how much time we've lost as a family through no fault of your own. I don't know how I'll ever make it to you."

Bri placed her hands on top of his. "I don't want you to make it up to me, Dad. I want you to make it up to yourself."

CHAPTER 23

FEBRUARY 13TH

Two Months Later

Avery made his way to the dayroom, saw the unoccupied community phone and decided it was now or never. While he had the chance, he sat at the table in the far corner, unfurled a piece of paper from his pocket and reached for the handset.

Earlier in the week, he hedged his bets and put out feelers for any available housing options he could churn up. But as before, there was little progress to speak of and he didn't bother adding his name to any supposed waitlists.

He stared at the number momentarily before scooting his chair forward and punching it in. An all-too-familiar voice answered on the fourth ring.

"Hello?"

Avery squeezed the receiver. "Good morning, Austin. How are you?"

"Avery? What's going on, man? I hope you're doing well."

"I am, actually. Thanks for asking." He went quiet for a moment. "The reason I'm calling is to speak with Uncle Earl. Any chance he's around?"

"I think he's upstairs. Let me go and gra—"

"Before you do that"—Avery shifted in his seat—"Since I got you on the line, I want to make amends and apologize for the things I said and did. A lot has changed in the past two months, and not to make excuses for my behavior, but the delusions and paranoia are long gone. You didn't deserve to be on the receiving end of that and I'm sorry you got dragged into it."

"I appreciate it," Austin said, "but I know you were having a rough go at it. You don't owe me an apology."

"Actually, I really do." Avery switched the phone to his other ear. "Just because I was exhibiting symptoms doesn't mean I'm not accountable for how I interact with people. You took the brunt of my paranoia through no fault of your own, and it wasn't fair, especially when you have your own issues you're working through."

"Again, I don't hold it against you. I know it's nothing personal, but if it helps, I accept your apology. Also, Uncle Earl just came downstairs if you still want to talk to him."

"If he's free, that'd be great."

"You got it. Hang tight." There was a loud click as Austin set the phone down, followed by a long pause.

"I thought I told you that whatever you're selling, we no like," Uncle Earl said, laughing into the phone.

"I see your sense of humor hasn't changed much," Avery said. "What a shame."

"Ain't that the truth." A calmness came over Uncle Earl's voice. "It's good to hear from you, Avery. What are you up to these days?"

"I'm back at the hospital and doing outpatient at Hina Makai. One more month and I graduate from IOP, then I'll be looking to move out."

"That's killer. Good for you for not giving up."

"Well, I have a lot of support and people who refuse to give up on me." Someone tapped Avery on his shoulder to ask how much longer he'd be and Avery brushed him away. "Which is sort of why I'm reaching out. I wanted to apologize for what happened and ask if there's any way we can talk about the possibility of me moving in again?"

"I'm really glad to hear you're doing well, but knowing what I now know, I don't think that's a—"

"Before you say no, I want you to know that I've put a lot of thought into this and have a revised relapse prevention plan designed to stave off psychiatric decomposition. I'm thinking Lauren can do weekly house visits to hold me accountable and I can cover monthly blood draws at the hospital to verify med compliance. On top of that, I'm going to keep working with my sponsor once I complete IOP, attend at least three AA meetings a week, and will meet with my substance abuse counselor at least twice a month."

There was a long pause. "That sounds like a really solid plan, but unfortunately I can't bring you back. You've had your fair share of chances, and I have to consider the safety of everyone who lives here."

"What if I provide proof of attendance from every meeting?"

"I appreciate the thought, but frankly, I'm the House Prez, not a babysitter."

Avery's grip loosened on the phone. "I'm confused. I thought I met the criteria to reapply since I've been sober for over a month."

"In most cases that is true, but I'm looking at the totality of the circumstances. And in this situation, we're simply not equipped to provide the level of care you deserve in the event you need it." Uncle Earl sighed into the phone and dropped his voice. "You know, between you and me, it's not so much the relapse that bothers me as much as you cutting your meds. If it's happened before, it can happen again, and had you asked for help beforehand, I would have moved heaven and hell to help you, but unfortunately you didn't. I simply can't afford to find out what might happen again if history repeats itself."

Avery closed his eyes and nodded. "I get it and understand where you're coming from. But if for any reason you decide to change your mind and take it to a house vote, please let me know."

"I will, but just so you know, we don't have any beds available anyway."

"Then I guess it wasn't meant to be," Avery said.

"Come on. Don't sound so depressed."

Avery stared at his scratched-out list of numbers. "Easy for you to say."

"Look, nobody's ever drowned in their own sweat. If you want something bad enough and will work for it, you'll make it happen. I know you're trying to make it sound like we're your last shot, but we're just one house on one street. This isn't the end of the road for you unless you throw it in park and give up right here. But that's not you, now is it? I know you better than that. I know *you're* better than that."

Avery pressed the receiver to his cheek as the muscles in his jaw coiled. "You're right. I'll keep playing my cards and see what unfolds."

"Which is about all you can do," Uncle Earl said. "Good luck out there."

"Actually, before you go, can I ask you something?"

"What's up?"

"Did you ever find out whose drugs those were?"

"You know, someone popped dirty a few days later, and while I can't say for certain those drugs belonged to him, I also wouldn't put it past him."

"Seriously? Can I ask who?"

"Believe it or not, it was Gil."

Lauren folded her hands on her lap and stared across her desk at Avery. Somewhere behind him, Gail hunched over her keyboard and pecked away at a treatment plan, one finger at a time.

"So it sounds like the sober house is off the table," Lauren said, "but we sort of saw that coming, didn't we?"

"I had a sinking suspicion, but still held out hope."

"Hope is good, but so is having options that are actionable." Lauren's chair squeaked as she rocked forward. "So let's talk about options."

Avery shrugged and scanned the collage of selfies on her wall, each an image of Lauren and a client on move-out day. He pulled at his chin when he saw their photo.

"You should take me down from your board," he said. "I don't deserve to be up there."

Lauren kept her eyes trained on him. "Don't look at it like that. Moving out is always a milestone to celebrate, and besides, you aren't the only one who had to come back."

His eyes moved away from the photos. "If you say so."

"Trust me, this isn't the end and there are always other options. Uncle Earl may not be willing to take you back, but there are other sober homes out there. Have you tried reaching out to any of them?"

"I've been working the phones all week. I'm on a few wait-lists—or so I'm told—but we both know what that means."

"Still better than nothing. What about a shared living situation? I know co-living isn't preferred since you never know who you'll get stuck with, or even if they're sober, but it's still a start."

"No luck so far and I've tried all the numbers you gave me." He unfolded his list and placed it on her desk. "What about mental health housing? Aren't there places designed to take people like me?"

"You're thinking of supported housing, but frankly you're too independent to qualify for that living arrangement and level of care. They also have long waitlists and prioritize taking in people from off the street who don't have any housing at all." Lauren clicked her pen and tapped it against her thigh. "I don't know if you and Bri have ever broached this discussion, but what about moving in with her?"

Avery shook his head. "I've thought about it, but she's got enough on her hands and I don't want to be a burden. Not to mention, I'd hate for Micah to see me at my worst if it ever came down to that. He's never known that part of me and I intend to keep it that way."

"But could that work to your benefit?"

"I'm not willing to find out. I know how much it hurt Bri to see me like that, and I'm not willing to do that to him. I'd rather stay here."

"Well, that's not really an option, at least not for the long term. But Bri is a great support person so let's not rule her out completely."

"What other options do I have?" Avery asked. "What about living on my own?"

Lauren rubbed her brow and stared at Avery. "What about it?"

"Is it on the table? Say I found another job and could swing it, would you be open to the idea?"

"You don't think Jas will rehire you?"

"She might be open to it, but if Emi is still there, it could be awkward."

"You still haven't spoken to her?"

Avery clenched his jaw. "No. I sent her that letter and left it at that."

"It's probably for the best, but a job's a job."

"I don't know. I'll think about it." Avery leaned forward in his chair. "So what do you think about me getting my own place?"

Lauren's face went slack and she didn't try to hide it. "It's a possibility but not preferred. Living alone has its own pitfalls and I'd much rather see you approach this with someone else. That way you can support one another and hold each other accountable. Also, I'd want to be certain you could afford it on your own without the benefit of subsidized housing because that's no easy task."

Avery didn't want to admit it, but he knew she was right.

"Do you think I'm still on track to move out once I complete IOP?"

"As long as you keep doing what you're doing and we're able to secure you housing, I don't see why not."

"In that case, is there anyone else who's on track to move out in the near future?"

"Funny you should ask." Lauren clicked her pen once more and placed it on her desk. "So I don't have anyone currently scheduled to move out, but there is someone who probably could if they really wanted to."

Avery cocked his head. "I'm confused. What does that mean?"

"It means that I don't know how close you two are since you're no longer roommates, but when's the last time you've talked to Marv?"

Avery sat there in shock, unable to process what he had just heard.

"I don't understand," he said. "You said she left you a *house*?"

"Ssh," Marv said, his gaze darting around the game room. "And I didn't say a house," he whispered. "I said a condo, which includes her estate and some money. Now, are you going to move or what?"

Avery glanced at the chessboard and tried to recapture his train of thought. "Why didn't you think to say anything?"

"To who? Kalani?"

"You could have mentioned it to me."

"I could have, but by the time I learned my aunt named me her sole beneficiary and the will made it to probate, you were long gone and out of the picture."

"But I've been back for two months. You could have told me anytime, unless your plan all along was to keep it a secret."

"Well, I'm definitely not going to parade it around and get shook down day in and day out for money."

"Don't you think people will put two and two together once they see you preparing to move out?"

"Who said anything about me moving out?" Marv looked down at the board. "Speaking of moving . . ."

Avery's eyes dropped to the board and he nudged a pawn forward. "I'm confused. So you're just going to stay here and do what? Sit on an empty house?"

"It's a condo, and why would I pay insurance and property tax on a place I'll never occupy?" Marv moved his bishop but kept his hand on the piece. Then, satisfied it wasn't a blunder, he let go of the game piece and finalized his move. "I may be crazy, but I'm not that crazy. I plan to sell it."

"Why not put it to good use? Your aunt obviously left it to you for a reason. It sounds like she wanted to help you get back on your own two feet."

Marv shook his head. "I think she left it to me because she died a widow with no heirs. And if she thought she was doing me a favor, that just goes to show she didn't know a thing about me because I'm perfectly comfortable here."

"But you can be just as comfortable out there, not to mention help an old friend out while you're at it."

"Help an old friend how?"

"Here's a crazy idea: what if we moved in together and made our own sober home? We could make it a safe space and help one another reintegrate into society. You can even be the House Prez."

"After all the times I've told you otherwise, you still think I want to reintegrate into society? Don't you know there's nothing out there for me anymore?"

"But that's not true," Avery said. "You can make a life for yourself beyond these walls, Marv. We both can, and everything starts with stable housing."

Marv stared at the chessboard and shook his head. "There's

no normal life in the wake of a high-profile case like mine. People don't forgive or forget what happened just because they had something like a little time to heal. I know you think you understand where I'm coming from, but you don't have to worry about your past coming to haunt your future."

Avery sacrificed his knight and pressed his pawn up the board. "What if I told you there are two days in any week that there's no point in troubling yourself over?"

"You may not have to worry about yesterday and tomorrow, but I do." Marv brought his queen back to defend his king. "I can't afford for my past to repeat itself. No one can."

Avery advanced his pawn another square. "You're not a monster, Marv. Stop treating yourself like one."

"That's easy for you to say when no one out there holds your crime against you, and if my own flesh and blood wants nothing to do with me, what makes you think the community will?"

"Once again, you're not a monster, but until you make it a point to prove this to the world, how will they ever know?" Avery's pawn reached the other side of the board and he promoted it to a queen. "Check."

Marv blocked with his queen and Avery traded pieces, leaving two lonely kings on the board. "I don't care what they think of me."

"Look Marv, if you don't want to move out, that's your right, but as your friend, I want you to know that if you stay put, all you'll ever do is run in circles like a tiger in a cage. You're better than that. Besides, if you try it out and times get tough, you can always come back here. Make this place your safety net, but don't let it trap you like a web." Avery reached out and offered his hand. "All I'm asking you to do is think about it."

Marv stared at the stalemate and looked up. "If I promise to think about it, will you leave me alone?"

"Only one way to find out."

Marv rolled his eyes and shook Avery's hand.

CHAPTER 24
MARCH 14TH

One Month Later

Lauren handed Avery and Marv each a sheet of paper and rocked back in her office chair. "I know the two of you have lived together before, Marv—that's not my concern here. But rooming with someone inside of a closed ward where everything is handled for you is a different beast than living with them on your own." She then reached across her desk and handed both men a pencil. "So before I sign off on any living arrangement, the three of us are going to brainstorm until we're all on the same page. That way, there are no surprises moving forward. Best to hash out the details now and spare an argument down the road because arguments lead to resentments and you know what they say about resentments, right?"

Avery glanced at Marv. "That resentments are the number one offender."

"Exactly," Lauren said. "Now the goal here isn't to cover everything, but hopefully this gets the two of you thinking and communicating in a way that keeps the conversation going. Good housing is hard enough to come by and opportunities like this rarely come up so let's make the most of it. Think we can do that?"

Both men nodded.

"Great. I've actually had this conversation quite a few times and think a good place to start is house rules because everything seems to flow from there. Have you two talked about any house rules by chance?"

Avery shook his head.

"What kind of rules?" Marv asked.

"That's up for you two to decide, but it's best to work them out before you move in together, not after. For example, are you going to set a curfew that you both abide by?"

"A curfew?" Avery chuckled and shook his head. "I don't think that's necessary."

Lauren turned to Marv. "And you feel the same?"

Marv nodded.

"Good. Finding common ground is always a good start. What about a house policy on drugs and alcohol?"

Avery crossed his arms over his chest. "We're both clean and sober and on conditional release, so shouldn't that go without saying?"

"For you, yes, but what about your guests?" Lauren pointed to Marv. "Say he happens to have a guest over for dinner and she wants a little prosecco with her prosciutto? Are you cool with that?"

"I don't know what those are, but assuming one of them is a wine or a spirit . . . sure. Why not?"

"You really wouldn't care?" Marv asked. "I don't know how I feel about someone drinking in my home."

"See? That's something you two need to work out," Lauren said. "And speaking of guests, have you thought of a guest policy?"

"What do you mean?"

Lauren looked at Marv. "I've seen agreements where room-mates have no guests and others that limit visitors to Fridays and Saturdays only. Something else to think about is if either of you start dating, can your guests spend the night? If not, is there a set time they have to be out by?"

"I'm not too keen on the idea of overnighters," Marv said. "I really value my privacy."

"Me too, but if I'm paying rent . . ." Avery shrugged and turned away from Marv. "Or maybe you're right and no overnighters are a good thing for now. It's not like I'm looking to date again anytime soon."

"I don't blame you," Lauren said, "especially if dating is a known risk factor."

"As far as I'm concerned, Emi and I are done," Avery said. "Which reminds me, I still haven't heard back from Jas about getting a reference. Maybe I should drop in this afternoon if that's okay with you?"

"Sounds like a good idea. You never know what can happen."

"Do you think I should ask for my job back?"

"That's up to you," Lauren said, "but I know it's hard to find a supportive boss and you'll need to find a job at some point. But back to rent; have you both settled on how much and when?"

Both men nodded.

"Good. So why don't you each start jotting down any rules or nonstarters you have for each other. Then we can compare what you come up with and see if there's any crossover or conflict."

Both men pulled their seats forward and started scribbling away.

"While you're at it, it's also a good time to think of responsibilities and what's expected of one another. I know you've lived together before, but you haven't had dishes to wash or even laundry to do. Also, what about groceries? Are you planning on pooling money or buying your own food? And are you going to cook meals together or be on your own? What's the plan if you have a disagreement, and how do you stop small issues from spiraling out of control?"

Marv put down his pencil and faced Avery. "What do you think?"

"It's a lot to process, but whatever you want to do is good for me. We've both come this far, I'm sure we can make it work."

Lauren smiled. "I do too. And it's worth mentioning you have a lot going for each other. It's nice you both know where the other is coming from and how to get help in a psychiatric emergency. You can support each other and be part of the other's relapse prevention plan." She checked her watch and pushed her chair back. "Why don't you both find time to finalize your house rules and we'll review it tomorrow? If the plan is to move out in three days, we don't have a moment to waste."

"So we're approved to move out?" Avery asked.

Lauren nodded. "You've been approved. The treatment team thinks it's a great fit, and I notified law enforcement last month."

Marv scooted forward in his chair. "So it's really happening?"

"Unless one of you gets cold feet in the next three days, hell yeah, it's happening."

Jas looked him in the eyes and smiled. "If you need time to think about it," she said, "you can—"

"No, it's not that," Avery said. "I just don't know how to thank you."

She placed her elbows on her desk and leaned forward. "You don't have to thank me because a job is a job and it works both ways. You working here makes my life easier because you're good at what you do and have a lot to offer."

"That means a lot and I really appreciate it, especially since I keep hearing good employers are hard to come by."

"Not as hard to come by as good employees. So when can you start?"

"I move out in three days, but I can probably get approval to start as early as tomorrow."

Jas twisted a bangle on her wrist. "Why don't you start on

Monday? That way, you can get settled in first and ease into it. We've been here for three generations; it's not like we're going anywhere soon."

Avery shrugged. "That works too."

"Perfect. It's good to have you back."

Avery rose and tucked in his chair. "Thanks again. See you in a few days."

Jas smiled and got up. "There is one more thing before you go, but I'm not sure how to frame it."

"Is it about Emi?"

She shrugged. "I pride myself on being as hands off as possible, but I also want to see you succeed. So I guess what I'm saying is I understand if any scheduling conflicts arise or accommodations are needed."

"Thanks, but I don't think that will be necessary. Work comes first, and I can work with anyone."

"I don't doubt that you can. Just know that if things change, my door is always open."

"Understood. Thanks again and see you on Monday." Avery stepped out of Jas' office, closed her door behind him and paused. In the short time he was in her office, the declining sun had dipped behind the Ko'olaus and torched the belly of each cloud. Slanted rays crested over the mountain range like the hills were ablaze, piercing through the front door and turning the fresh air golden.

Avery looked across the way and noticed Emi hunched behind the cash register, closing out the till. When he first arrived, her attention was on a customer so they settled for trading glances instead of words. But now, with the open sign switched off and the front door locked, he brushed past a budding Spathiphyllum and approached the register.

He waited for her to finish counting through a stack of twenties.

"Long time," he said.

Emi picked up a pen and marked the amount on a POS

report.

"Is it a bad time to talk?" he asked.

She shook her head and placed her pen down. "No, I just didn't want to forget the count since my memory's not what it used to be."

Avery smiled. "Any chance you remember receiving a package from me?"

A thin smile crossed her lips. "I do, and thank you for the gift."

"Did you like it?"

"I loved the drawing and agree it's perfect as it is." She stuffed the stack of twenties into a money pouch and zipped it shut. "As for the note, it was bittersweet, but I understand where you're coming from and why you'd feel that way. You should also know I enjoyed our time together, and I only hope that you don't hold it against me."

Avery glanced over his shoulder to make sure they were still alone. "Hold what against you?"

She stacked the remaining bills and credit card receipts and weighed them down with a stapler. "I hope you don't blame me for your relapse."

He shook his head. "No one is responsible for my decisions but me, so no, I don't hold it against you. If anything, I learned a lot from our time together and will be better for it."

Emi smiled. "Me too, and though I would have preferred a different ending, at least I have a better understanding of just how complicated it can be to successfully transition off one's meds."

Avery cocked his head. "You don't think it was a mistake to encourage someone like me to get off their meds?"

"I think it was a mistake to plant the seed without having a solid plan in place. I think there's a right way and wrong way to do it, and now my fear is that based on this one experience, you'll never believe you can do it successfully."

Avery stared at her, saying nothing.

"Please don't look at me like that," Emi said. "Because I've actually talked to people who have successfully freed themselves of their antipsychotic medications."

"What people?"

"There's an entire community out there and the information is free to anyone who wants it. If you're interested, I can invite you into a Facebook support group and you can see for yourself that you're not alone."

He shook his head. "That's okay, but thanks for offering."

"Anytime," she said, looking him up and down. "But if you change your mind, please speak up because I know that the longer you take meds like Zyprexa, the harder it is to come off of them. That said, I'm not trying to change your mind because while I care about you, you have to do what you believe is right. Just know that if you change your mind, you don't have to do it alone."

"I appreciate it."

"I saw you met with Jas. I take it you came to grab your last check?"

"No, she mailed that to me a while back. I actually came to ask her to be a reference, and you won't believe this, but she offered me my job back."

Emi jutted her chin out. "Oh, I believe it. That's Jas for you."

"I definitely wasn't expecting that."

"Me neither," Emi said. "So what'd you say?"

Avery shrugged. "Not much. I thanked her for a second chance and can't wait to start on Monday."

"That fast, huh? Good for you."

"Thanks." Avery turned and motioned for the door. "I should probably get going. Do you mind locking up behind me?"

"No, not at all." Emi circled the counter and stole a hug as she saw him out.

CHAPTER 25
MARCH 17TH

Lauren stretched her seatbelt across her lap and glanced in her rearview mirror. "Last call before we leave; are you sure you didn't forget anything?"

Marv patted his bags in the backseat. "Not that I know of, but then again, say I forgot something, how would I even know?"

"Touché. Did you at least say your goodbyes to everyone you needed to?"

"Not really. I was hoping to give everyone the slip and ride off into the sunset like 'prot.'"

"You mean 'prot' as in the quote unquote spaceman from that Kevin Spacey movie."

"Yeah. K-PAX. We only watch it every other week."

"Oof," Lauren said, rolling her eyes. "Too soon."

Marv cocked his head. "Too soon for what?"

"Let's just say it's probably not the best reference to make, but you get a pass since you don't get out much." She glanced at Marv. "Either way, I thought he hitched a ride home on a beam of light, not the sunset?"

"So I heard, but I guess we'll never truly know, will we?"

Lauren let out a small laugh. "Whatever it was, I'll always support any effort to vacate a place in style. It seems to be a long-forgotten art." She leaned over and elbowed Avery. "What about you?"

"I'm not one for goodbyes, so no grand exit here, though it would have been nice to see Sam and thank him for all the work he's done for me. I take it he's off today?"

"Actually, he's out for the rest of the week, but I'll pass the message along. That is unless you prefer to tell him yourself when you return for your weekly UDS."

Avery thought for a moment. "Maybe it's best for him to hear it from me."

"I'm sure he'd like that. I know he's thrilled for you to move on with your life, even if a part of him will be sad to see you go."

"What about me?" Marv asked.

Lauren grabbed the back of Avery's headrest and looked over her shoulder as she backed out. "I'm sure he'll also miss seeing your bubbly mug around here as well."

"How touching, but I was asking if I also have to return every week for a UDS?"

"Oh, right." She threw it in gear and eyed him in the mirror. "No, I don't think so because you don't have a substance history and you're not coming off a recent relapse. Let's start you off on randos for now and take it from there."

Lauren eased over a speed bump, rolled to a stop at the security gate and waited for Cap to finish logging in a new visitor. When he was done, he turned around, slid his window open and returned Lauren's smile.

"Well, well, well," he said, his eyes drifting toward the backseat. "Happy Aloha Friday. Is this what I think it is?" He wagged his finger at the bags next to Marv.

Lauren drummed her hands against her steering wheel. "I have two discharges with me: Avery West and Marvin Miller."

"As in Marvin Miller, the one who would never move out, not in a million years and not even then?"

Marv shrugged. "What can I say?"

"Wow. Good on you." Cap mouthed their names as he jotted

them on his clipboard, then set it aside and motioned for Marv to roll down his window. "A word of advice," he said over the engine rumble. "You both have come a long way to make it to this point, and while you have a lot to be proud of, all of that effort is now officially behind you. Today is a new day and the real work starts right here, right now. So stay strong, take care of yourself and have faith that Big Braddah will take care of the rest." He sat back down on his stool and hit a button which buzzed the gate open with a lurch.

"So where to now?" Avery asked as they rode away. "Straight to the house?"

Marv leaned forward and stuck his head between the two front seats. "It's a condo."

"Seatbelt," Lauren said, easing off the gas and nudging him backward. "And no, we have a few stops to make first."

"What kind of stops?" Marv asked.

"We talked about this. We need to swing by the food stamp and welfare office, then check in with Medicaid to let them know you're both no longer at the hospital. While we're at it, you also have an appointment with social security to get your disability going."

Avery tapped his wallet through his pants. "I still have my EBT card."

"Good, though they turned it off once you returned to the hospital."

"Seriously?"

"Yeah, because your stay with us was over thirty days."

"That's annoying."

"That's also the law."

"Hey Lauren, how long will this all take?"

"It shouldn't be too bad, Marv." She coasted to a red light and shifted into neutral. "Look, I know it sounds like a lot to get through and you're both excited to move in, but trust me, this is the last stretch and I've done this so many times it's like muscle memory."

"And then we're home free?"

Lauren nodded and hit the gas. "That's the plan, unless either of you have any other pit stops to make. Maybe we'll buzz the hardware store and you can get some copies of your key made?"

"Definitely, and it probably wouldn't hurt to do some grocery shopping to hold us over for the weekend," Avery said, "assuming we have time."

"Good call," Marv said, then looked around the backseat. "Though I'm not sure how much more we can pack in here."

"Worse comes to worst we can always drop your stuff off at the condo and make a separate grocery run if need be. It's not a big deal."

"Thanks, but I wouldn't want to make you go out of your way for us, not any more than you have to." Avery glanced at Marv, then back at Lauren. "You've already done so much, and I know you have better things to do."

"Not today I don't." Lauren hit her blinker and hooked a right. "Move out day is the culmination of years of effort and it doesn't get much bigger than this. Getting you both settled in and started off on the right foot is my number one priority today. I say that especially for you, Marv, since you haven't been through this process before."

"I don't expect any issues settling in," Marv said. "I mean, you've seen the place; Aunt Carolyn didn't just leave me a condo, she left me everything that comes with it. I've got more buttons and marbles and Precious Moments™ figurines than I know what to do with."

"How lovely, though I'm thinking more about the basics like bedsheets, shower curtains and silverware. You'd be surprised at some of the things that trip people up when they first move into a place and find themselves starting over from scratch."

"Well, we have all that covered too, not to mention more quilts, puzzles, coasters and Sunday dresses that I know what to do with."

"Good, because the games will keep you out of trouble and

the last thing I need is for either of you to have a meltdown over what to wear to church." Lauren laughed and pulled into a parking garage. "Seriously though, what a kind gesture of her to help you put your life back together. We all need all the help we can get."

"Speaking of which, I promise to help out any way I can," Avery said. "Dishes, cooking, laundry—you opened up your home to me, and that means more than you'll ever know."

Marv reached for the handle and looked back. "I appreciate that, but how many times are you going to make me say it before I lose my mind? It's not a house; it's a *condo*."

Avery plopped his bag in front of the door next to Marvs. "I know you said it was nice, but you didn't mention anything about us having the penthouse."

Marv knocked a flake of paint free as he gripped a wrought-iron railing and watched it tumble toward the ground. Down below, Lauren leaned on her rear bumper, phone pressed to her ear, standing guard by the Jeep and all their worldly belongings. "I'm pretty sure this is just the second story, but call it what you want." He removed a paper bag from his pocket, tore open the stapled top and shook out a spare key. "After you."

"I think you should do the honors," Avery said. "This is your condo, after all. I'm just a guest."

"A guest?" Marv stuck his key in the door and pressed it open. "Guests, by definition, don't pay rent."

Marv opened the door, slung his bag inside and then stepped aside to let Avery do the same. Avery poked his head in the space and caught a passing whiff of potpourri in a draft of musty air. Natural light spilled through a draped window in the corner and warmed an armchair sitting next to a bookshelf, home to more Tchotchkes than books. A hand-woven Persian rug. An authentic cuckoo clock from the Black Forest in Baden-Württemberg. A collection of paintings on the walls where rivers snaked through idyllic snow-capped valleys, each home to a neighbor-less cabin.

The kitchen had everything but style, being a closed-in galley with delaminating countertops and oak cabinets that stopped closing properly ages ago. Mugs hung from hooks and magnets from afar spoke of travels and tourist traps off the beaten path. Depression-era glassware and vintage Pyrex were on display as far as the eye could see. All the appliances were on their way out and bent over the oven handle lay an unused embroidered hand towel.

"Come on, you can check it out later," Marv said. "Let's offload the rest so Lauren can get out of here."

Avery backed out of the door, locked it behind him and then started down the walkway alongside Marv. "Looks nice in there," he said. "Quaint and homely."

"You think?" Marv was first down the steps and stopped at the landing. "I think it gives me the creeps."

"Why's that?" Avery asked. "Wait . . . she didn't die in there, did she?"

"No. She died from COPD in hospice care."

"That's good," Avery said. "I mean, not good that she died, but good that we don't have to worry about the place being haunted. The hospital was chilly enough."

Marv rolled his eyes. "You really believe in that shit? Vengeful spirits with nothing better to do than make you as miserable as them?"

"Sure I do. Why? You don't?"

Marv shook his head. "Can't afford to. The last thing I need is my past coming back to haunt me. I both like and need my sleep."

Avery watched Marv turn around and navigate down the stairs, then followed in his footsteps. Lauren ended her call as they approached and began passing out bags of groceries from the backseat.

"Pretty amazing how life works out sometimes, isn't it?"

Lauren handed Marv a paper sack and looked up at the apartment. "Does everything look good up there? Keys work? Utilities are on? No squatters or infestation of rabid trash pandas?"

Marv smiled. "I haven't checked under the beds and am afraid to open the fridge, but other than that, it seems cozy."

"Good." She glanced at Avery. "So, no issues settling in, then?"

"Not that I see."

"Wonderful. Now, what else? You've both been discharged with two weeks' worth of meds, so there's no rush to get to the pharmacy. And Avery, be sure to keep an ear out for a call from Dr. Nagasaki. If you don't hear from his office in say, three days, call me so we can schedule your intake." Lauren closed her door and leaned against the Jeep. "Actually, if anything comes up, you both have my number, which means I'm only ever a call away. And yes, you can call me anytime, for any reason."

"But what if you don't pick up?" asked Avery.

"It depends on the emergency but don't forget, you always have each other. Like it or not, you're in this together, but knowing you both you're going to be just fine. I'm proud of both of you and I mean it when I say I can't wait to see where life takes you." Lauren opened her driver's door and hoisted herself into the seat. "Oh, and Marv . . . I know you already know this, but don't forget that your no contact orders include any and all forms of social media."

"Social what?"

"Exactly." Lauren smiled and started her Jeep.

"Wait. Now that I'm out, what am I supposed to do if any of them contact me?"

Lauren leaned out of the window. "You think they will?"

"I don't know. That's why I asked."

"If something ever comes up, you need to report it to protect yourself."

"Report it? That's it?"

"And don't engage. I hate to say it, but that's about all you can do."

"But what happens to them?"

"I don't know. I don't supervise them; I supervise you. Just don't engage and we'll cross that bridge if we need to. Can you do that?"

Marv shrugged and took a step back.

"Enjoy your weekend you two. You deserve it."

"Wait," Avery called out, then threw an arm around Marv. "Aren't you forgetting something?" He knuckled Marv in the ribs and motioned for Lauren to join them for a photo.

CHAPTER 26
MARCH 20TH

A passing scatter pelted the pavement and it didn't take long for Avery to take the hint, shut off his hose and give up on watering the plants. He found cover under the nearest eave, but before he got settled, he heard someone dragging their feet and turned to see Kevin approaching.

Kevin wiped water off the bill of his hat and shook his hand dry. "That came out of nowhere."

"It always does."

Kevin craned his neck and studied the misty sky. "You know, I learned in class last week that Hawaiians view each passing rain as a blessing. Any truth to that?"

"Yes, though I think a lot of cultures see it that way." Avery watched the rain come down and listened to it corkscrew through the downspouts. "A lot of ancient civilizations based their survival on a deep understanding and connection to the land and elements. For example, do you know that in ʻōlelo Hawaiʻi, there are over two hundred names just for the varying rains?"

"How is that even possible?"

Avery shrugged. "We're talking about a culture that's deeply tapped into their surroundings. There are names for different rains coming from different directions and from different places. Names for rains with different colors and intensity, that come on suddenly or spill into a valley in a churning fog. Rains that tell when fish are running and when it's time to pull nets to catch them. Rains that let farmers know when to plant and when certain fruits will ripen. Even cleansing rains that traverse the spirit world and carry loved ones to the other side."

"And here my haole ass figured this rain came to bless your return to work, but I guess that's me being small-minded."

"I don't see it that way. Sometimes in life, things happen for more than one reason." Avery stuck his hand and let the falling rain bounce off his palm.

"It's good having you back since I'm always learning something from you."

"If you think that's impressive, don't even get me started on the winds or tides."

Kevin checked his phone and gave Avery a nudge. "Speaking of getting started, it's about that time. Have a good first day back." He clapped Avery on the back and darted toward the garden shed through the rain.

Wiping his shoes on a doormat, Avery entered the nursery and joined Emi behind the counter. Through the gaps in signage taped to the front door, he could see a handful of customers milling about under the metal awning, waiting to be let in.

"Should we let them in?" he asked. "What's an extra five minutes?"

"We can," Emi said, "but before we do, I wanted to ask you something."

"What's up?"

She finished changing the till roll in her printer and leaned against the counter. "Any chance you had time to think about what we talked about?"

"You mean about me going off my meds?"

"Not necessarily going off, but maybe talking to others who have. They can walk you through how to—"

"Let me stop you right there." Avery looked around to make sure they were alone. "Perhaps I didn't make myself clear before, so let me do it now. I'm here for an honest day's work—not free medical advice—so we're not going to keep doing this, okay? I appreciate your concern, but from here on out, I only take medical advice from my doctors."

"You know I only bring this up because—"

"You care about me? If that's true, you sure have a funny way of showing it." He held up his palms. "Out of curiosity, do you know the definition of the word 'insanity?'"

"Avery, this isn't about—"

"It's doing the same thing over and over and over again and expecting different results. I'm not doing that again. I've learned my lesson, and while there may come a time where switching meds or tapering off of them makes sense, that conversation needs to happen between me and my medical team. Now, if you don't mind, can we please get back to work?"

Avery walked over, unlocked the front door and held it open for the customers to string in. They filed in one after another, then split off in different directions, shaking themselves dry from head to tail. A familiar face carrying a plant in a trash bag dripping with water brought up the rear.

"You again?" she said. "I thought they got rid of you."

"Good morning to you as well," Avery said. "Let me guess . . . another return?" He reached out to take the bag from her, but she refused.

The woman walked over to the cash register and plopped the plant in front of Emi. "Some indoor plant this turned out to be." She undid the knot and shimmied off the trash bag. "Thanks to you all, my kitchen is now infested with an army of devilish little ghost ants."

"Oh no," Emi said, poking her finger in the soil of the breadfruit tree. "I'm sorry to hear that. Are you certain they came from this plant?"

"Well, they didn't come from nowhere." The woman handed Emi a folded receipt. "This time, I think I'll take a full refund instead of an exchange."

"Of course."

"And before I forget, since the colony has since branched out into satellite nests, I'd like to talk with someone about having an exterminator treat my house."

Avery stepped forward. "Wait, didn't you pick those out yourself? Did you not give them a once-over for pests before you left with them?"

"Excuse me, I'm a customer . . . not an entomologist. I don't know the first thing about pests and insects."

"Well, good thing I do, and as far as ants go, they aren't necessarily a bad thing for your plant as far as damage is concerned. They'll help aerate the soil and create tunnels that carry water to the roots."

The woman turned her back toward him and leaned on the counter. "Wasn't he fired?" she asked Emi, loud enough for Avery to hear.

Emi motioned for Avery to stay back and then turned to the woman. "No Ma'am, he wasn't. I'll also add that perhaps more than anybody here, he knows exactly what he's talking about."

The woman held out a flat palm to receive her refund. "What a shame," she said, stuffing her change into her wallet. "Now what can we do about covering an exterminator?"

"The thing to understand is that nursery pests are always present," Emi said. "There's simply no way for us to guarantee that any plant we sell will be pest free. We do our best to mitigate them, but as you know, our plants are mostly grown outdoors where ants and other pests live."

"Are you going to answer my question or just talk down to me?"

"My apologies; I didn't mean to come off that way." Emi

thought for a moment. "I doubt our owner would cover extermination of any sort because it sets a bad precedent. What she probably would do though is offer a complimentary case of TERRO® Liquid Ant Killer, which will eliminate the nest and make this issue a thing of the past." Emi crouched down and grabbed a box from under the counter. "Here, take this on us. It's safe, foolproof and also what many exterminators use themselves."

The woman reached out and took the box. "I'll give it a go, but if for any reason this doesn't work, best believe I'll be back."

Emi smiled. "I think you'll be pleasantly surprised. Have a nice day."

Without another word, the woman headed for the exit. Avery stepped aside to move out of her way and turned to watch her leave. When she was out of earshot, he turned to face Emi. "The things I'd like to say to that woman."

"Tell me about it. She's the worst, but what can you do about it?"

Avery shrugged. "Nothing. She's not worth it and fortunately for her, I need this job."

"And even if you spoke your mind, she'll never change," Emi said. "Some people are just like that; so set in their ways that all you can do is bite your tongue and be grateful that at the end of the day, you don't have to lie down next to them."

Avery and Bri sat across from one another in a diner booth near a foggy window that faced a sparse and unsightly parking lot. Outside, swollen drops of rain dimpled shallow puddles, disturbing reflections of the overblown streetlights above.

Bri slid the menu to the edge of the table.

"Something wrong?" Avery asked. "Not hungry?"

"No, I am. I just already know what I want." She rested her hands on the table, one on the other. With a sour face, she peeled her palm away from the surface, poured water into a napkin and scrubbed the sticky surface.

"Good to go?" he asked.

She nodded. "I wanted to tell you I'm glad to hear how you stuck up for yourself today. Nothing against Emi, but you shouldn't ever have to defend yourself against her or anyone. I don't know where her savior-complex comes from, but from everything I've heard, she's dangerous for you to be around."

Avery raised his glass to his lips, swallowed loudly and wiped his mouth. "She's harmless as long as I put my needs first."

"But if she's as persistent as you say she is, how can you not be concerned? It only takes one slip up and things go downhill fast."

"Bri, I put an end to it this morning. She won't be needling away at me any longer."

A young server in his early twenties approached the table and pointed at Avery's menu with a pen. "Need more time, or are we ready to order?"

Avery nodded. "I think we're good." He motioned for Bri to order first.

"Just my usual," she said. "And it's just me tonight. The little sly mongoose is at his friend's house."

"Perfect. And will this be together or separate?"

"Together," Avery said firmly. "And I'll take the check."

"Of course. And what are you having, sir?"

"I think I'll try the Loco Moco."

"Excellent choice. White or brown rice?"

"White's fine."

"Tossed or mac salad?"

"Let's go with the mac."

"Anything to drink?"

"Decaf, if you have it."

"Cream? Sugar?"

"No thank you."

"You got it." The server scribbled a note, snapped his book closed and took the menus with him.

"Where were we?" Avery asked.

"You were hoping to calm my nerves about Emi, but I'm still not convinced." Bri scooted forward on the bench. "Do you know what bothers me the most about her? I don't understand her motivations. That she would even think about bringing up your treatment plan after everything that happened. It boggles my mind. Who does something like that?"

"A lot of people because there's an entire generation out there with zero trust in psychiatric institutions and practices."

"But why? Where does that come from?"

"I want to say ignorance, but honestly, the entertainment industry is largely to blame."

"Because books and movies demonize schizophrenia?"

"Worse. They've broken our trust in the system. Take One Flew Over the Cuckoo's Nest for example. Ever read or seen it?"

"Can't say I have."

"You should; it's a great movie, even if some say it caused irreparable damage to the psychiatric community."

"What kind of damage?"

"It first started in the sixties with the publication of the book, which focused heavily on abuses like electro-shock therapy. A year later, President Kennedy passed the Community Mental Health Act, which paved the way for deinstitutionalization, a movement advocating the removal of people from state-run institutions. But the problem with discharging the gravely disabled to homes not equipped to provide proper care is that too many of them wound up on the streets or in jail."

Avery paused and thanked the server as he delivered his coffee.

"So that was the beginning of the end," he continued. "A decade later, the film was released and swept the Academy Awards, leaving appalled moviegoers calling for the immediate closures of hospitals in their communities. Then came the recovery movement, followed by the managed care movement, followed by a mental illness crisis that we are still recovering from today."

"And all of this from one book?"

Avery shook his head. "To be fair, it was more of a perfect storm because there were other factors at play. The mental health crisis was a long time coming and things like overmedicating patients and drugs like Thorazine being lauded as a cure-all didn't help." Avery leaned back as the server returned with their plates. "To bring it back to people who think like Emi, the take-away is that books, like movies, have the power to sway people's minds and influence an entire culture—and not always for the best. Now that's not to say Emi doesn't have good intentions as I'm sure she genuinely wants to see me have all the freedom, dignity and autonomy life has to offer. But the problem is that until there's a cure, there's unlikely to be a 'magic pill' that replaces meds where I can ride off into the sunset without a care in the world."

Bri twirled a ball of spaghetti onto her fork and raised it to her mouth. "You should probably eat before your food gets cold."

Avery picked up his knife and sliced through his burger patty. He took a bite and mulled it over. When he was mostly done chewing, he covered his mouth and said, "Not bad," then reached for the salt.

"Told you." Bri dabbed the corner of her mouth and took a sip of water. "My only concern is I don't want to see you moving backward. Emi sounds like the type to do her own research on conspiracy theories inside of an echo chamber. You don't need—"

"Pardon my reach." As the server stretched for Avery's mug to refill it, he frowned at the barely touched plate beside it. "Something wrong with your meal?"

"No, not at all. I just got lost in conversation with my good company over here." Avery flashed his eyebrows, swirled a bite of egg in his gravy and shoved it into his mouth.

"Good to know. I hope your dinner is as tasty as it looks."

Bri watched the server walk away and put down her utensils. "What I was trying to say is you don't need that negativity in your life. You deserve to be happy and I don't want to see anyone impede that."

He chewed on his food as one does when they'd rather not swallow their words. When he was finished, he laid his fork across his plate, swirled his ice in his cup and took two long drinks of water. "I hear what you're saying," he said, "but remember, I was the one who flushed my meds, not Emi. She can say or think or feel however she wants about me, but the only way I'll ever learn from my decisions is if I accept responsibility for them. Now, what do you say about enjoying our dinner together and not wasting any more energy on this?"

"Sure, but before we change the subject, can I ask you a favor?"

"Anything."

"If anything like this ever comes up again, will you promise to let me know? I want to be here for you, but I can't turn things around if I'm kept out of the loop."

"Of course," Avery said. "You have my word."

"I appreciate that." Bri poked around her spaghetti and smiled at him. "I also appreciate the fact that you're taking Tristan out to an AA meeting later tonight."

Avery stopped sawing away at his hamburger patty. "You know about that?"

"He messaged me this afternoon to let me know he's excited to get you plugged into his support group."

"Did he?"

Bri grew quiet. "Is something wrong?"

Avery shifted in his seat. "I just find it odd that he'd mention it, especially to you. '*Anonymity is the spiritual foundation of all our traditions.'* He should know that without me having to remind him."

"You think he's using this as a ploy to weasel his way back into our lives?"

"That's the problem with having trust issues; I don't know what to believe."

"Well, I don't think that's what he's after; he knows where we stand and that I've moved on. But either way, it's not like he's wasting his time. At least he's getting the help he needs and is working on himself, and that's all I could ever ask of him." She finished off her water and stuffed her napkin into the cup. "Actually, between you and me, that's about all I could ever ask of anyone."

It was long past his bedtime when Avery tugged the yellow wire to request a stop as the bus hung a left onto his street. He gave it a second as the brakes squealed then rose to his feet and navigated the narrow aisle toward the exit. The driver lurched to a stop and a sleeping rider across the aisle slumped forward. Mindful of his next step, Avery exited the parted doors and entered the dead of night.

Rain and darkness blurred his vision as the bus revved away. He checked both ways for headlights and crossed the street, but a misstep plunked his shoe halfway into an unseen puddle. Rainwater flooded his insole and with a quiet curse, Avery shook his sneaker and picked up the pace.

Hustling through the rain and being careful not to slip, he reminded himself that if recovery were easy, everyone and their mother would do it. He asked himself what was a block and a half jaunt through a rainy night compared to the depravity and insanity of his drinking? At least he had a warm shower and a clean bed waiting for him. What was an hour of his time to support the father of his grandson when the AA meeting they had just attended helped himself all the same?

Avery made it to cover and stood at the bottom of the staircase in a pool of his own making. He wiped his face dry, shook his clothes, grabbed the handrail and pulled himself up the steps.

Turning onto the walkway, he fished his keys out of his pocket and spotted two neighbors walking toward him. One of the men puffed a cigarette. His friend nudged him when he spotted the address on Avery's door.

"Evening," Avery said as he approached them in front of his door and stepped aside to let them pass. "Glad to see at least someone is staying dry tonight."

The man who was smoking stopped walking and took another drag, then flicked his cigarette over the edge, spiraling it into the night. "This you?" he asked.

Avery nodded and stuck his key into the door to unlock it. "Just moved in a few days ago."

"You did? From where?"

Avery shot a glance at the second man who squinted back at him. The look put him on edge, and with the men standing side by side, he saw in their facial structures they were related. Avery cut his eyes toward the rainy bleakness. "We lived down the road but wanted to upgrade."

"So you have a roommate then?"

He hesitated, then nodded. "And what about you two? I take it we're neighbors?"

The first man stuck another cigarette between his lips and lit it. He took a deep drag and blew it out above Avery's head.

Avery pulled the door closed and widened his stance. "Why do I have the feeling you're not here to lend me sugar or bring me pie?"

The man shook his head slowly. "No. No pie. We're here to welcome Marv to the neighborhood. We're here to tell him it's a nice place to live and that we have every intention of keeping it that way."

Without taking his eyes off the men, Avery shoved his key into the door and locked it. "I think you need to leave."

"I don't care what you think. We're not going anywhere. Not until we speak with Marv."

"Listen, I don't know who you are, but—"

"Marv knows who we are, and if he's home, we'd like a word."

"I have a better idea," Avery said. "Why don't the two of you hele on so I won't have to call the cops."

"The cops? The cops won't do shit, just like they didn't lift a finger when Marv murdered our aunt."

Avery held up one hand to keep them at bay and pulled out his phone.

"Make that call and you're going over this railing," the man said steadily. "And trust me, we already checked for cameras." He took another drag and approached Avery, exhaling smoke through his nostrils. "That sick fuck set fire to my aunt's house . . . with her still in it."

"I'm so sorry for what happened, but whatever you're thinking of doing right now, I promise it won't change the past."

"We're not here to change the past," the man said, turning to his brother. "We're here to make sure Marv doesn't hurt anyone else. The courts may have let him off easy, but we sure as hell won't. Now, where is he?"

"You're both making a mistake. This isn't how you—"

The man raised a fist and pounded on the door. "Marvin Miller? Are you in there? Your cousins are here to see you."

Avery heard the deadbolt unlock and the door swung open before he could warn his roommate.

"Well I'll be damned," the man said, stepping forward. "So it is true; the system really is broken."

Marv glanced at Avery while trying to press the door shut but the man braced it open with his foot. "Not so fast," he said. "We just want to talk. We're not here to hurt you, but that doesn't mean we won't."

The man's brother flanked him and cut off Avery from interfering. Marv immediately caved and let the door swing open.

"Do you know what happened a few days ago?" the man asked Marv, standing at the threshold. "Out of the blue, my mom received a victim notification that for some reason they let your crazy ass out. We all thought it was a mistake at first, especially after what I told you in court."

Marv stared at his cousin in silence.

"You do remember what I told you, don't you? I said, 'You destroyed our family and I'll be damned if you live to destroy another one.'" The man shook his head in disgust. "You have no idea how much pain you've caused this family, yet here you go again, reopening old wounds. Well, guess what? We're not doing that, not under my watch. Not today, tomorrow . . . not ever. Do you understand?"

Marv continued to stare into space.

The man turned to his brother, then back to Marv. "Let me spell it out for you. Tomorrow morning, you're going to get on the phone with whoever runs that hellhole you crawled out of and tell them that you've made a mistake, that you want to hurt yourself or others or whatever it takes to move back in. Do you understand? Because this is your only warning."

Marv stood there silently, his chest rising and falling with every heavy breath.

The man's eyes tightened. "What's wrong? The funny farm got you so doped up that you forgot how to talk?"

His brother laughed. "Maybe he's finally cracked and gone full blown catatonic?"

"Here's an idea," Avery said. "Maybe he's not engaging because the two of you aren't worth breaking a court order?"

"You need to get out of here," the man said. "This has nothing to do with you."

"This is my home and I'm not going anywhere."

The brother turned around and without warning, gave Avery a shove. "You heard what he said."

"Don't touch me again."

The brother took a step forward and smirked in Avery's face. "And what are you going to—"

Avery fired off a right cross that buckled the younger man and brought him to his knees. Avery grabbed his fist in pain and couldn't defend himself as the other man rushed him and socked him in his jaw. As his head hit the ground, his vision faded and the last thing he remembered was Marv jumping on the back of the man before everything went dark.

The following morning, Avery rolled over in bed and flexed his jaw in pain. He pressed his tongue against his teeth to check if any were loose, then felt for the lump on the back of his head when a searing bolt tore through his arm.

Avery inspected his right hand—which wasn't broken as far as he could tell—but the knuckle over his pinkie was severely swollen from his bad punch. He gently squeezed his metacarpal bone, and though it was painfully obvious something was wrong, he found fleeting relief in the pressure when he let go.

Laying back on his pillow, a part of him wished he had taken the time to ice his injury last night. But instead, he spent most of his waning energy on calming Marv after learning the damage he incurred while trying to protect him.

A dull shiner on Marv's cheek and pain in his ribs were his first complaints, followed by concerns over how long it would take before his cousins returned. Unfortunately, Avery didn't witness Marv's attack, having only returned from his daze in time to catch Marv's cousins taking off into the night. Marv was at his side on one knee, bracing a hand against the wall and cursing his luck. An elderly neighbor down the way yelled after the fleeing men, shaking her phone while threatening to call the cops if they even thought of circling back.

Marv was the first one up. Nursing his ribs, he helped Avery to his feet and apologized to their neighbor for the disturbance and unredeemable first impression. He made up some excuse and assured her the police had no place in a family quarrel, then took a moment to catch his breath and promised a further explanation in the morning. Satisfied, she tucked her phone away and locked her door behind her.

Following Marv inside, Avery did what he could to console him. He reminded Marv that he did nothing wrong as both men paced the living room. The discussion of filing a report came up along with ways it could backfire. Not long after they decided to forget it, Marv had enough and retreated to his room to lick his wounds.

Avery sat up in his bed and looked out the window. Not only had the rain run its course, but daybreak showed early promises of a picture-perfect day. With a few hours before work, he flexed his hand and decided to make Marv breakfast to let him know he wasn't alone.

After draining his bladder and washing his hands, Avery pulled eggs, butter, Portuguese sausage and other makings of a meat lover's omelet from the fridge. He grabbed a bowl from the cupboard and a pan from the cabinet, then thought it best to ask Marv how many eggs he wanted.

Avery knocked on Marv's door and called out to him. He gave it a moment before trying again, then pressed his ear to the door to listen for Marv's snoring. Hearing nothing, he wondered if Marv might be ignoring him on purpose, so he decided to let his cooking do the talking and hopefully coax him out of his shell.

On his way back to the kitchen, a handwritten note on the dining table caught his eye. Knowing it wasn't there the night before, he pressed his fists on the table and leaned over it.

Avery,
  Don't take this the wrong way, but my dumbass
should have trusted my gut all along. It was stupid to
believe moving out wasn't a mistake, and rather than
risk upsetting my family further, I've decided I'm going
back to where I feel safe. The alternative isn't worth it,
and I know you understand.
  I resign,
  —Marv
  P.S. Jeff and Kenny won't come back if I'm gone,
and though you're welcome to stay here if you want, I
wouldn't blame you if you left.

Avery reread the letter, closed his eyes and pounded his good fist on the table. He stood stewing for a moment, unsure of his next steps, then walked back into the kitchen and began returning ingredients to the fridge. Pulling out his phone, he searched his contacts for Bri's number and debated calling her long enough to realize he had no other choice.

Waving as he approached her truck, Avery opened the passenger door and hoisted himself into the seat. "Thanks again for coming on such short notice," he said. "I can't express how much it means to know that I can always count on you." He reached out to close the door and winced in pain.

Bri took her hands off the wheel and twisted in her seat. "Dad, what's wrong with your hand?"

"It's fine."

"Can I see?"

Avery sighed and placed his hand in hers. "I hurt it last night, but it's nothing I can't fix."

"I take it you hit something?" She touched the top of his knuckle, then read his eyes. "You hit someone, didn't you?"

He pulled his hand back. "More like I defended myself. But only after they laid their hands on me first."

"You didn't mention that on the phone," she said as they took off. "Who shoved you? Marv?"

"No, it was one of Marv's cousins and I didn't mention it because I didn't want to worry you. Two of them showed up last night hoping to scare him back to the hospital."

"And it worked?"

"That's what it sounds like, though Lauren won't confirm or deny it. But his stuff is gone and as far as I know, he has nowhere else to go or anyone who would take him in."

"But if he's your roommate—or I guess technically, your live-in landlord—don't you have a right to know what's going on with him and your housing?"

"Not if he's back in the hospital. If he's a patient again, he's protected by HIPAA and it's not that Lauren won't tell me anything, she can't tell me anything. I even read Marv's letter to her, but it didn't matter since it doesn't give her permission to speak with me about him."

"So assuming he's there and opts to stay, does this mean you lose your housing?"

"I'm not sure. He said in his letter I could stay there, but I don't know how long I can cover the utilities and maintenance fees on my own."

Bri glanced in the mirror and switched lanes. "I know I've said this before, but you can always stay with us if you need to."

"You're too sweet, but I wonder where exactly I'd sleep? On the couch? Or under Micah's bed?" Avery reached out and rubbed her shoulder. "I appreciate the offer, but that'd be a tight squeeze. The two of you need your space."

"Dad. We can make it work."

"I don't doubt that we can, but it's more than just not wanting to be a burden. Take a moment to imagine what would happen if things went south. Micah's never known that side of me and I'll do whatever it takes to keep it that way."

"Do you really think that's a possibility again? Especially if you had us around all the time?"

"It doesn't matter what I think; it's not a chance I'm willing to take," Avery said while cracking his window to get fresh air. "I've already suffered one child through that experience. I refuse to expose another."

"As long as you know the offer stands." Bri sped up to get around a trailer. "Then bring me up to speed. What's our plan for today? Show up unannounced and hope they let you in?"

"Something like that. I'm hoping Lauren spoke with Marv after I called and he granted her permission to speak with me."

"And if he didn't?"

"Then we ram the gate." Avery cracked a smile and a sharp pain ran through his jaw. "Let's just hope I can speak to Marv, because I don't have a better idea."

"But what if I do?" Bri pointed to his hand. "Let's swing by my clinic and get your hand checked out while we wait to hear from Lauren. It's on the way and shouldn't take long."

"I would, but I have work in a few hours and Marv needs me now. My hand isn't going anywhere, but him moving back is a huge mistake."

"You're talking like you've got your mind made up."

"I can't stand by and watch a friend get bullied like this, especially after he jumped to my defense."

As the two headed to the hospital, Avery brought Bri up to speed on everything that had happened, except for him being concussed. She focused on her driving and listened quietly until Avery mentioned their decision not to involve law enforcement. Refusing to make a record of the incident was a mistake in her view, especially when the odds of the situation escalating seemed probable without intervention. Avery didn't attempt to change her mind or defend their decision, except to say that it was what Marv wanted in the end.

Bri turned onto the narrow road that led to the hospital. It was a trip she was all too familiar with but one she had never made with her dad. Telephone poles zipped by, their lines sagging under the weight of beautiful but invasive vines. Then, distantly, the sally port came into view and Bri eased up on the pedal.

"Just pull up like you always do," Avery instructed as the window slid open and a palm waved for them to stop.

"Back so soon?" Cap asked.

Avery leaned over Bri's lap and smiled. "Morning, Cap. How's it going?"

"Better than I deserve. Thanks for asking." He nodded at Bri as his eyes drifted to the backseat. "No Micah today?"

Bri returned his smile and shook her head. "He's in school."

"As he should be. So what can I do for the two of you today?"

Avery cleared his throat. "I'm hoping to speak with Marv. Any chance you saw him this morning?"

Cap hooked his thumbs on his belt and smirked. "Nice try, but anyone who's been doing this job as long as I have knows it's best to stay out of these things. But give me a sec and I'll call Lauren to let her know you're here."

Avery thanked Cap as he retreated into his guard shack and hoped for the best. He considered any excuses Marv would conjure not to speak with him, but beyond some sense of misplaced shame, he couldn't think of another one.

Cap hung up his phone and leaned out of his window. "Avery, you're in luck; Lauren said she'll meet you at the door." He frowned at Bri as the gate lurched open. "But if you don't mind, you'll need to wait in the car."

"I'm more than happy to."

Bri rolled through the parking lot and pulled into the first open space. She wished her dad luck as he stepped out of the truck, then waved to Lauren as she appeared near the entrance.

"That was kind of her to bring you here," Lauren told Avery

as he approached. She held the door open and followed him into the corridor. "As I'm sure you guessed, Marv is here and yes, he granted me permission to speak with you."

"How's he holding up?"

"Other than a couple of bruised ribs and maybe a bruised ego, he's hanging in there."

Avery watched Lauren breeze past the steel door to the Step-Down Ward and did a double take. "He's not in high security, is he?"

"No," she said over her shoulder. "I asked him to meet with you in the courtyard. I figured we'd skip the headache of cutting through the ward and give you both some privacy."

"If that's the case, can I ask a small favor?"

Lauren stopped walking and spun around. "What's that?"

"Any chance you can grab us the chess set from the game room? I've learned over the years that Marv only seems to open up when his mind is preoccupied."

"I can do that as long as it's not being used." Lauren reached the end of the corridor and unlocked a steel door that led to the courtyard.

"Before you open that, can I ask if you have any advice on what I should say to him?"

Lauren stepped forward and looked him in the eye. "Normally, I say that honesty is the best policy, but you should read the situation and go with whatever feels right. Just remember that neither of you could have predicted or prevented what happened last night. I'd also add that Marv made his choice and only he can change his mind. That said, the best thing you can do is to show him through your actions and results that a life outside of here is not only possible, but the best thing for you. Does that make sense?"

Avery smiled and nodded.

"Perfect. Give me a few, and I'll bring the game out to you."

Avery thanked her and heard the sharp click of the door

locking behind him. Across the way, Marv sat alone at a table, mindlessly mixing his coffee with a disposable stirrer.

It was a beautiful day, Avery thought, despite the circumstances. The sun was out but not scorching and overbearing, and rustling tradewinds made the morning feel right. Avery's feathered friends were also back, flying through the courtyard and trilling from the rooftops.

Marv noticed Avery approaching and shaded his eyes. "Why'd I have a feeling I'd see you here today?"

"Because we're friends," Avery said. "And what kind of friend would I be if I didn't check on you after what we just went through?" He sat down at the table, made himself comfortable and then asked, "Why didn't you talk to me before you left?"

Marv placed his coffee stirrer on the table. "Because I knew you'd try to talk me out of it."

"Is that such a bad thing?"

"Maybe not for you it isn't, but you saw my family and what they think of me. Why on earth would I want to live in a world where I need to look over my shoulder every day?"

"But you wouldn't have to. What they did was not only wrong, but illegal. You could fight back and put an end to this if you really wanted to."

Marv glanced over his shoulder. "Correct me if I'm wrong, but I'm pretty sure I did just end it."

"But you didn't make this decision. This is you folding and caving. This is you tossing your hands up and throwing in the towel."

"I'm a lover, Avery, not a fighter. And like I told you before, this is my family and my kuleana to deal with. I'll respect their wishes because I've already put them through enough."

"But what about your aunt's wishes? Obviously, she left you her home for a reason. Don't you think she wanted to see you move out of here and on with your life?"

"I have no idea what she wanted and neither do you. For all I know, she probably left me her place to spite someone in the family. I wouldn't be surprised if I'm just a pawn in her end game." Marv noticed Avery looking past him and turned to see Lauren approaching.

"Not to interrupt," she said, "but here you go." She placed the chessboard next to Avery and patted him on the back.

Marv waited for Lauren to walk away, then pointed at the weathered box, its torn corners repaired repeatedly with masking tape. "What's that for?"

"Let's just say for old times' sake." Avery pulled the cover off the box and laid it on the table.

"I don't think so," Marv said. "As of this moment, I'm officially retired."

"Retired from what? Chess? Come on, Marv. I came all the way out here. The least you can do is—"

"Lose to you? Or have you back me into a corner where there's no escape or be chased around the board in circles? Or maybe the plan is to pin or trap me and make me some pawn in your grand design?" He shook his head. "I don't think so. I've been playing against you ever since you stepped foot on this ward and I'm done spinning my wheels."

"Marv. It's just a game."

"Is it really a game if you're no longer having fun?"

Avery placed the cover on the box and set it aside. "You know what? Forget about the game. Let's talk about where we go from here. If you end up deciding to call this place home, where does that leave me?"

"I've already moved out, so the decision's made." Marv took a sip of coffee and stared at Avery. "And as for where it leaves you, I have to say I haven't thought that far ahead. But like I said in my letter, I have no problem with you staying there in my absence. All I ask is that you take care of the place and treat it like it's your own with the understanding a day may come when I choose to sell it out from under you."

"Or choose to move back in?"

"Did I say that?"

"No, but I was hoping you misspoke." Avery exhaled sharply and looked around the courtyard. "My only problem with staying there—other than you staying here—is that in the long run, I'm not convinced I can afford it on my own."

"So find a roommate. You're a social butterfly and know how to make friends. I'm sure there are tons of senior citizens who'd love to call that place home."

Avery chuckled. "I'm sure there are, but as it turns out I think I'm allergic to cat ladies. Besides, if I'm going to live with anyone, it's going to be someone who understands where I'm coming from and what I'm going through."

Marv laughed and grabbed his side in pain. "Then why not find someone from here?"

"If only it were that easy."

Marv finished his coffee and nodded toward the greenhouse. "Maybe it is."

Avery entered the greenhouse and inhaled the earthy aroma of moist soil warmed by the sun, countered with the sweet fragrances of flowers and lemon-scented leaves. Benny looked up from his book and dog-eared a page.

"I thought you moved out?"

"I did but felt compelled to check in on some friends." Avery wiped his feet on the disinfectant mat and cocked his head to read the book. "Now that's a book."

"Is it? I found it in my neighbor's Little Free Library. I take it you've read it?" Benny flipped the book to show off the image of a dark road on the cover.

"'If trouble comes when you least expect it, then maybe it's best to always expect it.'"

"That sounds like a quote."

Avery shrugged. "For some reason, it always stuck with me."

"I take it that's from this book?"

Avery nodded.

"I haven't gotten that far and honestly don't know if I will. I'm not sure if some authors set out to break the reader, but this one comes closer than just about any I've ever read."

"He'll do that to you as long as you let him, but is that such a bad thing? Sometimes in life, we all need to be broken a bit in order to heal correctly."

Benny blew his breath out and flipped through the pages. "Ain't that the truth. Is that another quote?"

"Not that I know of. Enjoy the read." Avery moved past him and headed toward the back where Kalani was working. At an almost imperceptible level, he made out the honeyed voice of Luciano Pavarotti.

"Morning, Boss."

"I'm not your boss, though I see you've now leveled up to opera?"

"Is that what this is called?" Kalani pointed to a stack of CDs next to the stereo. "Lauren loaned me some new music to mix things up. I can't stand it, but I think the plants dig it so I leave it on repeat and tune it out. Do you think it makes a difference?"

Avery looked around and nodded as he admired Kalani's efforts. The greenhouse was everything he hoped it to be; a breath of fresh air and a beautiful space for anyone to call their own. Things were different but different in a way that only happens when one rises to the occasion, meets the day or embraces responsibility for all it's worth.

Kalani tugged off his gloves one finger at a time and placed them on the table. "I've done good, haven't I?"

Avery turned back to him and shook his head. "No. I think you've done great, and that's coming from someone who knows how much effort it takes to make this look so effortless. There's no denying you have a green thumb."

Kalani cocked an eyebrow. "What's that mean?"

"You've never heard that saying? It means you're a natural at gardening and working with plants."

"Where's it come from?"

Avery shrugged. "Have you ever noticed how earthenware pots left outside tend to grow algae on them? Handle enough of them long enough, and you'll stain your fingers and thumbs green. But since we only work with plastic nursery pots here, you'll just have to take my word for it until you find out for yourself."

Kalani smirked and glanced at his hands. "Interesting, but I don't know if I'd agree that I'm a natural."

"And why's that?"

"Because I think I can excel anywhere I go. Don't you remember me saying how much I hated working in the laundry room? I couldn't wait to leave that dead-end job because I couldn't stand the monotony of the same routine with the same results. Collecting, sorting, loading, unloading, folding, ironing, delivering"—Kalani blew out his breath—"I know that someone has to do that job, but I'm telling you that someone's not me. There was zero room for creativity and trying new things. That's what I was missing, and that's what I've found here."

"So if I hear what you're saying, you're happy here?"

"As happy as I can be with all things considered."

"Then, as far as I'm concerned, my job here is done. I'll leave you to your work."

Kalani crossed his arms over his chest. "Why'd you really come here?"

"To see how things are going with you and to make sure the late blight wasn't giving you any more headaches."

"I mean why'd you come back to the hospital? I saw you and Marv talking outside. What happened between you two?"

Avery went quiet for a moment. "Without putting words into his mouth, let's just say Marv has decided he's happier here."

"And you?"

Avery turned to look out the window. "To be honest, I'm not happy anywhere, but at least I know I have a life out there waiting for me. It may not be perfect, but it's the only one I have and I intend to make the most of it." For reasons unknown, his words brought a smile to his face. He turned to Kalani and asked, "What about you? What are your plans moving forward?"

"Nothing against this place, but I look forward to moving out the moment my time comes in a few months. I still need to find a place to live and save up first and last month's rent, but that buys me time to find a job. Like I said earlier, I can excel anywhere. It's just getting the chance to prove that to someone."

"What if I said you already did?"

Kalani cocked his head. "Already did what?"

"What if I told you that you already proved it to someone? I've seen what you've done here and know what you're capable of. I'm happy to vouch for you to my boss, and can almost guarantee she'll bring you on to the team. I also just so happen to have a place for you to stay that's move-in ready where you don't need to put a deposit. All you have to do is say the word and get it cleared with your treatment team."

Kalani's mouth fell open. "You would do that for me?"

"I would, but let's be honest—it helps me out too. I need a roommate and who better than someone who knows where I'm coming from?"

"I don't know what to say except thank you for thinking of me."

"Don't thank me," Avery said. "Thank Marv."

CHAPTER 28

MARCH 28TH

One Week Later

Avery leaned forward to get a better look at the photo of him and Marv outside their condo, then searched the rest of her photo wall. "It looks to me like you ended up taking my picture down after all."

Lauren rotated in her chair to admire the photos. "It's not that I took you down, I just updated your picture," she said. "You're still up there, see? Besides, you were blinking in the first photo so you should thank me."

"It's weird that I've looked at these photos for years, and now I'm wondering how many of those men and women are moving out for their second or third time?"

Lauren turned back and interlocked her hands on her desk. *"That's classified. See, I could tell you. But then I'd have to kill you.'"*

"In that case, I'll just assume the worst. I'm okay with not knowing."

"Speaking of knowing, you know what I'm dying to know? How are things going now that Marv's not there?"

"No one told me that living alone could be so lonely, but on the bright side at least I get to walk around naked and not wonder who ate my ice cream."

She let a smile slip. "Were I you, I'd work to get that all out of your system now because in three weeks that's all going to change."

"Kalani got approved to move out?"

"Law enforcement's been notified and now all that's left to do is to find him a job, unless you come bearing good news?"

He sat up a little taller. "I was hoping to tell him in person, but Jas said she'll give him a shot. It's a full-time position too, and she's willing to work around his schedule if need be."

"That's wonderful. Do you think I should send her flowers or—"

"I think she's probably good on flowers." Avery laughed at the idea and relaxed a little.

"Have they returned?" she asked.

"You mean Marv's cousins? Yeah, they did. Someone came knocking a few days ago. It was late and I don't know what I was thinking, but I opened the door. There were more of them this time and I told them Marv doesn't live there anymore. I let them know they got what they wanted and to fuck off. I know it's none of my business, but I can't have them coming around anymore looking for trouble. I hope you're not mad."

"No, not at all. That's your home too, and I'd have told them the same thing were I not bound by HIPAA. But there's also something I'd have told you."

"What's that?"

"Correct me if I'm wrong, but isn't this the first test you've had since moving out again?"

"You mean a test as in a challenge?"

"Exactly. If this is the first time something messed up has happened to you since moving out again, it's worth noting you didn't drink, flip out or go off the deep end. You responded by using your tools to stay the course, which means you're doing it, Avery; you're living life on life's terms. You should be proud."

"I don't know about being proud, but there's no way in hell I'd give them the satisfaction of sending me back the way I came. I've learned my lesson, and I'm not coming back here. Not for them. Not for anyone else."

"I hope that includes Emi."

"Who?" Avery asked, raising an eyebrow.

"Exactly."

"It's like I told you before, I'm no longer messing with her. And you'll be happy to know that—in no uncertain terms—I told her to leave Kalani alone too."

"How confident are you that the message got through?"

Avery shrugged. "I still don't understand women, so just to be safe I had a word with Jas and she's there if I need her."

"Good call. Jas sounds like a wonderful ally to have in your corner and the bigger your support system, the better."

Avery glanced at the door. "That reminds me, any chance I can check in with Marv before I leave? It'd be good to see him."

"Of course, but let's take care of business first. Are you able to piss right now?" She picked up her phone and texted as she talked. "Sam will take you so you can submit your drug test and if he has time, I'm sure he'll run by the greenhouse."

"Then after that I can see Marv?"

Lauren smiled. "Marv's in the greenhouse learning the ropes as we speak. Someone has to take the reins with Kalani leaving."

Avery scratched his jaw, then folded both arms across his chest. "Marv's in the greenhouse? You mean our greenhouse?"

"Is there another one I don't know about?"

"No, but . . ." Avery leaned forward. "Not that I think it's a terribly bad idea, but he doesn't know the first thing about plants."

"Neither did Kalani and look how well he turned out. Look, let's not forget that Marv was once your roommate; I'm sure there's been some observational learning going down over the years."

"Yeah, but . . . Marv's in the green—"

"It'll be good for him, Avery. Besides, a good treatment plan is individualized and Marv will benefit from vocational rehabilitation, especially compared to plopping him back in the same classes he could probably teach. Plus, if he embraces the opportunity, he can learn he's more than capable of taking care of something other than himself. Handling responsibility will be good for him."

Lauren waved at someone behind him, and Avery turned in his seat to see Sam near the doorway, making small talk with Gail. Sam took Lauren's cue and approached swinging a specimen cup in a Ziploc bag.

"Are we good to go?" Sam asked.

Avery pressed out of his seat, said his goodbyes and followed Sam into the corridor. They walked side by side in silence, rounded a corner and stopped outside the bathroom. Avery stepped inside to handle his business and handed Sam a half-filled specimen cup with dark yellow urine when he was done.

"You might want to think about drinking more water," Sam said. "Give those kidneys a rest."

"I try, but sometimes I get so busy I forget."

"Just keep at it. It's the thought that counts." He sealed the cup in his bag and motioned down the hall. "Lauren texted me something about the greenhouse. I take it that's our next stop?"

Avery nodded. "If you don't mind."

"Not at all."

The two men made their way outside, cut through the courtyard and paused at the door.

"You coming in?" Avery asked.

Sam held up the urine sample and shook his head. "Let me run to drop this off with the lab. If you're done before I'm back, do me a favor and don't wander off."

"Take your time," Avery said as he stepped inside the greenhouse. "I've got a lot to pass on."

"You must really love this place to keep coming back the way you do," Benny said, bookmarking his page with his thumb.

"Call it a force of habit." Avery pointed at Benny's book. "I see you moved on?"

"Actually, no. I took your advice and finished it."

"Are you glad you did?"

"I don't know if 'glad' is the first word I'd pick, but it definitely moved me, just not sure in which way."

Avery nodded, wiped his feet dry and patted Benny's shoulder as he brushed by. "I see they'll let anyone in here these days," Avery joked as he approached the workbench.

Kalani looked up from a checklist and smiled. "Morning, Boss."

"How many times do we have to go through this? I'm not your boss, remember?" Avery sat down on a stool and brushed some dirt off the table. "Jas is."

"Jas is?"

"Yes, Jas. She's the owner of Back to Eden and she can't wait for you to start. Congratulations and welcome to the 'ohana."

Kalani glanced at Marv. "I don't even know what to say. Thank you!"

"Don't thank me. All I did was vouch for you and promise her she won't regret it. So no pressure."

"Thank you so much. When do I start?"

"Whenever you're ready to move out, so a few weeks."

"Perfect. That should be plenty of time to get through everything here."

Avery nudged Marv. "You taking it all in?"

"Just what I can, but it's a lot to go through. Playlists and planting and pruning and—"

"Relax and take a deep breath," Avery said. "Yes, it's a lot to learn, but you've got a great teacher for the next few weeks, and then I'm back every week for the foreseeable future. You're not alone."

"Don't forget Benny's always here too," Kalani said.

"That might be a stretch," Avery whispered. "Benny doesn't like to admit it, but my guess is he's asleep about half the time."

"I don't blame him." Marv pointed at the stereo. "You guys are out here bumping Schumann and Tchaikovsky and—"

"That's all this guy," Avery said, glancing at Kalani. "But that's the beauty in this line of work, Marv. You're working with nature and nature is working with you, so go for whatever feels natural. Make this place your own and see what happens. My guess is you'll grow in ways you can't imagine, and whether or not you ever decide to leave this place, I can promise you this: you can and you will be better for it."

Marv dropped his elbows onto the table and leaned forward. "That sounds beautiful and all, but what I really want to know is how many times you practiced that speech on your way over here?"

"Come on, Marv. You know me better than that." Avery glanced at Kalani and smiled. "Because if you think for a second that I'm going to be walking around here talking to myself, you might just be crazier than you look."

PAU

AFTERWORD
"I AM NOT MY DIAGNOSIS" A POEM BY SHAWNA VICKERY

I am not schizophrenic
I am not bipolar
I am not schizoaffective disorder
I am not anxiety
I am not CPTSD
I am not a drug addict
I am not an alcoholic
I am not my diagnosis
I am me
I am a human being
I am a daughter
I am a niece
I am a granddaughter
I am a friend
I am a lover
I am a sister
I am an aunt
I am not my diagnosis
I try and live life to the fullest
But sometimes it's the dullest
The voices say I'm not worthy

They say I'll never be enough
I hear that woman screaming but she is never found
I hear those sirens coming but they never arrive
I am not my diagnosis
I get up but feel tired
I go to bed but and I'm wired
Sleep? Not tonight
My mind won't get right
So much noise
So much chatter
I wonder if I'll ever get better
I am not my diagnosis
I get by day by day
Wondering if I'll survive to the next day
Sometimes I want to die
Sometimes I want to thrive
Sometimes I just exist
I am not my diagnosis
I feel love
I feel anger
I feel happiness
I feel content
I feel passion
I feel all my emotions
They control me
They take over my life
I wear them on my sleeve for all to see
I am not my diagnosis
I am me
I am a human being
And I am free

MAHALO NUI LOA
THANK YOU!

If you enjoyed this book, and feel inspired to share, please help spread the word by leaving an honest review on the book's page at Amazon.com, Bookbub.com and/or Goodreads.com.

As a full-time *independent* author, reviews and ratings often translate to more exposure. It doesn't have to be a tome—even a few words will do. This affords me more time to write and promote this book, which also helps to put this message into more hands.

To leave a review, please visit:
https://mybook.to/lateblight

Mahalo for your continued support!

ACKNOWLEDGMENTS

Mahalo to the following for lending your experience, expertise and excitement to this project:

Ashli Quevedo for the wonderful recordings to aid in the audiobook production.

Aunty Chris Wilkinson for your early beta reading. Your excitement keeps me excited.

Elizabeth Reed for the endless late night writing sprints and constant book recs.

Elizabeth (@LucidWeavingCo) for the wall art in my new writer's studio.

Glen Dahlgren for always being there to bounce ideas off of.

Jessey Mills for not just being an editor, but a teacher and a great friend.

Jordan (Ko'olau Farmers) for taking the time to help me better understand how to deal with certain situations at work.

Keoni Kramer for lending your likeness to the cover and for being a stand-up guy.

Kevin (@EpicGardening) for answering so many questions about gardening and for being so cool about sharing your expertise.

Kourtney Ross Wytko for sparking this book and for carrying the fire. I learned so much writing this book and for that I am forever grateful.

Lucia Charman for letting me bounce ideas off you and for sharing so openly.

Riad (@GorillaBrigade) for the beautiful cover art. You're talented beyond measure.

Roberta Kresse for the beta reading and providing invaluable feedback.

Rosie Meleady for the late night writing sprints and endless laughs.

Ryan Haugen for loaning your talent and voice to this project.

Shawna Vickery for being a brilliant sensitivity reader and for the beautiful poem.

And to my loving family for everything.

KICKSTARTER BACKERS

A huge mahalo to the following Kickstarter backers who successfully funded the campaign to produce the audiobook version of this book:

Aaron Linsdau

Bobbie and Theodore Williams

Chris Kemp

Chris Simpson

Elizabeth Reed

Dan and Kate Stock

Denise Prins

Gay Mathews

Gates & Co.

Isadora O'Boto

Jamie Pacheco

Jeri and Gary Barnes

Jen, Jarred, and Bella Cutting

Jessey Mills

Kensi T

K.N. Ros

Michael Kitchens
My Kailua 'Ohana
Nick Oliveri
Rachel Sherck
Riad
Rose Combs and Family
Rosie Meleady
Ryan Haugen
Savannah Gilmore
Shawna Vickery
Sparkle Barnes
Stolen Stuff Hawai'i 'Ohana
The Creative Fund by BackerKit
The Chong 'Ohana
The Forkner 'Ohana
The Russell 'Ohana
The Wytko Family
And to everyone else who wished to keep their donations anonymous.

ABOUT THE AUTHOR

Jordan P. Barnes is a grateful alcoholic & addict in recovery and Sand Island Treatment Center is his home group. When he's not sharing his experience, strength and hope through writing or talking story, he enjoys bodysurfing and gardening.
Residing in beautiful Kailua, Hawai'i with his lovely wife Chelsea and two sons, Jordan has been sober from all mind and mood-altering substances since August 29th, 2011.
Jordan is a member of the Hawai'i Writers' Guild and his debut book, One Hit Away: A Memoir of Recovery won 2020's "Best Book of the Year" award from www.IndiesToday.com, was a B.R.A.G. Medallion Honoree as well as a finalist in both the 15th Annual National Indie Excellence Awards and the 2021 Independent Author Network Book of the Year Awards.

Learn more at:
www.JordanPBarnes.com

Subscribe to my YouTube channel:
www.youtube.com/OneHitAway

Follow me on Goodreads: www.goodreads.com/
jordan_p_barnes

Get the latest deals and new release alerts by following me on BookBub: www.bookbub.com/authors/jordan-barnes

Correspondence:

info@jordanpbarnes.com

Let's join forces:

JOIN ME ON PATREON

PATREON |

Want to support an Independent Author? I'm now on Patreon and offering a number of award tiers with some great BTS / Early access to my books!

What is Patreon? Patreon is *the best place for creators to provide exclusive access to their work and a deeper connection with their communities.*

Pick from multiple tiers with a variety of benefits, including:

- Early Access to Advanced Chapters
- Patron Shoutout in Publications
- Signed Books
- . . . and More!

www.Patreon.com / jordanbarnes

INTERVIEW - KOURTNEY WYTKO

During the run up to publishing Bridgetown: A Harm Reduction Novel, I reached out to my dear friend Jen Cutting (Supplies For Life) and asked if she could connect me with people in her circle who might be interested in giving feedback on an advanced reader copy. Jen doesn't know how to disappoint and connected me with some amazing people that helped get my book off the ground.

Kourtney Wytko was one of those people.

From the onset, Kourtney was pumped about Bridgetown and I quickly realized that the work she does is in the same vein as my fictional character Harley and the very real Haven Wheelock, MPH. A forensic therapist who works in a psychiatric facility, Kourtney has dedicated her life to a world I knew very little about, yet one that runs parallel to what I know and write, the common thread being substance use disorder and mental health. I hope you enjoy our following interview:

What's your name and what do you do?

My name is Kourtney Wytko, and I am a forensic therapist. I work with people who were found not guilty by reason of insanity (NGRI). I help them reintegrate into the community and then work with them to maintain stability in the community setting for the remainder of their supervision.

What drew you to this line of work?

Working in mental health was not like my lifelong dream, as I originally went to college to become a teacher. My bachelor's degree is in elementary education, but while teaching kindergarten, I became utterly disgusted that I made more money bartending 3 nights a week than by teaching. It also pained me that public education is so tied to standardized testing, and I hated that the first experience most of my students experience with school was one of failure based on a certain test. I had kids who didn't even know a single letter at the beginning of kindergarten who not only learned the alphabet but all the sounds, but since they didn't know certain words on a test, they were marked a failure. So on a whim, I applied to exactly one grad school (that only accepted 13 students to their program) and told myself that if it was meant to be, it was meant to be. Turns out I was accepted and once I started grad school, I got a work-study job at the state psychiatric facility. I continued bartending, and when I graduated from grad school, the hospital offered me a full-time job and I have been there ever since. I spent the first 5 years of my career working with civilly committed people and have been working with the NGRI population since 2012.

Before I embarked on this journey, you sent me a massive box of books with titles such as The Center Cannot Hold, No One Cares About Crazy People, Mad in America, The Collected Schizophrenias, and more. You're obviously a reader. What should be on everyone's TBR list?

I am definitely a big reader and was happy to send you what I had because I love sharing books with people. I think those books you listed are all great and I think people should read them. Everything is Fine: A Memoir by Vince Granata is an excellent look at a family where one brother commits a crime and is found NGRI and what that looks like for them. Brain on Fire: My Month of Madness by Susannah Cahalan is another good one that looks at the difference privilege can make in receiving good treatment.

Another important book is Tattoos on the Heart: The Power of Boundless Compassion by Father Greg Boyle (calm down, I'm not promoting religion; I just adore his approach). He talks about radical kinship and just loving people where they are. I have found that to be the most therapeutic thing I can do. Just show someone that they are worthy of love just as they are. Someone giving a genuine fuck about you can be life changing. Then there is All the Young Men: How One Woman Risked It All to Care for the Dying by Ruth Coker Burks. In this book, she tells how she became the caregiver and advocate for so many HIV-positive men at the beginning of the AIDS crisis in the South. And once again, she was someone who cared so deeply about people that many others viewed as "throwaway people." Both books are incredible and had a profound impact on me. They really touched me and shaped how I try to serve my dudes.

And last but not least, I think everyone needs to read One Hit Away: A Memoir of Recovery and Bridgetown: A Harm Reduction Novel by Jordan P. Barnes. These books humanize addiction and harm reduction which is something we need more of. You better not take that part out, Jordan!

Some argue that One Flew Over the Cuckoo's Nest led to a massive pushback in our country (i.e. Trans-institutionalization) where many hospitals and asylums were shuttered and patients were displaced from care. This led to a slippery slope where massive numbers of the gravely disabled wound up in jail or on the streets. Are we still reeling from this lack of care?

The issue of de-institutionalization/trans-institutionalization is so multifaceted I'm not even gonna act like I can cover all aspects. This is a gross oversimplification, but yes, we are absolutely still feeling it. Prisons are the most prominent mental health provider in America, and that's fucked up in so many ways. Also, in my experience, social services are the first place we cut funding and the last place we give it to. In mental health, we are constantly being asked to do more and more with fewer resources and more people who need services. Although I think the idea of people receiving services in their community (as opposed to a state hospital) is a beautiful goal, in most cases the resources are unavailable to meet the ever-growing need.

I've read stories where certain laws and politics seem to interfere with family members getting their loved ones the care they need. Has that been your experience?

I think this is a really complicated question. If a person is unwilling to get help, family members and loved ones often feel at a loss for what to do. So as a result, they want a way for their loved one to be forced to get help. The commitment laws vary from state to state, but basically a person who is in a mental health crisis can be held against their will (involuntary commitment) if they are a danger to themselves, a danger to others, or gravely disabled. Some criteria must be met to prove this. One of the reasons these criteria were put into place was because, back in the day, people's families could just dump someone off at a mental institution for acting odd, promiscuous, or even running a big mouth. The story of actress Frances Farmer is an excellent example of this. So I think it's a topic that requires a tricky balance between patients' rights and getting people the care they need.

If you could author one bill for the POTUS (President of the United States) to sign into law, what would that be and why?

I have a mile-long list of bills I would want the POTUS to sign into law (like literally so many), but my number one request would be to require **mandatory mental health classes in every high school.** I would even go so far as to make it a graduation requirement. And the curriculum would be designed by mental health professionals who work in "the system" and people on the receiving end of mental healthcare. My best friend Jen (who is also a mental health professional) and I speak to health classes at our local high school a couple times a year, yet despite there being a mental health unit in class, the real issues of mental health and mental illness aren't adequately covered. I have had so many of my dudes tell me they had no clue what was happening when they first experienced symptoms of their mental illness because they had no clue what mental illness looked like. And that goes for most people in society. I firmly believe that if people knew what was happening and what to do, they could get help a lot sooner and, in turn, prevent a lot of tragedy.

In the book Crazy: A Father's Search Through America's Mental Health Madness, Pete Earley recounts his frustration with the system as he fights to get his son with schizophrenia help. What is the biggest obstacle to getting help for those in need?

I know people will say that they frequently tried to get their loved one help and the loved one refused. While I think that definitely is a big obstacle, in my experience it's not the biggest one. When navigating the mental healthcare system in America, I believe the biggest obstacle is not knowing how it works or what to do. The system is complicated, and there are so few providers who all have months-long wait lists, and they may or may not take your insurance. Primary care physicians rarely feel confident in diagnosing or prescribing medications for mental health issues. The list goes on and on. I get about 5-10 calls per week from people who don't know where to turn for help, both for mental health and substance abuse resources. I help as much as possible, but so many people don't have a Kourtney or homie hookup they can call who knows how to navigate the system. Making the mental healthcare system more accessible for all would be game changing.

State Hospitals have long been villains in books and movies, portrayed as dark, dank, scary places rife with abuses. How has that stigma affected the work you do?

In my experience, state hospitals are villainized in many ways, and based on the history of mental health institutions in America, much of that is deserved. This country has treated people terribly, and all those wrongs are inexcusable. The thing I notice even more though is the stigma around working with the population I serve. Stand next to me while I tell someone what I do for a living, and you will see a variety of horrified reactions. And that has affected me profoundly and created a desire to educate people about mental health, addiction and NGRI. Everyone is one bad day away from a completely different reality and I don't think enough people realize that. Any of us could be in my dude's shoes tomorrow. The population I serve are amazing people who have done some tragic things, and I believe the more we educate people on mental illness, the better off we all will be.

MENTAL HEALTH RESOURCES

Substance Abuse and Mental Health Services Administration (SAMHSA)
www.SAMHSA.gov

SAMHSA's National Helpline: 1-800-662-HELP (4357)

Health Resources and Services Administration (HRSA)
www.HRSA.gov

Centers for Medicare & Medicaid Services (CMS)
www.CMS.gov

The National Library of Medicine (NLM) MedlinePlus
www.MedlinePlus.gov

CPSIA information can be obtained
at www.ICGtesting.com
Printed in the USA
BVHW042010060223
657986BV00004B/53

9 781734 716696